Gianrico Carofiglio, born in 1961, is an anti-Mafia judge in the southern Italian city of Bari. He has been responsible for some of the most important indictments in the region involving organized crime, corruption and the traffic in human beings. *Involuntary Witness* is his debut novel and has won a number of literary awards such as the Marisa Rusconi and Rhegium Julii prizes. It is a best-seller in Italy and the basis for a television series there.

INVOLUNTARY WITNESS

Gianrico Carofiglio

Translated from the Italian
by Patrick Creagh

BITTER LEMON PRESS
LONDON

BITTER LEMON PRESS

First published in the United Kingdom in 2005 by
Bitter Lemon Press, 37 Arundel Gardens, London W11 2LW

www.bitterlemonpress.com

First published in Italian as *Testimone Inconsapevole* by
Sellerio editore, Palermo, 2002

This edition is published with the financial assistance of the
Italian Ministry of Foreign Affairs

© Sellerio editore, Palermo, 2002
English translation © Patrick Creagh, 2005

Acknowledgements
P. 86: 'The Boxer', Words & Music by Paul Simon, © Copyright 1968
Paul Simon. Used by permission of Music Sales Limited. All Rights
Reserved. International Copyright Secured. P. 71 'The River' by Bruce
Springsteen. Copyright 1980 Bruce Springsteen. All rights reserved.
Reprinted by permission. P. 85: 'Please Forgive Me', © David Gray,
1998, reprinted with kind permission of Chrysalis Music Ltd'.
Extracts from the English translation of Antoine Saint-Exupéry's *Le
Petit Prince* (The Little Prince) on pages 98, 100 are © Katherine
Woods, 1945.

A CIP record for this book is available from the British Library

ISBN 1–904738–07–9

Typeset by RefineCatch Limited, Broad Street, Bungay, Suffolk
Printed and bound by
WS Bookwell, Finland

What the caterpillar thinks is the end of the world, the rest of the world calls a butterfly

Lao-tzu, *The Way of Virtue*

Part One

1

I well remember the day – or rather the afternoon – before it all began.

I'd been in the office for a quarter of an hour and had absolutely no wish to work. I had already checked my e-mails and the post, straightened a few stray papers, made a couple of pointless telephone calls. In short, I had run out of pretexts, so I'd lit a cigarette.

I would just quietly enjoy this cigarette and then start work.

After the cigarette I'd have found some other excuse. Maybe I'd go out, remembering a book I had to get from Feltrinelli's that, one way or another, I'd too often put off buying.

While I was smoking, the telephone rang. It was the internal line, my secretary ringing from the waiting room.

She had a gentleman there who had no appointment but said it was urgent.

Practically no one ever has an appointment. People go to a criminal lawyer when they have serious, urgent problems, or at least are convinced they do. Which comes to the same thing of course.

In any case, in my office the routine went as follows: my secretary called me, in the presence of the person who urgently needed to see a lawyer. If I was busy – for example, with another client – I made them wait until I was finished.

If I was not busy, as on that afternoon, I made them wait all the same.

I wanted them to know that this office is for working in, and that I receive clients only if the matter is urgent.

I told Maria Teresa to inform the gentleman that I could see him in ten minutes, but couldn't spare him much time because I had an important meeting.

People think that lawyers often have important meetings.

Ten minutes later the gentleman entered. He had long black hair, a long black beard and goggling eyes. He sat down and leaned towards me, with his elbows on the desk.

For a moment I was certain that he would say, "I have just killed my wife and mother-in-law. They're downstairs in the back of the car. Luckily I have an estate car. What are *we* going to do about it, Avvocato?"

Nothing of the sort. He had a van from which he sold grilled frankfurters and hamburgers. The health inspectors had confiscated it because hygienic conditions inside it were pretty much those of the sewers of Benares.

This bearded character wanted his van back. He knew that I was a smart lawyer because he had been told so by one of his mates, a client of mine. With a kind of sickening conspiratorial smirk, he gave me the name of a drug pusher for whom I had managed to negotiate a disgracefully light sentence.

I demanded an exorbitant advance, and from his trouser pocket he produced a roll of 50,000- and 100,000- lire notes.

Please don't give me the ones with mayonnaise stains, I prayed resignedly.

He thumbed out the sum I had asked for, and left

me the confiscation document and all the other documents. No, he didn't want a receipt: what would I do with it, Avvocato? Another conspiratorial smirk. We tax evaders understand one another, don't we?

Years before, I had quite enjoyed my work. Now, on the contrary, it made me feel slightly sick. And when I came across people like this hamburger merchant I felt sicker still.

I felt I deserved a meal of frankfurters served by this Rasputin and to land up in Casualty. In wait for me there I would find Dr Carrassi.

Dr Carrassi, second-in-command in the Casualty Department, had killed off a 21-year-old girl with peritonitis by misdiagnosing it as period pains.

His lawyer – yours truly – got him off without the loss of a day's work or a penny of his salary. It wasn't a difficult case. The public prosecutor was an idiot and counsel for the family a terminal illiterate.

When he was acquitted, Carrassi gave me a hug. He had bad breath, he was sweating and he was under the impression that justice had been done.

Leaving the courtroom I avoided the eyes of the girl's parents.

The bearded character left and I, choking down nausea, prepared the appeal against the confiscation of his precious meals-on-wheels.

Then I went home.

On Friday evenings we usually went to the cinema, followed by dinner in a restaurant, always with the same bunch of friends.

I never took any part in choosing the cinema or the restaurant. I did whatever Sara and the others decided and spent the evening in a state of suspended animation, waiting for it to end. Unless it turned out to be a film I really liked, but that happened increasingly rarely.

When I got home that evening Sara was already dressed to go out. I said I needed at least a quarter of an hour, just time for a shower and change of clothes.

Ah, she was going out with her own friends, was she? Which friends? The ones from the photography course. She might have told me earlier, and I'd have got myself organized. She'd told me the day before and it wasn't her fault if I didn't listen to what she said. Oh, all right, there's no need to get in a huff. I'd have tried to arrange something for myself, if I'd had time. No, I had no intention of making her feel guilty, I only wanted to say just exactly what I had said. Very well, let's just stop bickering.

She went out and I stayed at home. I thought of calling the usual friends and going out with them. Then it seemed to me absurdly difficult to explain why Sara wasn't there and where she had gone, and I thought they would give me funny looks, so I dropped the idea.

I tried calling up a girl who at that time I sometimes used to see on the sly, but she, almost whispering into her mobile, told me she was with her boyfriend. What did I expect on a Friday? I felt at a loose end, but then I thought I'd rent a good thriller, get out a frozen pizza and a big bottle of cold beer and, one way or another, that Friday evening would pass.

I chose *Black Rain*, even though I'd already seen it twice. I saw it a third time and still liked it. I ate the pizza and drank all the beer. On top of that I had a whisky and smoked several cigarettes. I flipped between television channels, discovering that the local stations had taken to showing hard porn again. This made me realize that it was one in the morning, so I went to bed.

I don't know when I got to sleep and I don't know when Sara came in, because I didn't hear her.

When I woke next morning she was already up. I took my sleepy face into the kitchen and she, without a word, poured me a cup of American coffee. Both of us have always liked American coffee, really weak.

I took two sips and was just about to ask her what time she had got back the night before when she told me she wanted a separation.

She said it just like that: "Guido, I want a separation."

After a long, deafening silence I was forced to ask the most banal of questions.

Why?

She told me why. She was perfectly calm and implacable. Maybe I thought she hadn't noticed how my life had been in the last . . . let's say two years. She, on the other hand, had noticed and she hadn't liked it. What had humiliated her most was not my *infidelity* – and the word struck me in the face like spittle – but the fact that I had shown real disrespect by treating her like a fool. She didn't know if I had always been like this or had become so. She didn't know which alternative she preferred and perhaps she didn't even care.

She was telling me that I had become a mediocrity and may have been one all along. And she had no wish to live with a mediocrity. Not any longer.

Like a real mediocrity, I found nothing better to do than ask her if there was someone else. She simply said no and that in any case, from that moment on, it was no business of mine.

Quite.

This conversation didn't last long after that, and ten days later I was out of the house.

2

So, I was – politely – given the push, and my life changed. Not for the better either, though I didn't realize this at once.

On the contrary, for the first few months I had a feeling of relief and, towards Sara, one that almost amounted to gratitude. For the courage that she had shown and I had always lacked.

In short, she had pulled my chestnuts out of the fire, as the saying goes.

I had so often thought that we couldn't go on in that situation, that I ought to do something. I ought to take the initiative, find a solution, speak out honestly. Do something.

However, being a coward, I had done nothing, apart from grasping whatever clandestine chances had come my way.

Thinking it over, of course, the things she had said that morning stung me badly. She had treated me as a mediocrity and, like a little coward, I had taken it all lying down.

Actually, in the days that followed that Saturday, and in fact when I had already gone to live in my new home, I thought more than once of what I might have answered, just to keep some shred of dignity.

I thought of things such as "I don't wish to deny my responsibility, but remember that the blame is never all on one side." Things like that.

Luckily this happened only, as I say, some days later.

That Saturday morning I kept my mouth shut and at least avoided making myself ridiculous.

In any case, after a while I dropped all that and was left only with a few pangs, inside. Whenever I wondered where Sara might be at that moment, what she was doing and with *whom* she was doing it.

I was very good at anaesthetizing these pangs, quelling them quickly. I forced them back inside where they had come from, pushing them down, hiding them deeper.

For several months I lived a wild life, that of a born-again single. What they call life in the fast lane.

I kept outlandish company, went to fatuous parties, drank too much, smoked too much and all that.

I went out every evening. The idea of staying at home alone was intolerable.

Naturally, I had a few girlfriends.

I don't remember a single conversation I had with any one of those girls.

In the midst of all this came the hearing to legalize our separation by mutual consent. There were no problems. Sara had stayed on in the flat, which was hers. I had tried to maintain a dignified attitude by refusing to remove any furniture, household appliances, and in fact anything except my books, and not all of those.

We met in the anteroom of the judge appointed by the court dealing with separations. It was the first time I had seen her since leaving home. She had cut her hair and had a slight tan, and I wondered where she might have gone to acquire her tan and with *whom* she might have gone to acquire it.

These weren't pleasant thoughts.

Before I could say a word she came up and gave me a peck on the cheek. This, more than anything else, gave me a sense of the irremediable. Just after my thirty-eighth birthday I was discovering for the first time that things really do come to an end.

The judge tried to persuade us to make it up, as he is obliged to by law. We were extremely polite and civil. Only Sara spoke, and even then very little. We had made up our minds, she said. It was a step we were taking calmly and with mutual respect.

I kept silent, nodded, and felt I was definitely playing a supporting role in the movie. It was all over very quickly, since there were no problems with money, property or children.

As soon as we left the judge's room she gave me another kiss, this time almost at the corner of my mouth. "Ciao," she said.

"Ciao," said I, when she had already turned and was walking away.

"Ciao," I said again to the air, after smoking a cigarette while slouching against the wall.

I left the law courts when I noticed the looks I was getting from passing clerks.

Outside it was spring.

3

Spring rapidly turned to summer, but the days still ran by all exactly the same.

The nights too were all the same. Dark.

Until one morning in June.

I was in the lift, just back from the law courts and on my way up to my office on the eighth floor when suddenly, and for no reason, I was seized by panic.

Once out of the lift I stood on the landing for God knows how long, panting, in a cold sweat, feeling sick, eyes riveted on a fire extinguisher. And full of terror.

"Are you all right, Avvocato?" The voice of Signor Strisciuglio, a former clerk in the Inland Revenue and tenant of the other apartment on my floor, was a little puzzled, a little worried.

"I'm all right, thank you. I'm completely out of my mind, but I don't think this is a problem. And how are you?"

That's a lie. I said I'd had a slight dizzy spell but that now everything was fine, thank you, good day.

Naturally, everything was not fine, as I would come to realize all too well in the days and months that followed.

In the first place, not knowing what had happened to me that morning in the lift, I began to be obsessed with the idea that it might happen again.

So I stopped using the lift. It was a stupid decision that only made matters worse.

A few days later, instead of recovering, I began to fear that I might be seized by panic anywhere, at any time.

When I had worried myself enough, I managed to bring on another attack, this time in the street. It was less violent than the first but the after-effects were even more devastating.

For at least a month I lived in constant terror of a fresh panic attack. It's laughable, looking back on it now. I lived in terror of being assailed by terror.

I thought that when it happened again, I might go mad and perhaps even die. Die mad.

This led me, with superstitious dismay, to remember an occurrence of many years before.

I was at university and had received a letter, written on squared paper in a loopy, almost childish hand.

Dear Friend

When you have read this letter make ten copies in your own handwriting and send them to ten friends. This is the original Chain Letter: if you keep it going, your life will be blessed with good luck, money, love, peace and joy, but if you break it, the most terrible misfortunes may befall you. A young married woman who had for two years longed for a child without managing to become pregnant copied the letter and sent it to ten friends. Three days later she learned that she was expecting. A humble post-office clerk copied the letter, sent it to ten friends and relations, and a week later won masses of money on the lottery.

On the other hand, a high-school teacher received this letter, laughed and tore it up. A few days later he had an accident, broke a leg and was also evicted from his home.

One housewife got the letter and decided not to break the chain. But unfortunately she lost the letter and, as a result, did break the chain. A few days later she contracted meningitis, and though she survived she remained an invalid for the rest of her life.

A certain doctor, on receipt of the letter, tore it up, exclaiming in contemptuous tones that one shouldn't believe in such superstitions. In the course of the next few months he was sacked from the clinic where he worked, his wife left him, he fell ill, and in the end he died mad.

Don't break the chain!

I read the letter to my friends, who found it highly diverting. When they had got over laughing they asked me if I intended to tear it up and die mad. Or else sit down and diligently make ten copies in elegant hand-writing, something that they would not fail to keep reminding me of – rather rudely, I presume – for at least the next ten years.

This got on my nerves. I thought they wouldn't have been such Children of the Enlightenment if they had received the letter themselves, but told them that of course I'd tear it up. They insisted that I do it in front of them. They insinuated that I might have had second thoughts and, once safe from prying eyes, might make the famous ten copies etc.

In short, I was forced to tear it up, and when I'd done so the biggest joker of the three of them said that, whatever happened, I needn't worry: when the time came, they would see to it that I was admitted to a comfortable loony-bin.

Some eighteen years later I found myself thinking – seriously – that the prophecy was coming true.

In any case, the fear of having another panic attack and going mad was not my only problem.

I began to suffer from insomnia. I lay awake almost all night every night, falling asleep only just before dawn.

Rarely did I get to sleep at a more normal time, but even then I unfailingly woke two hours later and was unable to stay in bed. If I tried to, I was assailed by the saddest, most unbearable thoughts. About how I had wasted my life, about my childhood. And about Sara.

So I was forced to get up and wander about the apartment. I smoked, drank, watched television, turned on my mobile in the absurd hope that someone might call me in the middle of the night.

I began to be worried that people might notice the condition I was in.

Above all, I began to worry that I might totally lose control of my actions, and in such a state I spent the entire summer.

When August came, I didn't find anyone to go on holiday with – to tell the truth, I didn't try to – and I wasn't brave enough to go off alone. So I mooned about, parking myself in the holiday homes and the *trulli* of friends, either at the sea or in the country. I'm sure I didn't make myself very popular during these peregrinations.

People would ask me if I was a bit under the weather, and I would say, yes, a little, and as a rule we didn't pursue the matter. After a very few days I'd realize it was time to pack my bags and find another bolt hole, trying as far as possible to put off going back to town.

In September, as things got no better, and especially as I couldn't bear the sleepless nights, I went to my doctor, who was also a friend of mine. I wanted something to help me sleep.

He examined me, asked me to describe my symptoms, took my blood pressure, shone a torch in my eyes, made me do slightly demented exercises to test my balance, and at the end said that I'd do well to see a *specialist*.

"Eh? What do you mean? What kind of specialist?"

"Well . . . a specialist in these problems."

"*What* problems? Give me something to make me sleep and let's have done with it."

"Listen, Guido, the situation is a bit more complicated than that. You have a very strained look. I don't like the way you keep glancing around. I don't like the way you move. I don't like the way you're breathing. I have to tell you, you are not a well man. You must consult a specialist."

"You mean a . . ." My mouth was dry. A thousand incoherent thoughts went through my head. Perhaps he means I should go and see a consultant. Or a homeopath. Or a masseur. Even an Ayurvedic practitioner.

Oh, that's fine if I have to go to a consultant, masseur, Ayurvedic practitioner, homeopath. To hell with it, that's no problem, I'll go. I'm not one to shirk treatment, not I.

I'm not a bit scared because . . . *a psychiatrist?* Did you say a PSYCHIATRIST?

I wanted to cry. I'd gone mad and now even a doctor said so. The prophecy was coming true.

I said, all right, all right, and now could he give me that damned sleeping pill, and I'd think about it. Yes, all right, I had no intention of underestimating the problem, see you soon, no no, there's no need to give me the name of a – mouth very dry indeed – of one of those. I'll call you and you can tell me then.

And I ran for it, steering clear of the lift.

4

My doctor had agreed to prescribe something to help me sleep, and with those pills the situation seemed to improve. A little.

My mood was still mouse-grey but at least I wasn't dragging myself around like a ghost, dead of insomnia.

All the same, my output of work and my professional reliability were dangerously below safety level. There were a number of people whose freedom depended on my work and my powers of concentration. I imagine they would have been interested to learn that I spent the afternoons absent-mindedly leafing through their files, that I couldn't care less about them and the contents of their files, that I went into court totally unprepared, that the outcome of the trials was to all intents and purposes left to chance and that, in a word, their destiny lay in the hands of an irresponsible nutcase.

When I was obliged to receive clients the situation was surreal.

The clients talked. I paid no attention whatever, but I nodded. They talked on, reassured. At the end I shook them by the hand with an understanding smile.

They seemed pleased that their lawyer had given them their head in that way, without interrupting. He had evidently understood their problem and requirements.

I was a really decent sort, was the opinion confided to my secretary by a pensioner who wanted to sue her neighbour for putting obscene notes in her letter box. I didn't even seem to be a lawyer at all, she said. How true.

The clients were satisfied and I, at the best of times, had only a vague notion of the problem. Together we proceeded on our way towards catastrophe.

It was during this phase – after I had managed to get some sleep for a few nights running – that a new factor intervened. I began to burst into tears. At first it happened at home, in the evening as soon as I got back or when I first got up in the morning. Later, it happened outside as well. As I was walking along the street, my thoughts went berserk and I began to cry. I did, however, manage to control the situation, both at home and – more important – in the street, even if each time it was a little more difficult. I concentrated all my attention on my shoes or on the number plates of cars, and, above all, avoided looking into the faces of the passers-by, who, I was convinced, would be aware of what was happening to me.

Finally it happened to me in the office. It was one afternoon and I was speaking to my secretary about something when I felt the tears welling up and a painful sensation in my throat.

I set myself to staring dully at a small patch of damp on the wall, answering meanwhile by simply nodding, scared stiff lest Maria Teresa should realize what was going on.

In fact she realized perfectly well, suddenly remembered that she had some photocopies to make and very tactfully left the room.

Only a few seconds later I burst into tears, and it was no easy matter to stop.

I felt it was not a good idea to wait for a repetition, in the middle of a trial for example.

Next day I called my doctor and got him to give me the name of that specialist.

5

The psychiatrist was tall, massive and imposing, bearded and with hands like shovels. I could just see him immobilizing a raving lunatic and forcing him into a straitjacket.

He was kindly enough, considering his beard and bulk. He got me to tell him everything and kept nodding his head. This seemed reassuring. Then it occurred to me that I too used to nod my head while clients were talking and I felt somewhat less reassured.

However, he said that I was suffering from a particular form of adjustment disturbance. The separation had worked in my psyche like a time bomb and after a while had caused something to snap. Caused, in fact, a series of ruptures. I had made a mistake in neglecting the problem for so many months. There had been a degeneration of the adjustment disturbance, which was in danger of evolving into a depressive state of moderate gravity. Such situations ought not to be underestimated. There was no need to worry, though, because the fact of having come to a psychiatrist was in itself a positive sign of self-awareness and a prelude to recovery. I was certainly in need of pharmaceutical treatment, but, all in all, after a few months the situation would be decidedly improved.

A pause and a piercing look. They must have been part of the therapy.

Then he began writing, filling a page of his prescription pad with anxiolytics and antidepressants.

I was to take the stuff for two months. I must try to find distractions. I must avoid dwelling on myself. I must attempt to see the positive side of things and avoid thinking there was no way out of my situation. I must hand over 300,000 lire, there was no question of a receipt and we'd meet in two months' time for a check-up.

From the doorway as he showed me out, he advised me against reading the descriptive leaflets enclosed with the drugs. He was a real authority on the human psyche.

I hunted for a chemist's a long way from the centre of town, to avoid meeting anyone I knew. I didn't want a client or colleague of mine present when the chemist yelled out to the assistant in the back some such phrase as "Look in the psychotropic cupboard and see if we have extra-strong psychiatric Valium for this gentleman."

After cruising around a bit in the car, I selected somewhere in Japigia, on the outskirts of the city. The chemist was a bony young woman with a rather unsociable air, and I handed her the prescription with averted eyes. I felt as much at my ease as a priest in a porn shop.

The bony chemist was already making out the bill when I recited my little speech: "While I'm here I'll get something for myself as well. Have you some effervescent vitamin C?"

She looked at me for a second, without a word. She knew the script. Then she gave me the vitamin C along with the rest. I paid and fled like a thief.

When I got home I unwrapped the package, opened the boxes and read the enclosed leaflets. I found them all interesting, but my attention was irresistibly drawn to the side-effects of the antidepressant. Trittico with a trazodone base.

The patient began with simple dizzy spells, passing swiftly on to dryness of the mouth, blurred vision, constipation, urinary retention, tremors and alteration of the libido.

It occurred to me that I had already seen to altering my libido on my own, then I went on reading. I thus discovered that a limited number of men who take trazodone develop a tendency to long, painful erections, what is known as priapism.

This problem might even require an emergency surgical operation, which in turn might result in permanent sexual impairment.

But the end was reassuring. The risk of fatal overdose of trazodone was, fortunately, lower than that resulting from the use of tricyclic antidepressants.

Having finished reading, I fell to meditating.

What do you do in the case of a prolonged and painful erection? Do you go to a hospital holding the thing in your hand? Do you put on *very* comfortable underpants? What do you say to the doctor? What does permanent sexual impairment amount to?

And again, how much does one need for a fatal overdose of trazodone? Are two pills enough? Or does it require the whole packet?

I found no answers to these questions, but the Trittico ended up down the bog, along with the rest of the medicines prescribed by my psychiatrist. My ex-psychiatrist.

I conscientiously emptied all the packets and pulled the chain. Into the rubbish bin went the boxes, phials, ampoules and descriptive leaflets.

That done, I poured myself an ample half-glass of

whisky – *avoid alcoholic beverages* – and put *Chariots of Fire* into the video machine. One of the few cassettes I had brought away with me.

When the first pictures started coming, I lit up a Marlboro – *avoid nicotine, especially in the evening* – and for the first time in a very long while I almost felt in a good mood.

6

When I was a boy I used to box.

My grandfather took me along to a gym after seeing me come home with my face swollen from the beating it had taken. Administered by a fellow bigger – and nastier – than me.

I was fourteen then, very skinny, with a nose red and shiny from acne. I was in the fourth form at grammar school, and was perfectly convinced that there was no such thing as happiness. For me, at any rate.

The gym was in a damp basement. The instructor was a lean man approaching seventy, with arms still lean and muscular and a face like Buster Keaton's. He was a friend of my grandfather.

I have a precise recollection of the moment we entered it, at the foot of some narrow, ill-lit steps. There was not a voice to be heard, only the dull thud of fists hitting the punch bag, the rap of skipping ropes, the rhythm of the punch ball. There was a smell I can't describe, but it is there in my nostrils now, as I write, and a thrill runs through me.

That I was going in for boxing was long kept secret from my mother. She only learned it when, at the age of seventeen and a half, I won the welterweight silver medal in the regional junior championships.

My grandfather, however, never got to see me on that pasteboard podium.

Three months previously he had been walking through a pine wood with his Alsatian when at a certain moment he stopped and calmly sat down on a bench.

A lad who was nearby reported that, after stroking the dog, he had leaned his head on the back of the bench in an unusual fashion.

The carabinieri had to shoot the dog before they could approach the body and identify him as Guido Guerrieri, former Professor of Medieval Philosophy.

My grandfather.

I won other medals after those regional championships. Even a bronze as a middleweight in the Italian university championships.

I never had a deadly punch, but I'd acquired a good technique, and I was tall and lean, with a longer reach than others at my weight.

Shortly before I took my degree I gave it up, because boxing is something you can keep up for long only if you are a champion, or if you have something to prove.

I was not a champion and it seemed to me I had already proved what I had to prove.

Having decided to get along without modern psychiatry, I searched my mind for some alternative. And I found what I needed was a spot of fisticuffs.

Thinking it over, I realized that it had been one of the few solid things in my life. The smell of glove leather, the punches given and taken, the hot shower afterwards, when you discovered that for two whole hours not a single thought had passed through your head.

The fear as you were walking towards the ring, the fear behind your expressionless eyes, behind the expressionless eyes of your opponent. Dancing, jumping, trying to dodge, giving and taking 'em, with arms so weary you can't keep your guard up, breathing through your mouth, praying it'll end because you can't take it any longer, wanting to punch but being unable to, thinking you don't care whether you win or lose as long as it ends, thinking you want to throw yourself on the ground but you don't, and you don't know what's keeping you on your feet or why and then the bell rings and you think you've lost and you don't care and then the referee raises your arm and you realize you've won and nothing exists at that moment, nothing exists *but* that moment. No one can take it away from you. Never ever.

I searched for a gym that catered for boxing. The old basement of nearly twenty-five years before was long gone. The instructor was dead. I consulted the Yellow Pages and saw that the city was full of gyms for the martial arts of Japan, Thailand, Korea, China and even Vietnam. The choice was vast: judo, ju-jitsu, aikido, karate, Thai boxing, taekwondo, tai chi chuan, wing chun, kendo, viet vo dao.

Boxing seemed to have simply vanished, but I didn't give up. I rang the local office of the Olympic Committee and asked if there were any gyms in Bari that did boxing. The chap at the other end was very efficient and helpful. Yes, there were two boxing clubs in Bari, one near the new stadium, housed by the council, and the other, which used the gym of a secondary school just round the corner from where I lived.

I went to take a look at it and found that the instructor was an acquaintance of mine from the old gym. Pino. But to remember his surname was obviously beyond me. He had started at the basement shortly before I gave up. He was a heavyweight with not much technique but really powerful fists. He'd even had a few bouts as a professional, without great success. Now he had a number of occupations: boxing instructor, bouncer in discothèques, head of security at rock concerts, mass events, festivals and the like.

He was glad to see me, and of course I could sign up, I was his guest, he wouldn't hear of my paying. And in any case a lawyer might always come in useful.

In short, starting the following week, every Monday and Thursday I left the office at half-past six, by seven I was in the gym, and for nearly two hours I was boxing away.

This made me feel a little better. Not what you might call well, but a little better. I skipped, did the knee-bends, abdominal exercises, punched the punchbag, and fought a few rounds with lads twenty years younger than myself.

Some nights I managed to get some sleep on my own, without pills. Others not.

Sometimes I even managed to sleep for five or six hours at a stretch.

Some evenings I went out with friends and felt almost relaxed.

I still burst into tears, but less often, and in any case I managed to keep it under control.

I went on not taking the lift, but this wasn't a great problem and nobody noticed anyway.

I passed almost unscathed through the Christmas holidays, even if one day, perhaps the 29th or 30th, I saw Sara in the street in the middle of town. She was with a woman friend and a man I had never seen. He could well have been the friend's fiancé, or her uncle, or a gay as far as I knew. All the same, I was convinced at once that he was Sara's new boyfriend.

We waved to each other from opposite pavements. I went on another step or so and then realized that I was holding my breath. My diaphragm was obstructed. I felt something, something hot, rising up in me to spread across my whole face, into the roots of my hair. My mind was a blank for several minutes.

I had trouble breathing for the rest of the day and got no sleep that night.

Then even that passed.

After the Christmas holidays I started working again, at least a little. I recognized the catastrophe that was threatening my practice and above all my unsuspecting clients and, ploddingly, I attempted to regain a modicum of control over the situation.

I began once more to prepare for trials, began to listen – a little – to what my clients were saying, I began to listen to what my secretary was saying.

Slowly, in jerks, like a worn-out jalopy, my life began to get moving again.

Part Two

7

It was a February afternoon, but it wasn't cold. It had never been cold, that winter.

I passed the bar downstairs from the office but didn't go in. I was ashamed to ask for a decaffeinated coffee, so I went to a dismal bar five blocks away.

Ever since I'd started suffering from insomnia I didn't drink proper coffee in the afternoon. I had tried barley coffee a few times, but it really was too disgusting. But decaffeinated coffee seemed like real. The main thing is not to be seen ordering it.

I had always looked with a certain condescension on people who ordered the decaffeinated stuff. I didn't want the same sort of looks to be cast at me now. At least, not by people I knew. I therefore avoided my usual bar in the afternoons.

I drank the coffee, lit a Marlboro and smoked it seated at an ancient Formica-topped table. Then back five blocks and up to the office.

As far as I could remember, it was due to be a rather quiet afternoon: only one appointment. With Signora Cassano, due for trial the next day for maltreating her husband.

According to the indictment, this gentleman had for years come home from work to hear himself called, at the best, a shitty down-and-out failure. For years he had been forced to hand over his wages, allowed to keep only some loose change for cigarettes and other personal expenses. For years he had been humiliated

31

at family gatherings and before his few friends. On numerous occasions he had been slapped about and she had even spat in his face.

One day he could stand it no longer. He had plucked up the courage to leave home and had denounced her, asking for a separation and damages.

She had chosen me to represent her, and that afternoon I was expecting her for us to settle the details of the defence.

When I got to the office Maria Teresa told me that the harridan had not yet arrived. On the other hand a black woman had been waiting for me for at least half an hour. She didn't have an appointment but – she said – the matter was very important. As always.

She was in the waiting room. I peered through the crack in the door and saw an imposing young woman, with a face both beautiful and austere. She can't have been over thirty.

I told Maria Teresa to show her into my room in two minutes' time. I took off my jacket, reached my desk, lit a cigarette, and the woman entered.

She waited for me to ask her to take a seat and in an almost accentless voice said, "Thank you, Avvocato." With foreign clients I was always in doubt as to whether to use *tu* or *lei*. Many of them do not understand the *lei* form, and the conversation becomes surreal.

From the way this woman said "Thank you, Avvocato" I knew I could address her as *lei* without any fear of not being understood.

When I asked her what the problem was she handed me some stapled sheets headed "Office of the Magistrate in Charge of Preliminary Investigations, Order for Precautionary Detention".

Drugs, was my immediate thought. Her man was a

pusher. Then, almost as quickly, that seemed to me impossible.

We all of us go by stereotypes. Anyone who denies it is a liar. The first stereotype had suggested the following sequence: African, precautionary detention, drugs. It is usually for this reason that Africans get arrested.

But straight away the second stereotype came into play. The woman had an aristocratic look and didn't seem like a drug-pusher's moll.

I was right. Her partner had not been arrested for drugs but for the kidnap and murder of a nine-year-old boy.

The charges stated were brief, bureaucratic and blood-curdling.

Abdou Thiam, Senegalese citizen, stood accused:

a) *of the offence as under Art. 603 of the Penal Code for having deliberately deprived of his personal liberty Francesco Rubino, the latter being under age, inducing him by subterfuge to follow him and thereafter restraining him against his will.*

b) *of the offence as under Art. 575 of the Penal Code for having caused the death of the said minor Francesco Rubino, exercising on him unascertained acts of violence and subsequently suffocating him by means and methods equally unascertained.*
Both offences committed in the rural district of Monopoli between 5 and 7 August 1999.

c) *of the offence as under Art. 412 of the Penal Code for having concealed the body of the minor Francesco Rubino by throwing it down a well.*

Polignano Rural District, 7 August 1999.

Francesco, nine years old, had disappeared one afternoon while playing football on his own in a yard in front of the seaside villa of his grandparents in Monopoli, to the south of Bari.

Two days later the boy's body had been found at the bottom of a well some twelve miles further north, in the countryside near Polignano.

The police doctor who had performed the autopsy had been unable either to confirm or to exclude the possibility that the child had been subjected to sexual violence.

I knew that police doctor. He wouldn't have been up to saying whether a child – or even an adult or a senior citizen – had been subjected to sexual violence even if he had been eyewitness to the rape.

The investigations were in any case based from the first on the assumption of murder with a sexual motive. The paedophiliac track.

Four days after the discovery of the body the carabinieri and the public prosecutor had triumphantly announced at a press conference that the case was solved.

The culprit was Abdou Thiam, a 31-year-old Senegalese pedlar. He was in Italy with a valid residence permit and had a few previous convictions for dealing in counterfeit goods. In other words, apart from regular wares he sold fake Vuittons, fake Hogans, fake Cartiers. In summer on the beaches, in winter in the streets and markets.

According to the investigators, the evidence against him was overwhelming. Numerous witnesses had declared that they had seen him talking on the beach to little Francesco on more than one occasion and at some length. The owner of a bar very near the house belonging to the child's grandparents had seen

Abdou pass on foot only a few minutes before the boy disappeared, and without his usual sack of more or less fake merchandise.

Questioned by the carabinieri, the Senegalese who shared lodgings with Abdou had stated that during those days – he was not able to say on exactly *which* day – the subject under inquiry had taken his car to be washed. As far as he remembered, that was the first time it had happened. Evidently, the prosecution considered this useful evidence: to eliminate every possible trace, the man had had his car washed with a view to frustrating the investigation.

Another Senegalese, also a pedlar, had stated that the day after the little boy's disappearance Abdou had not been seen on the usual beach. This too was considered – and rightly – a suspicious circumstance.

Abdou was interrogated by the public prosecutor and fell into numerous, grave contradictions. At the conclusion of the interrogation he was detained on the charges of unlawful restraint and murder. They did not accuse him of rape because there was no proof that the child had been violated.

The carabinieri had searched his room and found books for children, all of them in the original languages. Three books in the Harry Potter series, *The Little Prince, Pinocchio, Doctor Dolittle* and others. Most important of all, they had found and confiscated a photograph of the boy on the beach in swimming trunks.

In the detainment order which the woman had handed me across the desk, the books and the photograph were considered "significant facts in support of the circumstantial framework".

When I raised my eyes to look at the woman – Abajaje Deheba was her name – she began to speak.

In his own country, Senegal, Abdou was a

schoolteacher and earned the equivalent of about 200,000 lire a month. Selling handbags, shoes and wallets, he earned ten times as much. He spoke three languages, wanted to study psychology and wanted to stay in Italy.

She herself was an agronomist and came from Aswan, Nubia. Egypt. On the border with Sudan.

She had been in Bari for nearly a year and a half and was towards the end of a postgraduate course in the management of soil and irrigation resources. When she returned to her own country she would be employed by the government on a project to bring water to the Sahara and transform sand dunes into cultivable land.

I asked her what Bari had to do with the irrigation of the desert.

In Bari, she explained, there was an institute of advanced studies and research in agronomy. It was called the Centre Internationale Hautes Études Agronomiques Méditerranées, and it attracted postgraduate students from all the emerging countries of the Mediterranean. Lebanese, Tunisians, Moroccans, Maltese, Jordanians, Syrians, Turks, Egyptians, Palestinians. They lived in a dormitory annexe of the institute, studied all day, and at night went swarming about the city.

She had met Abdou at a concert. In a nightspot in the old city – she told me the name but I didn't know it – where Greeks, blacks, Asians, North Africans and even a few Italians gathered every evening.

It was a concert of the traditional Wolof music of Senegal, and Abdou was playing the drums, along with some compatriots of his.

She paused for a few seconds, her gaze fixed somewhere outside my room, outside my offices. Elsewhere.

Then she started again and I realized she was not really speaking to me.

Abdou was a teacher, she said without looking at me.

He was a teacher even though now he was selling handbags. He loved children and was incapable of doing harm to any one of them.

It was at this point that Abajaje Deheba's firmly controlled voice cracked. That face of a Nubian princess contracted with the effort of fighting back tears.

She succeeded, but she was silent for a very long minute.

Immediately after the arrest they had hired a lawyer, and she gave me the name of one I knew all too well. On one occasion, chatting away, he had boasted of declaring an income of only eighteen million lire.

Ten million he had demanded simply to make the petition to the Provincial Appeals Court. Abdou's friends had passed the hat round and put together nearly the whole sum. My so-called colleague was satisfied and pocketed the money. In cash and in advance. No receipt, of course.

The petition was refused. To go to appeal again would cost twenty million. They didn't have twenty million so Abdou had remained in prison.

Now that the trial was approaching they had decided to come to me. A young member of the Senegalese community knew me – the woman gave me a name that meant nothing to me – and also knew that I wasn't one to make a fuss about money, and that in any case, to be going on with, they could give me two million, which was what they had managed to collect.

Abajaje Deheba opened her bag, drew out a bundle of banknotes fastened with an elastic band, laid it on the desk and pushed it towards me. There was no question of my being able to refuse or discuss the matter. I said I would get my secretary to make out a receipt for that advance. No thank you, she didn't want a receipt, she wouldn't know what to do with it. What she wanted was for me to go at once and see Abdou in prison.

I told her I couldn't do that, that Signor Thiam would have to appoint me, if only by making a declaration in the prison register. Very well, she said, she would tell him when they next spoke. She rose to her feet, held out her hand – she hadn't done so when she came in – and looked me in the eye. "Abdou didn't do what they say he did."

Her handshake was as firm as I expected it to be.

When I opened the door I heard my secretary trying to explain to a Signora Cassano distinctly annoyed at having to wait that the Avvocato had had an emergency visit and would see her just as soon as possible.

I could imagine my client's thoughts when she saw Abajaje Deheba pass by, and realized that she had been made to wait on account of a *nigger*.

She entered the room and gave me a look of disgust. I'm sure she would have spat in *my* face if she could have.

The next day she was found guilty, and for the appeal she went to another lawyer. Naturally she didn't pay the remainder of my fee, but maybe she had a point: I hadn't exactly done my best to get her off.

8

I parked the car illegally, as usual on a Friday. On visiting days you can't find a legal space anywhere near the prison.

Friday is visiting day.

However, this isn't a problem, because you are unlikely to get fined. No traffic warden is too keen on having words with relatives visiting the prisoners; as a rule, no traffic warden is too keen on being on duty at all in the prison neighbourhood.

So I parked illegally on a pavement, climbed out of the car, straightened my tie, took a cigarette from the packet, put it in my mouth without lighting it and set off for the entrance.

The warder at the door knew me, so I didn't have to show my lawyer's card.

I went through the usual metal gates, then the gratings, then still more gates. Finally I reached the room reserved for lawyers.

I am convinced that in all prisons they go out of their way to choose the room that is coldest in winter and hottest in summer.

It was winter, and even though outside the air was mild, in that room, furnished with a table, two upright chairs and a broken-down armchair, there was a mortifying chill.

Lawyers are not much loved in prisons.

Lawyers are not much loved in general.

While they were off fetching Abdou Thiam I lit the

cigarette and, just for something to do, rummaged in my bag and pulled out the precautionary detention order.

Once again I read that "the impressive probative material acquired against Abdou Thiam forms a reassuring picture serving not only to justify the restraint of personal liberty at the present stage of proceedings but also, in prospect, to allow for reasonable predictions of a conviction in the forthcoming trial."

In plain words: Abdou was up to his neck in evidence against him, must be arrested and kept in custody, and when the trial came up would certainly be found guilty.

While I was reading, the door opened and a warder ushered in my client.

Abdou Thiam was a strikingly handsome man, with the face of a film star and liquid eyes. Sad and far away.

He remained standing near the door until I went up, gave him my hand and told him I was his lawyer.

A person's handshake says a lot of things, if one takes the trouble to pay attention to it. Abdou's handshake told me he didn't trust me, and that perhaps he no longer trusted anyone at all.

We sat ourselves down on the two chairs and I realized almost at once that it was not going to be an easy conversation.

Abdou spoke Italian well, even if not in the well-nigh perfect, accentless manner of Abajaje. In any case, it came naturally to me to address him as *tu*, and he replied in kind.

We hurried over the matter of how they were treating him and whether there was anything he needed. Then, since I had not yet examined the file, I tried to persuade him to give me his version of the whole story, with a view to starting to get my bearings.

He was not collaborative. He spoke apathetically, without looking at me, giving vague answers to my questions. It almost seemed as if the matter was of no concern to him.

This very soon got on my nerves, not least because behind that absurd vagueness I could clearly perceive a hostile attitude. Towards me.

I made an effort to conceal my irritation.

"Well then, Abdou, let us get things straight between us. I am your lawyer. You appointed me yourself" – I produced the telegram that had arrived from the prison the previous day and waved it about for a moment – "and I am here to help you, or to try to do so. For this I need your assistance. Otherwise I can do nothing. Do you follow me?"

Until then he had been bent slightly forward, looking at the table. Before answering, he straightened up and looked me in the face.

"I only sent that telegram because Abajaje told me to. Maybe you will try to do something, like the other lawyer, or maybe not. But I'll stay here whatever happens. When the trial comes up I'll be found guilty. We all know that. Abajaje thinks you are different from the other lawyer and really can do something. I don't believe it."

"Listen to me, Abdou," I said, forcing myself again to keep my voice calm, "if you cut yourself and the wound is deep and bleeds a lot, what do you do?" I didn't wait for an answer. "You go to a doctor and have it stitched up, don't you? You don't know how to stitch a wound because you're not a doctor."

This seemed to me an appropriate metaphor to explain to him that there are times when one simply has to avail oneself of a specialist, and that in this case the specialist was me.

"I know how to put in stitches because I was an army nurse during military service."

At that point I gave up trying to appear calm. It was obviously useless.

"Listen here and listen carefully. Listen very carefully indeed, because if you give me another crappy answer like that I'll walk out of here, call your woman, give her back the money – what there is of it – and you can find yourself another lawyer. Otherwise the court will appoint a counsel who won't do a damn thing for you unless you pay him. And he probably won't do anything even if you do pay him, seeing what you can afford. Obviously, if you are behaving in this idiotic manner because you really did kill that boy and want to pay for it, well, all the more reason for me to drop the matter . . ."

Silence.

Then, for the first time since we had been together in that room, Abdou Thiam looked at me as if I really existed. In a low voice, he spoke.

"I didn't kill Ciccio. He was my friend."

I held still briefly, to regain my balance.

It was as if I had hurled myself bodily at a door in an attempt to burst through, and someone on the other side had calmly opened it. I took a deep breath and had a hankering for a cigarette. I drew a soft packet from my coat pocket and offered it to Abdou. He said nothing, but took one and waited for me to light it for him. Then I lit my own.

"All right, Abdou. I'll have to read the prosecution's documents, but first I must have a clear picture of everything you remember about those days. Can we begin to talk about them?"

He was silent a while before nodding.

"When did you learn about the boy's disappearance?"

42

He took a long drag at the cigarette before replying.

"I learned that the boy had disappeared when they arrested me."

"Do you remember what you did on the day the boy disappeared?"

"I went to Naples to pick up my supplies. I said this when they questioned me. I mean, I said I'd been to Naples, but I didn't say I had been to buy handbags, so as not to make trouble for the people who sold me them."

"You went there alone?"

"Yes."

"When did you get back from Naples?"

"In the afternoon, the evening. I don't remember exactly."

"And the next day?"

"I don't remember. I went to some beach but I don't remember which."

"Do you remember anyone you met? I mean both on 5 August and on the following morning. Someone who might remember having seen you and whom we can call as a witness."

"Where were you that morning, Avvocato?"

I was in the shit, was the answer I would have liked to give. I was in the shit also the morning before and the morning after. I'm pretty much still in it. Just a little bit less.

This was of no interest to Abdou, however, and I said nothing. I rubbed my forehead, then passed a hand across my face and finally lit another cigarette.

"OK. You're right. It isn't easy to remember an afternoon, a morning or a day that's just the same as so many others. However, we have to make an effort to reconstruct those days. Now would you like to tell me something about the boy? You knew him?"

"Certainly I knew him. Since last year. That is, ever since I worked that beach."

"Do you remember when it was you last saw him?"

"No. Not exactly. But I saw him every time I went to that beach. He was always with either his grandparents or his mother. Occasionally with an aunt and uncle."

"Have you ever seen him near his grandparents' house, or anywhere other than the beach? Have you ever visited his grandparents' house?"

"I don't even know where his grandparents' house is, and I've only seen the boy on that beach."

"The owner of the Bar Maracaibo says that he saw you on the afternoon the boy disappeared, that you didn't have your bag of goods, and that you were heading towards the grandparents' house."

"I don't know which house that is," he repeated irritably, "and that afternoon I didn't go to Monopoli. When I got back from Naples, I stayed in Bari. I don't remember what I did but I didn't go to Monopoli."

With an angry movement he seized the packet of cigarettes and matches, still on the table, and lit up again.

I let him take a few puffs in peace, then went on.

"How did you come to have a photograph of the boy at home?"

"It was Ciccio who wanted to give me that photo. An uncle of his, I think, had a Polaroid and took several photos at the beach. The boy gave me one of them. We were friends. Every time I passed I stopped to talk to him. He wanted to know about Africa, about the animals, if I'd ever seen any lions. That sort of thing. I was happy when he gave me the photo because we were friends. What's more, at home I had masses of photos, lots of them of people on the beach, because I am friends with lots of clients. The carabinieri took only

44

that one. It's plain that this way it looks like evidence against me. Why didn't they take all the photos? Why did they take only a few books? I didn't have only children's books. I have manuals, history books, books on psychology, but they took only the children's books. Obviously this makes me out to be a maniac. What's the word? A paedophile."

"Did you tell these things to the magistrate?"

"Avvocato, do you know the state I was in when they took me before the magistrate? I couldn't breathe from the beating I'd taken, I was deaf in one ear. First I was beaten up by the carabinieri, then I was beaten up by the warders as soon as I got to prison. In fact, it was the warders who told me it was much better for me to say nothing to the magistrate. Then the lawyer told me I mustn't answer questions, as there was a risk it would only complicate matters, and I'd already made a mistake by answering the public prosecutor. He needed to study the documents carefully first. So I went before the magistrate and told him I didn't want to reply. But even when I did answer, it made no difference, because the magistrate took no notice of what I said. In any case, I stayed in prison."

I waited a second or two before speaking again.

"Where are all your things, the ones you mentioned, the books, the photos, everything?"

"I don't know. They cleared out my room and the landlord has let it to someone else. You'll have to ask Abajaje."

We were silent for a few minutes, with me trying to sort out the information I had received, him I don't know where.

Then I spoke again.

"All right, that's enough for today. Tomorrow, or rather on Monday, I'll go to the prosecutor's office

45

and see when we can make a copy of the documents. Then I'll study them, and as soon as I've got my ideas a bit clearer I'll come back and see you and we'll try to organize a defence strategy that makes sense . . ."

I left the sentence in the air, as if there were something to be added to it.

Abdou noticed, and gave me a faintly questioning look. Then he nodded. He hesitated a moment, but he was the first to hold out his hand and shake mine. His grasp differed slightly, only slightly, from the one of an hour before.

Then I opened the door and called the warder who was to take him back to his cell, in the special section reserved for rapists, child abusers and those who had turned state's evidence. All of them subjects who wouldn't have lasted long in the company of the other prisoners.

I picked up the cigarette packet and realized it was empty.

9

On Monday I woke up at about half-past five. As usual.

In the early days I'd tried to stay in bed, hoping to get back to sleep. But I did not get back to sleep, and ended up wrapped in sad and obsessive thoughts.

I therefore realized that it was better not to stay in bed, and to content myself with four or five hours of sleep. When things went well.

So I acquired the habit of getting up as soon as I woke. I would do some exercises, have a shower, shave, make breakfast, tidy the apartment. In short, I spent a good hour and a half managing to think about practically nothing.

Then I would go out and there would be the daylight, and I'd take a long walk. This too helped me not to think.

And so I did that morning. I got to the office at about eight, glanced at my memo pad and put it into my briefcase along with a few pens, some official forms, my mobile. I scribbled a note to my secretary and left it on her desk.

Then I set out for the law courts. Getting up so early and arriving so early at the law courts had certain advantages. The offices were practically deserted, so it was possible to get through chancellery matters more quickly.

I had a hearing that morning, but first I had to go and talk to Prosecutor Cervellati. The public prosecutor engaged on Abdou's case.

He was not exactly the most congenial man of law in the judiciary offices.

He was neither tall nor short. Not thin, but not exactly fat. His paunch was in any case always covered, summer and winter alike, with a horrible brown waist-coat. Thick glasses, very little hair, and what there was of it always a shade too long, grey jackets, grey socks, grey complexion.

On one occasion a friendly female colleague of mine, speaking of Cervellati, called him "a man in a singlet". I asked her what she meant and she explained that this was a category of human being that she had come up with herself.

A man in a (metaphorical) singlet is first of all one who, at the height of summer, when it's 95 degrees in the shade, wears a (real) singlet under his shirt, "because it absorbs the sweat and so I don't catch my death of cold from all these draughts". An extreme variant of this category is constituted by those who wear singlets even under a T-shirt.

A man in a singlet has an imitation-leather pouch for his mobile, with a hook to attach it to his belt. In the afternoon he gets home and puts on pyjamas. He keeps his old e-tacs mobile because those are the ones that still work best. He sucks mints to sweeten his breath, uses talcum powder and mouthwash.

Sometimes he has a condom hidden in his wallet, but he never uses it and sooner or later his wife discovers it and gives him hell.

A man in a singlet uses phrases such as: nowadays it's impossible to park in the centre of town; nowadays the young have no interests except discothèques and video games; I have nothing against homosexuals/gays/queers/faggots/fairies as long as they leave me alone; if someone is a homosexual/gay/queer/

faggot/fairy, he can do as he pleases but he can't be a schoolteacher; sincerest condolences; there's no difference between right and left wing, they're all thieves; I know when the weather's going to change because I get a pain in my elbow/knee/ankle/corns; we learn by our mistakes; at the end of the day; I don't talk behind people's backs, I say it straight out; only fools work; worse than wetting your bed; don't dig your grave with your knife and fork; where there's life there's hope; it seems like yesterday; I must decide to learn how to use the Internet/go to the gym/go on a diet/get my bicycle going/give up smoking etc., etc., etc.

It goes without saying that a man in a singlet says there are no longer any intermediate seasons and that the dry heat/cold is no problem, it's not so much the heat/cold, it's the humidity.

The man in a singlet's swearwords: oh sugar, shoot, drat it, oh flip, bloomin' heck, well I'll be jiggered, ruddy hell, for Pete's sake, naff off, eff off.

Anyone who knew him would have agreed. Cervellati was a man in a singlet.

One of his few merits was that of being in the office every morning by half-past eight. Unlike almost all his colleagues.

I knocked at his door, heard no invitation to come in, opened the door and looked in.

Cervellati raised his eyes from a tattered dossier on a desk covered with other rather grubby dossiers, codices, files, an ashtray with half a Tuscan cigar that had gone out. As usual the room stank a bit: dust and stale cigar smoke.

"Good morning, Mr Prosecutor," I said with all the fake affability I could muster.

"Good morning, Avvocato." He did not ask me to

come in. Behind his glasses and the barrier of dossiers his face was devoid of any expression.

I entered the room, asking if I could come in and not expecting an answer, which indeed I never got.

"Mr Prosecutor, I have been appointed by Signor Thiam, whom you will certainly remember —"

"You mean the nigger who killed the boy in Monopoli."

Evidently he did remember. In a few days' time he would announce that the preliminary investigations were concluded and I would be able to view the documents and make copies. He had no doubt at all that I would ask for the shortened procedure, which would save time for everyone. Perhaps I had not noticed, by a mere oversight, that the charge did not contain the aggravating circumstances of "the teleological nexus" that could trigger a life sentence. If we opted for the shortened procedure, without those aggravating circumstances, my client could get off with as little as twenty years. If we went to the Assize Court he – Cervellati – would have to include those circumstances in the charge and for Abdou Thiam the door to life imprisonment would stand wide open.

He declared his innocence? So did they all.

He thought of me as a serious person and was sure I would not conceive any wrong ideas, such as going to the Assizes in the absurd hope of getting an acquittal. Abdou Thiam would be found guilty anyway, and a court of judges and jury would tear him to shreds. In any case he – Cervellati – had no intention of wasting weeks or even months in the Assize Court.

The shortened procedure is one of the things which in the trade are known as special procedures. As a rule, when the public prosecutor concludes the inquiries in a murder case he asks the judge for the preliminary hearing to commit the accused for trial.

The preliminary hearing serves to verify whether there are sufficient prerequisites for a trial, which, in the case of murder, falls within the competence of the Court of Assizes, composed of both professional judges and a sworn-in jury. If the judge for the preliminary hearing considers that these prerequisites exist, he orders the committal for trial.

The accused, however, has an opportunity to avoid being sent up to the Court of Assizes and to get himself a simplified trial, and this is the shortened procedure.

At the preliminary hearing he can ask, either directly or through his defending counsel, that the trial be determined within what is called the state of the acts. This means that the judge for the preliminary hearing, basing his judgement on the documents provided by the public prosecutor, decides whether there is sufficient evidence to convict the accused. If he finds that such evidence exists, he finds the accused guilty.

It is a far swifter procedure than a normal trial. No witnesses are heard and, except in rare instances, no new evidence is acquired. The public is not admitted and the case is decided by one judge sitting alone. In short, it is an abbreviated procedure that saves the state a great deal of time and money.

Of course, the accused also has an interest in choosing this kind of trial. If convicted, he has the right to a considerable reduction in his sentence. To put it in a nutshell, the state saves money and the accused saves years in prison.

This shortened procedure has another advantage. It is ideal when the accused hasn't much money and cannot afford long hearings, witnesses, experts, examinations and cross-examinations, summings-up, lengthy harangues and so on and so forth.

Opting for the shortened procedure, the accused clearly loses numerous chances of being acquitted, because everything is based on the documents provided by the public prosecutor and the police, who, as a rule, work to get their man, not to let him go.

However, when for the accused the chances of acquittal are few or none even in a normal trial, then the reduced sentence is a really attractive prospect.

From all points of view, therefore, the shortened procedure seemed ideal for Abdou Thiam, who truly had very slim chances of being acquitted.

"Read the indictment and you'll see that it's better for all concerned to do it the short way," concluded Cervellati, dismissing me.

Outside it was raining. A fine, dense, perfectly odious rain.

I was just getting to my feet when Cervellati said it: "Nasty weather, this. I have no trouble with dry cold, perhaps with a fine sunset thrown in. It's this *damp* cold that gets into your bones . . ." He looked at me. I could have said quite a number of things, some of them even amusing from my point of view. Instead I gave a sigh: "It's the same as with heat, Mr Prosecutor. It's not so much the heat, it's the humidity."

10

After the meeting with Cervellati I attended a hearing and negotiated a settlement for a woman accused of fraudulent bankruptcy.

In point of fact, the woman had nothing to do with the bankruptcy, the insolvency, the firm or the law. The real owner of the firm was her husband, who had already gone bust once and had a record of swindling, embezzlement and indecent behaviour.

He had registered his fertilizer business in his wife's name, had made her sign masses of promissory notes, had not paid his workers, had not paid his electricity bills, had not paid his telephone bills, but *had* raided the till.

Naturally the firm had gone bust and the titular owner had been accused of fraudulent bankruptcy. The husband had chivalrously allowed justice to take its course and his wife to be found guilty, albeit with plea-bargaining.

I had been paid the week before, without submitting an invoice. With the money from the till or acquired from goodness knows what other swindle on the part of Signor De Carne.

One of the first things you learn as a criminal lawyer, especially when dealing with types like De Carne, is to get paid in advance.

Obviously you are almost always, or at least very often, paid with money obtained by criminal means.

It shouldn't really be mentioned, but when you

defend a professional pusher who pays you ten, twenty, even thirty million if you manage to get him out of prison, well, you're bound to have some vague doubt about the source of that money.

If you are defending a man arrested for persistent extortion in complicity with persons unknown, and his friends come to the office and tell you not to worry about the fee, they'll take care of it, here too you can make a guess that *that* fee will not be composed of spotlessly clean money.

Let me make it clear that I was no better than the rest of them, even if I did sometimes try to retain a morsel of dignity. Not with types like De Carne, however.

In short, I had in any case been paid in advance with money from an unknown – and dubious – source, I had concluded a decorous plea-bargaining that at least guaranteed the poor woman a suspended sentence, and as far as that morning was concerned I could go home.

I took advantage of a lull in the rain, did my shopping, reached my apartment and had hardly begun to make myself a salad when my mobile rang.

Yes, I was Guido. Of course I remembered her, Melissa. Yes, at dinner with Renato. It had been a very pleasant evening. Liar. No, I didn't mind that she'd got hold of my mobile number, far from it. Did I know who Acid Steel were? Sorry, I didn't. Ah, well there was a concert of this Acid Steel lot in Bari this evening. Well, near Bari anyway. Would I like to go along with her? Yes, but what about tickets? Ah, she had two tickets, in fact two invitations. Fine. Then it's agreed, tell me your address and I'll pick you up. You'll come here? Very well. Ah, you already know where I live. Very good, this evening at eight, yes, don't worry, I won't dress like a lawyer. Ciao. Ciao.

I remembered Melissa very well. About ten days previously my friend Renato, a former hippie now working in the art side of advertising, was celebrating his fortieth birthday. Melissa had arrived in the company of a stumpy little chartered accountant wearing black trousers, a black elasticated pullover, a black Armani-style jacket, and black hair long over the ears, non-existent on top.

She had not passed unobserved. Levantine face, five foot eight, quite unsettling curves. Even an apparently intelligent expression.

The accountant thought he had picked an ace that evening. But instead he had the two of spades with clubs as trumps. No sooner had she entered than Melissa was on friendly terms with practically every male at the party.

She had chatted with me too, no more and no less than with the others, it seemed to me. She had shown interest in the fact that I boxed. She had told me that she was studying biology, that she was going to do postgraduate studies in France, that I was a charming fellow, that I didn't seem like a lawyer at all and that we'd certainly be meeting again.

Then she went on to the next one.

Time was – a year before – when I would have dashed to retrieve her from the jungle of ill-intentioned males who populated the party. I would have thought up something, given her my mobile number, tried to invent excuses for meeting again as soon as possible. And the inky-cloaked accountant could drop dead. He, however, was actively engaged in knocking back one cocktail after another, so he would soon be dead of cirrhosis anyway.

But that evening I did nothing about it.

When the party ended I'd gone home and gone to

bed. When I woke up after the usual four hours, Melissa was already far, far away, practically invisible.

Now, ten days later, she called me on my mobile to invite me to a concert by Acid Steel, who were playing in Bari. Or rather, near Bari. Just like that.

I had an odd feeling. For a moment I was tempted to ring back and say no, I unfortunately had another engagement. Sorry, it had slipped my mind, perhaps some other time.

Then I said out loud, "Brother, you're going *really* mad. *Really* mad. You go to this bloody Acid Steel concert and let's put an end to this nonsense. You're thirty-eight years old and have a pretty long life-expectancy. D'you think you're going to spend it all like this? Go to this bloody concert and be thankful."

Melissa arrived punctually a few minutes after eight. She was on foot and her attire was an incitement to crime.

She said that her car wouldn't start but that she'd come into the centre anyway, and was wondering if we had time to get mine. We did. We got the car and set off in the direction of Taranto.

The concert was in a small, disused industrial warehouse out in the country between Turi and Rutigliano. I'd never have been able to get there on my own.

The atmosphere in the place was semi-clandestine. Some of the audience looked clandestine without the semi.

Luckily, one was not forbidden to smoke.

One was not forbidden to smoke *anything*.

And in fact they were smoking everything and drinking beer. The air was dense with the stench of smoke, beer, beery breath and sweaty armpits. No one was laughing and many seemed absorbed in a dark, mysterious ritual from which I – fortunately – was excluded.

I began to feel uneasy, and the impulse to make a run for it grew and grew.

Melissa talked to everyone and knew everyone. Or maybe she was simply doing a repeat performance of Renato's party. In that case, I thought, I was in the accountant's shoes. The impulse to cut and run redoubled. Worry. Worry. I felt prying eyes on me. More worry.

Then, luckily, Acid Steel started to play.

I have no wish to talk about the two hours of uninterrupted so-called music, partly because my most intense recollection is not the sounds but the smells. The beer, the cigarettes, the joints, the sweat and I don't know what else seemed more and more to fill the air of that gloomy warehouse. For a moment I even had the absurd notion that from one minute to the next it would explode, hurling that deadly cocktail of stenches off into space. The positive aspect of this eventuality was that Acid Steel – whose visible perspiration led one to suppose that they made a determining contribution to the fetor – would also be hurled into space and no one would hear of them ever again.

The warehouse did not explode. Melissa drank five or six beers and smoked several cigarettes. I am not sure that they were only cigarettes, because it was pesky dark and the source of the smells – including that of joints – was indefinable. At a certain point I seemed to see her wash down a few pills with her beer.

I confined myself to smoking my cigarettes and drinking the occasional sip of beer from the bottles Melissa handed me.

When the concert came to an end I refrained from buying the Acid Steel CD on sale at the exit.

Melissa greeted a bunch of characters with whom I feared we might have to spend the evening, but then she took my hand. In the darkness of the churned-up field that served as a car park I felt the blood rush to my face, and elsewhere.

"Shall we go and have a drink?" she gurgled in a strangely suggestive voice, meanwhile stroking the back of my hand with her thumb.

"Maybe we could *eat* something too." I was thinking of the pints of beer already swilling about inside her and of the other unspecified psychoactive substances circulating in her blood and among the neurones.

"You bet. I really feel like something sweet. A crêpe with Nutella or with cream and a dark chocolate sauce."

We returned to Bari and went to the Gauguin, where they made very good crêpes, were polite and nice, and had beautiful photographs on the walls. It was a place I had often been to when I was with Sara, and had not visited since. That evening was the first time.

No sooner inside than I was sorry I'd come. Familiar faces at every table. Some I had to greet, all knew who I was.

Between the tables, the owner and the waiters staring at us. Staring at *me*. I could hear the wheels turning in their heads. I *knew* they'd gossip about me now. I felt like a squalid forty-year-old who takes out teenagers.

Melissa, meanwhile, was relaxed and talking non-stop.

I chose a crêpe with ham, walnuts and mascarpone, plus a small bottle of beer. Melissa had two sweet crêpes, the first with Nutella, hazelnuts and banana, the second with ricotta, raisins and melted chocolate. She drank three glasses of Calvados. She talked a lot. Two or three times she touched my hand. Once, while talking, she suddenly stopped and gave me an intense look, almost imperceptibly biting her lower lip.

They're shooting with a hidden camera, I thought. This girl is an actress, there's a TV camera somewhere, now I'll say or do something ridiculous and someone will pop out and tell me to smile at the audience.

No one popped out. I paid the bill, we left, reached the car and I started up. Melissa said we could round off the evening by having a drink at her place.

"No thanks. You're an alcoholic and maybe something worse. I shall now take you home, *I won't come up*, and then I'll go home to bed." That's what I should have said.

"I'd love to. Maybe just a drop and then we'll get some sleep because tomorrow is a working day." I said exactly that: "maybe just a drop".

Melissa gave me a kiss on the corner of my mouth, lingering over it. She smelt of booze, smoke and a strong perfume that reminded me of something. Then she said that she didn't have much at home and so we'd better go to a bar and buy a few beers.

I wasn't entirely easy in my mind but I stopped in front of an all-night bar, got out and bought *two* beers. To prevent the situation from degenerating.

She lived in an old block of council flats near the television studios. The sort of building populated by five or six foreigners living in one room, old council tenants (a species on the verge of extinction) and students away from home. Melissa came from Minervino Murge.

The entrance had a very dim bulb that shed no light whatever. Melissa lived on the first floor and the stairs smelt of cat pee.

She opened the door and went in first, with me following her into the darkness. Stuffiness and stale cigarette smoke.

When the light went on I saw I was in a minute

hallway that gave onto a study-cum-bedroom on the left. On the right was a closed door that I took to be the bathroom.

"Where is the kitchen?" was my fatuous thought of the moment. And at the same instant she took me by the hand and led me into the bedroom/study/living room. There was a bed against the wall opposite the door, a desk, books everywhere. Books on shelves, stacks of books on the floor, books on the desk, books scattered here and there. There was an old radio–tape recorder, an ashtray containing two squashed filters, a few empty beer bottles and a nearly empty bottle of J&B whisky.

The books ought to have reassured me.

When I enter a house for the first time I check on whether there are books, if they are few, if they are many, if they are too neatly arranged – which is a bad sign – or if they are all over the place – which is a good sign, and so on.

The books in Melissa's tiny home should have given me a good impression. But they didn't.

"Do sit down," said Melissa, pointing to the bed.

I sat, she opened the beers, handed me one and drank more than half of hers without taking the neck of the bottle from her lips. I took a sip, just to show willing. My brain was searching frantically for an excuse to escape. After all, it was nearly two o'clock in the morning, I had to work the following day, we had had a pleasant evening, we would certainly be seeing each other again, don't worry I'll call you, and anyway I've got a slight headache. No, there's nothing the matter except the fact that you're an alcoholic, a drug addict, probably a nymphomaniac and I want to cry. I'll call you, really I will.

While I was struggling to think up something less

pathetic, Melissa – who in another single gulp had finished her beer – slipped off her panties (black) from under her skirt.

She didn't want to waste too much time on preliminaries and other boring formalities. So much was obvious.

And in fact there were no formalities.

I stayed in that place, what with this and that, until nearly daylight.

While she smoked and finished the bottle of whisky she recited the difficulties of living away from home with next to nothing coming from her parents. Of paying the month's rent, of eating – and of *drinking*, I thought – of buying cigarettes, clothes, paying for the mobile, having the odd evening out. And books, of course. The occasional job – hostess, public relations – hardly ever brought in enough.

That month, for example, she was already late with the rent, had an exam to prepare for, and the landlady waiting for nothing better than an excuse to chuck her out.

If she wouldn't be offended, I could lend her a little. No, she wouldn't be offended, but I had to promise that I'd make her pay it back. Of course, don't worry. No, I haven't got half a million in cash, but look, here's 220,000 in my wallet, I'll keep the twenty just in case. Don't worry about it, you'll let me have it back when you can, there's no hurry. I really must go now, because tomorrow, that is today, I have to work.

She gave me her mobile number. Of course I'll call you, I said, screwing up the slip of paper in my pocket, wrenching open the door and fleeing like a scalded cat.

Outside was a leaden dawn, a mouse-coloured sky. The puddles were so black they reflected nothing.

My eyes reflected nothing either.

There came to mind a film I had seen a couple of years before, *The Ghost and the Darkness*, a splendid yarn about big-game hunters and lions.

Val Kilmer asks Michael Douglas, "Have you ever failed?"

The reply: "Only in life."

The next day I changed my sim-card and mobile phone number.

11

The days that followed that night were not memorable.

About a week passed, then we were notified that the inquiries were concluded.

At eight-thirty next morning I was in Cervellati's secretariat to request copies of the file. I made the application, they told me that I could have copies within three days and I left the offices prey to pessimism.

On the Friday my secretary called at the public prosecutor's office, paid the fees, collected the copies and brought them to the office.

I spent Saturday and Sunday reading and re-reading those papers.

I read, smoked, and drank big cups of weak decaffeinated coffee.

I read, smoked, and what I read I didn't like a bit. Abdou Thiam was in a pretty pickle.

It was even worse than I'd thought when I read the detention order.

It looked like one of those cases without any prospects, in which going to the Assizes could lead only to a pointless massacre.

It looked as if Cervellati was right and that the only way of reducing the damage was to opt for the shortened procedure.

The thing that nailed my client most of all was the testimony of the barman. He had made a statement to the carabinieri the day before Abdou was arrested. He had been heard again, a few days later, by the public prosecutor in person.

A perfect witness – for the prosecution.

I read and re-read the two reports, on the look-out for any weak points, but I found almost nothing.

That of the carabinieri was a summary report written in the most classic police-station jargon.

On the 10th day of August 1999 at 19.30 hours, in the offices of the Operations Unit of the Carabinieri of Monopoli, before the undermentioned non-commissioned officers of the criminal police Sergeant-Major Lorussa Antonio, Sergeant Sciancalepore Pasquale and Lance-Corporal Amendolagine Francesco, all of whom are attached to the aforementioned Command, there appeared Antonio Renna, born Noci (Bari) 31.3.1953, resident in Monopoli, Contrada Gorgofreddo 133/c, who when properly questioned as to facts falling within his cognizance stated as follows:

Witness replied: I am the proprietor of the commercial premises denominated "Bar Maracaibo" situated in Contrada Capitolo, Monopoli. During the summer months my premises remain open from seven in the morning until nine at night. In the management of the aforesaid commercial concern I am assisted by my wife and two of my children.

Witness replied: I was acquainted with little Francesco Rubino and in particular with his grandparents, who are proprietors of a villa situated at a distance of approximately 300 yards from my bar. They have been spending holidays in Contrada Capitolo for many years. The grandfather of the child frequently visits my bar to purchase and consume a coffee and smoke a cigarette.

Witness replied: I am acquainted with the non-European citizen whom you inform me is named Abdou Thiam and whom I recognize in the photograph you have submitted for my inspection. He deals in counterfeit leather goods and passes nearly every day in front of my bar on his way to the beaches where he sells his wares. On occasion he visits my bar to take refreshment.

Witness replied: I recall having observed the aforesaid non-European citizen on the afternoon of the boy's disappearance. He passed in front of my commercial premises without the bag which he habitually carries with him and he was walking rapidly as if in haste. He did not stop at the bar.

Witness replied: The non-European citizen was proceeding in a northerly-southerly direction. In effect, he was coming from the direction of Monopoli and proceeding towards the beaches.

Witness replied: The house of the missing boy's grandparents is situated at about 300 yards south with respect to my bar. If I am not mistaken, it stands almost opposite Duna Beach.

Witness replied: I am unable to indicate with any precision the hour at which I saw the non-European citizen pass. It might be between 18.00 and 18.30 hours or perhaps even 19.00 hours.

Witness replied: I did not observe the non-European citizen pass on his way back in the opposite direction. That day I did not see him again at all.

Witness replied: If I remember rightly, I learned of the disappearance of the child the day subsequent to the fact. Before being summoned by you carabinieri I had not been aware of being in possession of information relevant to the inquiries, and that is to say it had not occurred to me to connect the passing of Thiam that afternoon with the disappearance of the child. If it had occurred to me, I would have presented myself of my own accord to collaborate with the law.

I have nothing more to add and in witness thereof I append my signature.

Cognizance is taken of the fact that the present statement, due to the unavailability of recording equipment, has been drawn up only in summary form.

Read, confirmed and undersigned.

The evidence given to Cervellati was complete, in the sense that it was recorded and stenotyped. Here the person in possession of the facts did not use improbable expressions such as "the aforesaid commercial premises" or "purchase and consume a coffee". But the upshot was the same.

On 13 August 1999 at 11.00 hours, in the offices of the Public Prosecutor, and before the Prosecutor Dr Giovanni Cervellati, assisted in the drafting of the present document by legal clerk Biancofiore Giuseppe, there appeared Antonio Renna, whose particulars are already documented.

It is here noted that the present statement will be documented in full by means of shorthand typing.

Question: Well then, Signor Renna, some days ago you made a statement to the carabinieri. The first thing I want to ask you is whether you confirm it. You remember what you said, don't you?

Answer: Yes, yes, sir.

Question: So you confirm it?

Answer: Yes, I confirm it.

Question: Let us, however, recapitulate what you said. In the first place, I take it you already knew the non-European citizen Abdou Thiam?

Answer: Yes, sir. Not by name, though. The name I learned from the carabinieri. I recognized him from the photograph they showed me.

Question: You know him because he often passed in front of your bar and on some occasions had something to drink. Is that so?

Answer: Yes, sir.

Question: Would you care to tell me about the day the child disappeared? That day, that afternoon or evening, you saw Thiam, didn't you?

Answer: Yes, sir. He passed my bar between half-past six and seven.

Question: Did he have his bag of goods?

Answer: No, he didn't have the bag and he was rushing along.

Question: Do you mean that he was running or that he was in a hurry?

Answer: No, he was hurrying. It wasn't that he was exactly running, but he was walking quickly.

Question: In which direction was he going?

Answer: Towards the beaches, which is more or less the direction to take to the child's grandparents' house —

Question: All right, towards the beaches. That means from north to south, if I have understood correctly.

Answer: Yes, from Monopoli towards the beaches.

Question: Did you see him pass on the way back?

Answer: No.

Question: You told the carabinieri that you knew the boy, and his family also, particularly the grandparents. Do you confirm this?

Answer: Yes, I confirm it. The grandparents have a villa 300 or 400 yards past my bar, more or less in the direction the young Moroccan was going.

Question: Moroccan?

Answer: Non-European citizen then. We use the word Moroccan for all these young niggers.

Question: Ah, I see. Do you recall any other detail, any other fact relevant to the inquiries?

Answer: No, sir, but in my opinion it absolutely must have been that Moroccan because —

Question: No, Signor Renna, you must not express personal opinions. If some other fact comes to mind well and good, if not we can bring this statement to an end. Does any other specific fact come to mind?

Answer: No.

Abdou's interrogation by the public prosecutor was little less than catastrophic.

It had taken place at night, in the carabinieri station in Bari, with a defence lawyer appointed by the court.

The report was a summary, without recording or stenotyped record.

On 11 August 1999, at 01.30 hours, in the offices of the Operations Unit of the Carabinieri of Bari, before the Public Prosecutor Dr Giovanni Cervellati, assisted in the drafting of the present statement by Sergeant Sciancalepore Pasquale, attached to the Carabinieri of Monopoli, there appeared Abdou Thiam, born 4 March 1968 in Dakar, Senegal, and domiciled in Bari, Via Ettore Fieramosca 162.

Note is made of the presence of Avvocato Giovanni Colella, appointed for this occasion by the court to defend the said Thiam, the latter not having chosen to appoint a lawyer of his own.

The Public Prosecutor charges the said Abdou Thiam with the offences of unlawful restraint and murder of Francesco Rubino and gives him a summary of the evidence against him.

He informs him that he has the right not to answer questions, but that the inquiries will continue even if he does not answer.

The suspect states: I intend to answer and expressly renounce any time for defence.

Counsel for defence has no observation to make.

In answer to questioning, the suspect replies: I deny the charges. I am not acquainted with any Francesco Rubino. This name means nothing to me.

Suspect replies: On the afternoon of August 5th I believe I went to Naples in my car. I went to visit some fellow country-men of mine whose names I am, however, unable to indicate. We met, as on other occasions, in the neighbourhood of the Central Station. I am unable to provide useful indications for the identification of these fellow countrymen of mine and I am unable to indicate anyone in a position to confirm that I was in Naples that day.

Suspect replies: I refuse to admit that I went to Monopoli that day. When I returned from Naples, I remained in Bari.

Suspect replies: I take cognizance of the fact that Your Excellency points out to me that the version I have provided appears totally unworthy of credit. I can only confirm that I went to Naples that day and never went at all to Monopoli or adjacent areas.

Suspect replies: I take cognizance of the fact that there is a witness who saw me in the vicinity of Capitolo on the very afternoon of August 5th. I take cognizance of Your Excellency's advice that I should make a confession. I take cognizance of the fact that by confessing I might mitigate my situation. I must, however, confirm that I did not commit the murder of which I am accused and do not understand how anyone says that they saw me on August 5th in the vicinity of Capitolo.

At this point it is placed on record that the suspect is shown a photograph found in his lodgings in the course of the search there carried out.

Having viewed the aforesaid photograph, Thiam states:

I know the boy portrayed in the photo but I learn only now that his name is Francesco Rubino. I knew him by the name of Ciccio.

When questioned, the suspect replies: It was the little boy who gave me the photograph. It wasn't me who took the snap. I don't even own a camera.

At 02.30 hours the taking of the record is suspended to enable the suspect to consult with his defence counsel.

At 03.20 hours the record is resumed.

When questioned, the suspect replies: Even after talking to the lawyer – who advised me to tell the truth – I have nothing to add to the statements I have already made.

The defence had no observations to make.
Read, confirmed and signed.

Two days after his arrest, the hearing took place before the magistrate in charge of preliminary investigations. Abdou had availed himself of the right not to reply.

Since then he had not been further interrogated.

I re-read the order for precautionary detention. I read the decision of the regional appeals court by which – rightly, in view of the evidence – Abdou's appeal was rejected.

I read and re-read every single document.

The statements of the habitués of that beach who said they had often seen Abdou stop and talk to the child. The statements of the Senegalese who spoke about the car-washing and the other Senegalese who had said that he had not seen Abdou at the usual beach the day after the child's disappearance.

The scene-of-the-crime report about the finding of the boy's body. The report of the search of Abdou's home and the list of books confiscated.

The report of the police doctor, which I leafed through swiftly, avoiding the photographs.

The upsetting, useless statements of the boy's parents and grandparents.

On the Sunday evening my eyes were smarting and I left the flat. The mistral was blowing and it was cold.

That pitiless cold peculiar to March, which makes spring seem a long way off.

I had thought of taking a stroll, but I changed my mind, fetched the car and headed north along the old State Road No. 16.

Bruce Springsteen was booming from the loud-speakers and in my head as I drove through the coastal towns, all deserted and swept by the north-west wind.

I stopped in front of the cathedral in Trani, facing the sea. I lit a cigarette. The harmonica screeched in my ears and in my soul.

The terrible words were written especially for my desperate solitude.

> *But I remember us riding in my brother's car*
> *Her body tan and wet down at the reservoir*
> *At night on them banks I'd lie awake*
> *And pull her close just to feel each breath she'd take*
> *Now those memories come back to haunt me*
> *They haunt me like a curse.*

At dawn I woke up shivering with cold, the taste of tobacco smoke in my mouth. My hand was still clutching the mobile, which I'd stared at interminably before falling asleep, thinking of calling Sara.

12

The code of criminal procedure requires that at least twenty days elapse between the announcement that inquiries have been concluded and the application for committal for trial. The public prosecutors nearly always take much longer. Months, sometimes.

Cervellati filed the request for committal on the twenty-first day. Obsessive punctuality was typical of him. You could accuse him of practically everything, but not of letting documents stack up on his desk.

The preliminary hearing was fixed for early May. The judge was Ms Carenza, and all in all it could have been worse.

Among us defence lawyers La Carenza was considered one of the good ones. The shortened procedure became an increasingly interesting possibility. Abdou really did have a chance of getting off with twenty years.

In about 2010, with good conduct, he would be out on parole.

While I was having these thoughts, still holding the note with the date of the hearing, I had an uneasy feeling. A feeling that stayed with me all day long, without my being able to find a reason for it.

The same uneasy feeling took hold of me when, a week later, I had to visit Abdou in prison to explain to him why it was to his advantage to accept the shortened procedure, take twenty years or so instead of life, and begin chalking up the days on the wall of his cell.

Abdou was, or seemed, thinner than last time. He

didn't want to tell me how he had come by the enormous bruise on his right cheekbone. As he listened to what I had to say, he looked at the grainy lines in the wooden table, without making a single gesture suggesting that he'd understood or wondered what I was talking about. Not so much as a nod. Nothing.

When I had finished explaining what was the best solution for his case, Abdou remained silent for several minutes. I offered him a Marlboro but he didn't take it. Instead he pulled out a packet of Diana Red and lit one of those.

He spoke only when he had finished the cigarette and the silence was becoming unbearable.

"If we choose the shortened procedure, have I any chance of being acquitted?"

He was just too intelligent. With the shortened procedure he would be found guilty for sure. I had not told him that but he knew implicitly.

I felt awkward as I replied.

"Technically, yes. Theoretically, yes."

"What does that mean?"

"It means that in theory the judge could acquit you, but on the basis of what is in the documents produced by the public prosecutor, which is what the judge will base her decision on if we opt for the shortened procedure, it is extremely unlikely."

I paused, and came to the conclusion that I didn't feel like beating about the bush.

"Let's say that it's practically impossible. On the other hand, with the shortened procedure you'd avoid —"

"Yes, I've understood that. I'd avoid a life sentence. In other words, if we choose the shortened procedure I am certain to be convicted but they'll give me a discount. Isn't that it?"

My embarrassment grew. I felt the blood rising to my face.

"Yes, that's it."

"And if we don't choose this shortened procedure, what happens then?"

"You will be committed for trial before the Court of Assizes. This means you will be tried in public before two judges, and six jurors, who are ordinary citizens. If you are found guilty by the Court of Assizes, you are in danger of life imprisonment."

"But I do have a chance of being acquitted?"

"A slender one."

"But more than with the shortened procedure?"

I didn't answer at once. I took a deep breath. I passed a hand across my face.

"More. Not much more, but more. Bear in mind the fact that with the shortened procedure you are practically certain of being found guilty, whereas before the Court of Assizes something can always happen. All the witnesses have to be questioned by the public prosecutor and then we can cross-examine them. That means that I, as your counsel, can cross-examine them. One of them might not confirm his evidence, one of them might contradict himself, some new factor might arise. But it is a very grave risk."

"What are my chances?"

"Hard to give a figure. A 5 or 10 per cent chance at the best."

"Why do you want to choose the shortened way?"

"What do you mean, why? Because it's the thing that suits the case best. With this judge you get off with the lightest possible sentence, and in —"

"I didn't do what they say I did."

I took another deep breath, got out a cigarette. I

didn't know what to say, so naturally I said the wrong thing.

"Listen, Abdou. I don't know what you've done. But for a lawyer it can be better not to know what his client has done. This helps him to be more lucid, to make better decisions without allowing himself to be influenced by emotion. Do you see what I'm getting at?"

Abdou gave an imperceptible nod. His eyes seemed to have sunk into their black orbits. Averting my gaze, I continued.

"If we don't opt for the shortened procedure, if we go before the Assize Court, it's as if we were playing cards with your life, with very few chances of winning. And then, to play it that way takes money, lots of money. A trial before the Assize Court takes a long time and costs a great deal."

I realized I had said something stupid even as the words were coming out of my mouth. And at the same time I realized why I was uneasy in my mind.

"You mean that because I can't pay enough money it's better to opt for the shortened procedure. Is that it?"

"I didn't say that." My tone of voice went up a notch.

"How much money does it take to have a trial before the Court of Assizes?"

"The money is not the problem. The problem is that if we go before the Assize Court you'll get a life sentence and your life is finished."

"My life is finished anyway if they convict me for killing a child. How much money?"

I suddenly felt dead tired. An enormous, irresistible weariness came over me. I let my shoulders slump and realized then how tense they had been until that moment.

"Not less than forty or fifty million. If we wanted to

make investigations for the defence – and in this case we would probably need them – a good deal more."

Abdou seemed stunned. He swallowed, with some difficulty, and gave the impression of wanting to say something but failing. Then he began to follow a train of thought from which I was excluded. He looked up, shook his head, then moved his lips in the recitation of some soundless, mysterious litany.

In the end he covered his face with his hands, rubbed them up and down two or three times, then lowered them and looked me in the face again. He said nothing.

I had an unbearable buzzing in my ears and spoke chiefly to drown it.

We didn't have to decide that very morning. There was still a month left before the preliminary hearing, when we might or might not opt for the shortened procedure. And then we had to talk to Abajaje. The question of money was the least of our problems. I would give the documents another reading, look for other rays of hope. Right now I had to be off, but we'd meet again soon. If he needed anything he could let me know, even by telegram.

Abdou said not a word. When I touched his shoulder in greeting I felt a body totally inert.

I escaped, pursued by his phantoms. And my own.

13

When I left home the next morning I realized there was a removal in progress. New tenants were moving in to our building. I registered the fact in my mind and uttered a quick prayer that we were not getting a family with Pomeranian dogs and rowdy children. Then my thoughts turned to other matters.

That day was to see the beginning of a trial that the newspapers had dubbed "Dogfighting".

To be exact, it was not the papers which called it that, but the police who had carried out the operation some ten months previously. The papers had confined themselves to repeating the code name for investigations into organized dogfights and the related clandestine betting ring.

It had all started with a denouncement by the Anti-Vivisection League and had continued because the inquiries had been entrusted to a truly exceptional policeman, Chief Inspector Carmelo Tancredi.

Inspector Tancredi had succeeded in infiltrating the clandestine betting ring, had attended the dogfights, made recordings, managed to find out where the breeders kept their animals, and noted how and where the bets changed hands. In short, he had nailed them.

He was a small man with a gaunt face and a large black moustache that looked completely out of place on it. He seemed the most innocuous person on earth.

He was, in fact, the most intelligent, honest and deadly cop I have ever met.

He worked in the sixth section of the flying squad. The one that dealt with sexual offences and everything that the other sections – the more important ones – wouldn't touch with a bargepole.

He had always refused to leave that job, even though they had often tried to induce him to transfer to the Criminalpol, the anti-drug section or even the Secret Service. All jobs in which he would have worked less for more pay.

On one occasion I'd had a visit from the parents of a nine-year-old child who had been sexually abused by his swimming instructor.

They wanted advice on whether or not to report the incident, on what they would be up against if they did, and especially what the child would be up against. I took them to Tancredi and saw how he spoke to the child, and saw how the child – who until then had answered in monosyllables, never raising his eyes – spoke in turn to Tancredi, looked him in the face and even began to smile.

The swimming instructor ended up behind bars and, what's more, stayed there. Just as ending up behind bars and staying there was the fate of most of the maniacs, rapists and child abusers who had had the bad luck to cross the path of Inspector Tancredi.

The organizers of the dogfights were similarly unlucky.

The first strike of the operation led to the seizure of eight pit-bull terriers, five Fila Brasileros, three Rottweilers and three bandogs, these last being a deadly cross between Alsatian and pit bull. They were all champions, each worth between twenty and a hundred million. The most priceless was a three-year-old bandog called Harley-Davidson. He had won twenty-seven fights, invariably killing his opponent. He was considered a sort of champion of southern Italy, and the inquiries established that there were preparations in hand for a contest for the All-Italy title against a pit bull which fought in the Province of Milan. A contest worth over half a billion lire in bets.

Dozens of videos of dogfights, not to mention fights between dogs and pumas, and even dogs and pigs, were confiscated as well. The owners of a kennels, where not only the animals but also arms and drugs were found, were arrested. Among those charged were a very well-known vet, a number of breeders and three people who had previously been arrested and found guilty on charges of association with the Mafia and trafficking in drugs. Needless to say, they had all been released, because the length of time for which they could be held had run out.

Anyway, that late March morning the trial resulting from Operation Dogfighting was scheduled to begin. The Anti-Vivisection League planned to start civil proceedings and had appointed me to represent them.

There were only two precedents of trials concerning cruelty to animals in which the Anti-Vivisection League and the Society for the Prevention of Cruelty to Dogs had been admitted as civil parties. The matter was anything but a walkover, so I'd had to work hard the previous afternoon to find convincing arguments to present in court. And to clear my mind of the meeting with Abdou.

Purely because I was well-prepared that morning and ready to do my job in a professional fashion, the preliminary hearing was immediately adjourned on account of – in the words of the same old formula that was always used – "the excessive workload involved in the hearing and the impossibility of concluding all the proceedings at today's date".

The adjournment was immediate, but it was ordered only after four hours of hearing. And waiting.

In short, at about half-past two in the afternoon, the judge read out the formula and adjourned the trial until December, since, as all the defendants were at liberty, there was no hurry.

I was used to it. I donned my raincoat, picked up my briefcase, made my way through the now deserted law courts and set off for home.

I was walking along Via Abate Gimma, towards Corso Cavour, when I heard myself called from behind, "Avvocato, Avvocato", in an accent from somewhere inland which I couldn't place.

There were two of them, and they seemed to have stepped straight out of a documentary on suburban thuggery. The smaller one came up very close and spoke, while the bigger one hung back a little and looked at me through half-closed eyes, as if measuring me up.

The small man was a friend of – he said the name – whom I knew well because he had been a client of mine.

His voice conveyed a forced, almost diplomatic politeness. I said I had no recollection of his friend and that if they wanted to speak about professional matters they could make an appointment and come to the office.

They had no wish to come to the office and, according to the small man, I should stay calm. Very calm. The diplomatic tone hadn't lasted long.

They knew that I intended to represent those arse-holes of the Anti-Vivisection League, but it was better for all concerned if I minded my own business.

I took a deep breath through the nose, at the same time placing my briefcase on the bonnet of a car, then pronounced the four syllables which, ever since I was a child, had always been the prelude to a street fight: "What if I don't?"

The small man opened with a wide, clumsy blow with his right. I parried with my left and almost simultaneously delivered a straight right to the face. He fell back, cursing and calling to his friend to give me the works.

The big man was a lumbering great oaf, six foot four and eighteen stone at a guess, much of it paunch. From the way he covered the space between us and squared up to attack, I realized he was a southpaw. And in fact he started with a left swing, which was probably his best punch. If the fist had connected, no doubt it would have hurt, but this lout was moving in slow motion. I parried with my right forearm and went instinctively for his liver with a left hook, doubling with a straight right to the chin.

The big man had a glass jaw. He stayed on his feet for a moment, motionless, with a queer look of surprise on his face. Then he fell.

I resisted the temptation to kick him in the face. Or to insult him; or to insult them both.

I picked up my briefcase and left, suddenly aware of the blood throbbing in my temples. The small man had stopped swearing.

I turned the corner, walked for another block and then stopped. They were not following. No one was following, and since it was three in the afternoon the street was deserted. Putting down my briefcase, I raised my hands in front of my face and saw they were trembling violently. My right hand was also beginning to hurt.

I remained like that for a few seconds, then I shrugged. An infantile smile flickered on my lips. I went on home.

14

The next day I found my car with four slashed tyres and a deep scratch – the work of a knife or a screwdriver – running the whole length of the body.

Rather than anger at the damage, I felt humiliated. I found myself reflecting on what it is like for someone to come home and find the place turned upside down by burglars. Next I thought of all the petty thieves I had defended and got off.

Lastly, it occurred to me that my brain was turning to pulp and I was becoming pathetic. So, luckily, I dropped moral speculation and made an attempt to be practical.

I called up a client of mine who had a certain reputation in criminal circles in Bari and the surrounding province. He came to the office and I told him the story, including the street-fight. I said I didn't want to go to the police or the carabinieri, but I would if these people forced my hand. In my opinion we were even. I would pay for the damage to the car and they, whoever they were, could nurse their bruises and leave me to get on with my work in peace.

My client said I was right. He also said that they really ought to pay to repair my car and provide new tyres. I said that I'd get the car done up and I didn't want new tyres.

It had occurred to me that neither did I want a summons for receiving stolen goods, seeing that they certainly wouldn't have gone and bought them from an authorized dealer. But this I didn't say.

All I wanted was for everyone to stay put and not go making trouble for anyone else. He didn't push the point, and gave me a nod signifying respect. A different kind of respect from that usually paid to a lawyer.

He said he'd let me know within two days.

He was as good as his word. He came back to the office two days later and mentioned a name that carried weight in certain circles. That person sent word offering his apologies for what had happened. It had been an accident – two accidents in fact, thought I, but let's not split hairs – that would not be repeated. He, however, was at my disposal should I need anything.

The story finished there.

Apart from the two million lire I had to fork out to put the car in order.

A few days later I discovered the identity of the new tenant in our building. Or rather, the tenant*ess.*

About half-past nine in the evening I had just come back from the gym and was about to thaw two chicken breasts, grill them and prepare a salad, when the bell rang.

I spent a few seconds wondering what had happened. Then it registered that it must be my own doorbell, and while on my way to answer it I realized that this must be the first time anyone had rung it since I'd been living here. I felt a pang of melancholy, then I opened the door.

At last she'd found someone in. It was the fourth time she'd tried my door but there was never any answer. Did I really live alone? She was the new tenant, on the seventh floor. She had introduced herself to all the other tenants in the building, I was the last. Her name was Margherita. Margherita, and I didn't catch the surname.

She gave me her hand across the invisible frontier of the doorway. It was a fine, masculine hand, large and strong.

Certain women – and especially certain men – give you a strong handshake but you realize at once that it's for show. They want to make themselves out to be decisive, no-nonsense people, but the strength is only in the hand and arm. What I mean is, it doesn't come from inside. Some people can actually crush your hand, but it's as if they were doing body-building.

There are others, if only a few, who when they shake your hand tell you that there's something behind the muscles. I held Margherita's hand for maybe a second or two more than necessary but she went on smiling.

Then I asked her awkwardly if she'd care to come in. No, thank you, she had just stopped by to introduce herself. She was actually on her way home after being out the whole day. She had a mass of things to do, what with having just moved in. When things were more organized, she'd ask me up for a cup of tea.

She had a good smell about her. A mixture of fresh air, dry and clean, a masculine, leathery smell.

"Don't be sad," she said as she made for the staircase.

Just like that.

When she was already out of sight I realized that I had never really looked at her. I went back inside, half closed my eyes and tried to reproduce her face in my mind. I couldn't do it. I wasn't sure I'd recognize her if I saw her in the street.

In the kitchen the chicken breasts had thawed in the microwave. But I no longer felt like having them simply grilled, so I got out a recipe book I kept in the kitchen but had never used.

Tasty chicken rissoles. That sounded just the job. At least, the name did. I read the recipe and was glad to see I had all the ingredients.

Before starting I opened a bottle of Salice Salentino, tasted it, and then looked for a CD to listen to while I was cooking.

White Ladder.

The syncopated rhythm of "Please Forgive Me" started and then, almost at once, came the voice of David Gray. I stayed near the speakers to listen until it got to the part of the song I liked best.

> *I won't ever have to lie*
> *I won't ever have to say goodbye . . .*
> *Every time I look at you*
> *Every time I look at you.*

Then I went back to the kitchen and got down to work.

I boiled the chicken and minced it, along with a couple of ounces of cooked ham that had been in the fridge for some days. Then I put the meat into a bowl together with an egg, some grated Parmesan, nutmeg, salt and black pepper. I stirred the mixture with a wooden spoon before kneading it with my hands, having added some breadcrumbs. I shaped the mixture into rissoles the size of an egg, then dipped them into beaten egg to which I'd added salt and a little wine, then rolled them in breadcrumbs to which I'd added another pinch of nutmeg, and finally sizzled them in olive oil over a moderate flame.

I drained the rissoles – which smelled delicious – on kitchen paper and prepared a salad with balsamic vinegar dressing. I laid the table with a cloth, real plates, real cutlery, and before sitting down to eat I went and changed the CD.

Simon and Garfunkel. *The Concert in Central Park.*

I pushed "skip" until number 16 came up. "The Boxer."

I stood and listened to it until the last verse. My favourite.

> *In the clearing stands a boxer*
> *And a fighter by his trade*
> *And he carries the reminders*
> *Of every glove that laid him down*
> *Or cut him, till he cried out*
> *In his anger and his shame*
> *I'm leaving, I am leaving*
> *But the fighter still remains . . .*

Then I turned off the CD player and went to eat.

The rissoles were excellent. So was the salad, while the wine had a bouquet and reflections danced in the glass.

I wasn't sad that evening.

15

"The fact is that we have opted for American-style trials, but we lack the preparation the Americans have. We lack the cultural basis for accusatory trials. Look at the questioning and cross-questioning in American or British trials. And then look at ours. They can do it, we can't. We never will be able to, because we are children of the Counter-Reformation. One cannot rebel against one's own cultural destiny."

Thus, during a pause in a trial in which we were fellow counsels for the defence, spake Avvocato Cesare Patrono. A Prince of the Forum. Mason and Millionaire.

I had heard him express that idea about a hundred times since the new code of criminal procedure had come into force in 1989.

It was to be understood that *others* couldn't do it. Other lawyers – certainly not him – and especially the public prosecutors.

Patrono liked to speak ill of everything and everyone. In conversations in the corridors – but even in court – he loved to humiliate his colleagues and, most of all, he loved to intimidate and embarrass magistrates.

For some unknown reason he had a liking for me. He was always cordial towards me and occasionally had me assist him in the defence, which was big business, from a financial standpoint.

He had just finished expressing his views on the current criminal procedure when there emerged from the courtroom, still wearing her robe, Alessandra Mantovani, Assistant Public Prosecutor.

She hailed from Verona, and had asked to be transferred to Bari to join her lover. Behind her in Verona she had left a rich husband and a very comfortable life.

As soon as she had moved to Bari her lover had left her. He explained that he needed his freedom, that things between them had gone well up to that point thanks to the distance, which prevented boredom and routine. That he needed time to think things over. In short, the whole classic load of shit.

Alessandra Mantovani had found herself in Bari, alone, with her bridges burnt behind her. She had stayed on without a murmur.

I liked her a lot. She was everything a good public prosecutor ought to be, or a good policeman, which comes to more or less the same thing.

In the first place she was intelligent and honest. Then she didn't like crooks – of any sort – but she didn't spend her time eating her heart out at the thought that most of them would get off scot-free. Above all, when she was wrong she was up to admitting it, without argument.

We had become friends, or something like it. Enough to lunch together sometimes, and occasionally tell each other something of our personal histories. Not enough for anything more to happen between us, even if our presumed affair was one of the many bits of gossip that did the rounds of the courthouse.

Patrono detested La Mantovani. Because she was a woman, because she was an investigating magistrate, because she was more intelligent and tougher than he was. Even though, naturally, he would never have admitted it.

"Here, Signora," – he called all women magistrates

Signora, not Dottoressa or Judge, to make them nervous and unsettle them – "come and listen to this story. It's the latest, really a peach."

La Mantovani stepped nearer and looked him in the eye, tilted her head to one side and said not a word. A slight nod – yes, go on and try to tell your story – and the ghost of a smile. It was not a warm smile. The mouth had moved but the eyes were utterly still. And cold.

Patrono told his story. It wasn't the latest, or even very recent.

It was the story of a young man of good family talking to a friend and telling him how he is about to marry an ex-prostitute. The youngster explains to his friend that his fiancée's ex-profession is no problem as far as he is concerned. No problem either are his fiancée's parents, who are drug pushers, thieves and pimps. Everything therefore seems hunky-dory, but the lad confides to his friend that he has one really big worry.

"What's that?" asks the friend.

How's he going to tell the bride's parents that his father is a magistrate?

Patrono had his snigger all to himself. Personally, I was embarrassed.

"I've got a rather good one too. About animals," said La Mantovani. "Snake and Fox are wandering in the woods. At a certain point it starts to rain and they both take shelter in an underground tunnel, going in at opposite ends. They begin making their way along the tunnel, where it's pitch dark, getting nearer and nearer each other until they meet. They actually bump into each other.

"The tunnel is very narrow and there's very little room for them to pass. In fact, for one to pass the other has to flatten himself against the wall, in other words give way.

89

"But neither of them is willing to give way and so they start to quarrel.

" 'Move over and let me pass.'

" 'Move over yourself.'

" 'Who d'you think you are?'

" 'Who *are* you anyway?'

" 'You tell me first.'

" 'No, my dear, you tell me first who *you* are.' And so on and so forth.

"In short, the situation seems to have reached an impasse and the two of them don't know how to get out of it, partly because neither wants to take the initiative of attacking the other, not knowing who he is up against.

"Fox then has an idea. 'Listen, it's no use going on quarrelling, because that way we'll be in here all day. Let's have a game to solve the problem. I'll stay still and you touch me and try to guess who I am. Then you stay still, and I'll touch you and try to guess who you are. Whoever finds out the identity of the other wins and can pass first. What d'you think of that?'

" 'It's an idea,' says Snake. 'I agree, but I have first guess.'

"So Snake, moving sinuously, starts touching Fox.

" 'Now then, what long, pointed ears you have, what a sharp muzzle, what soft fur, what a bushy tail . . . You must be Fox!'

"Fox is rather miffed, but has to admit that the other has got him.

" 'However, now it's my turn, because if I guess right we'll be even and we'll have to find another way of deciding who goes first.'

"And he starts to touch Snake, who in the meanwhile has stretched out on the floor of the tunnel.

" 'What a small head you have, you don't have

any ears, you're long and slimy . . . And you have no balls!

" 'You wouldn't by any chance be a lawyer?' "

I lowered my eyelids and laughed to myself. Patrono tried to laugh too, but failed. He came out with a sarcastic cackle and tried to say something, but nothing equal to the occasion occurred to him. He didn't know how to lose.

La Mantovani took off her robe, said she was going to her office, that we'd all be meeting when the hearing resumed and went her way.

Every so often, a real man, I thought.

16

Some days passed and then I got a telephone call from Abajaje.

She wanted to see me. Soon.

I told her she could come that very day, at eight in the evening, when the office closed. That way we'd be able to talk more calmly.

She arrived almost half an hour late, and this amazed me. It didn't fit with the image I'd formed of her.

When I heard the bell ring I was already beginning to think of leaving.

I crossed the empty offices, opened the door and saw her. In the middle of the unlit landing.

She came in, dragging a big box. It contained the books and a few other belongings of Abdou, including an envelope with several dozen photographs.

I told her we could go through and talk in my room, but she shook her head. She was in a hurry. She remained where she was, one step inside the door, opened her bag and took out a roll of banknotes similar to the one she produced the first time she came to the office.

She held out the money and, without looking me in the face, began talking quickly. This time her accent was very noticeable. As strong as a smell.

She had to leave. She had to return to Aswan. She was forced, she was forced – she said – to return to Egypt.

I asked when and why, and her explanation

became confused. Broken at times by words I didn't understand.

She had taken her final exams more than a week before. In theory she should have gone straight back, and in fact all the other scholarship holders had already left.

She had stayed on, asking for an extension of the grant, claiming that she had to do further work on some subjects. The extension had been refused and yesterday she had had a fax from her country ordering her to return. If she didn't do so, and at once, she would lose her position at the Ministry of Agriculture.

She had no choice, she said. Even if she stayed she could do nothing to help Abdou. Without money or a job.

Without anywhere to live, since they had already told her to vacate her room at the annexe as soon as possible.

She would go back to Nubia and try to obtain temporary leave. She would do everything she could to come back to Italy.

She had collected all the money she could to pay for Abdou's defence, meaning me. It came to nearly three million. I must do all I could, *all* I could to help him.

No, Abdou didn't know yet. She would tell him tomorrow, at visiting time.

However – she repeated, too quickly and without looking at me – she'd do everything she could to come back to Italy. Soon.

We both knew it wasn't true.

Curse it, I thought. Curse it, curse it, curse it.

I had an urge to insult her for leaving me alone with all the responsibility.

I didn't want that responsibility.

I had an urge to insult her because I saw myself

in her unexpected mediocrity, in her cowardice. I recognized myself with unbearable clarity.

There passed through my mind the time when Sara had talked about the possibility of having a baby. It was one October afternoon and I said that I didn't think the right moment had yet come. She looked at me and nodded without saying anything. She never mentioned it again.

I did not insult Abajaje. I listened to her justifications without saying a word.

When she had finished, she backed away, as if afraid of turning her back on me.

I was left standing near the door, with the cardboard box containing Abdou's things, holding the roll of banknotes. Then I picked up the telephone on my secretary's desk and without really thinking rang Sara's number, which had been my number.

It rang five times, then someone answered.

The voice was nasal, fairly young-sounding.

"Yes?" The tone was that of a man who feels at home. Maybe he's just back from work, and when the telephone rang he was loosening his tie, and now while he's answering he's taking off his jacket and tossing it onto a sofa.

For some unknown reason I didn't hang up.

"Is Stefania in?"

"No, there's no one here called Stefania. You've got the wrong number."

"Oh, I'm sorry. Could you please tell me what number I've rung?"

He told me and I even wrote it down. To be certain I'd heard right.

I looked for a long time at that piece of paper, my brain circling round and round a nasal voice, faceless, on the telephone in my own home.

17

"That was a lovely film this evening. What are the actors' names again?"

"Harry is Billy Crystal. Sally, Meg Ryan."

"Wait, how did it go . . . the bit with the dream about the Olympics?"

" 'Had my dream again where I'm making love, and the Olympic judges are watching. I'd nailed the compulsories, so this is it, the finals. I got a 9.8 from the Canadians, a perfect 10 from the Americans, and my mother, disguised as an East German judge, gave me 5.6.' "

She bursts out laughing. How I love her laugh, I thought.

A person's laugh is important because you can't cheat. To know if someone is genuine or fake, the only sure way is to watch – and listen to – his laugh. People who are really worthwhile are the ones who know how to laugh.

She made me jump by touching my arm.

"Tell me your three favourite films."

"*Chariots of Fire, Big Wednesday, Picnic at Hanging Rock.*"

"You're the first who's ever answered like that . . . quickly. Without thinking."

"This favourite film game is one I often play myself. So you might say I was ready for it. What are yours?"

"Number one is *Blade Runner*. No doubt about it."

" 'I've seen things you people wouldn't believe. Attack ships on fire off the shoulder of Orion. I watched C-beams glitter in the dark near the Tannhauser gate. And all those moments will be lost in time, like tears in rain. Time – to – die.' "

"Well done. It's said just like that. 'Time – to – die.' With the words spaced out. And then he releases the dove."

I nodded and she went on talking.

"I'll tell you the other films. *American Graffiti* and *Manhattan*. Tomorrow perhaps I'll tell you a couple of others – *Blade Runner* is a fixture – but that's them for today. I've often said *Metropolis*, for example."

"Why these for today?"

"I don't know. Come on, shall we go on playing?"

"All right. Let's try this game. An extraterrestrial arrives on our planet and you have to give him an example of what's best on earth, so as to persuade him to stay. You must offer him an object, a book, a song, a quote or, well there'd also be films but we've already done those."

"Good idea. I already know the quotation. It's Malraux: 'The homeland of a man who can choose is where the biggest clouds gather.' "

We remained for a moment in silence. When she was on the point of speaking, I interrupted her.

"You must do me a favour. Will you?"

"Yes. What is it?"

"If you fall madly in love with me, I'd like you to tell me at once. Don't trust me to know instinctively. Please. Is that all right with you?"

"Fair enough. Does the same hold good for me?"

"Yes, it does. And now tell me the other things for the Martian."

"The book is *The Catcher in the Rye*. I'm pretty doubtful about the song. 'Because the Night' by Patti Smith. Or else 'Suzanne' by Leonard Cohen. Or 'Ain't No Cure for Love', by Cohen again. I don't know. One of those. Perhaps."

"And the object?"

"A bicycle. Now tell me yours."

"The quote is really a quick exchange. From *On the Road*. It goes like this: 'We gotta go and never stop going till we get there.' The reply: 'Where we going, man?' 'I don't know but we gotta go.' "

"The book?"

"You're sure not to know it. It's *The Foreign Student*, by a French writer —"

"I've read it. It's the one about a young Frenchman who goes to study in an American college in the 50s."

"Nobody knows that book. You're the first. What a coincidence."

Her eyes flashed for a moment in the darkness of the car, like little knife blades.

We were parked on the cliffs, almost sheer above the sea at Polignano. Outside it was February and very cold.

Not inside the car though. Inside the car, that night, we seemed to be sheltered from everything.

"I'm glad I came out with you this evening. At the last moment I was about to call you and say I wasn't feeling up to it. Then I thought you must have already left home and that anyway it would be bad-mannered. So I said to myself: we'll go to the cinema and then I'll ask him to take me home and I'll get an early night."

"Why didn't you want to go out?"

"I don't want to talk about it now. I only wanted to tell you I'm glad I came. And I'm glad I didn't ask you to take me home right after the cinema. Let's play some more. I like it. Tell me the song and the object."

"The object is a fountain pen. The song is 'Pezzi di vetro.' "

97

"Can I say something about the book?"

"What is it?"

"I'm no longer sure about *The Catcher in the Rye*."

"You want to change?"

"Yes, I think so. *The Little Prince*. It seems more appropriate, maybe. What does the fox say to the little prince when he wants to be tamed?"

" 'The wheat fields have nothing to say to me. And that is sad. But you have hair that is the colour of gold. Think how wonderful that will be when you have tamed me! The grain, which is also golden, will bring me back the thought of you. And I shall love to listen to the wind in the wheat . . .' "

She turned and looked at me. In her eyes was a childlike wonder. She was very beautiful. "How do you manage to remember everything by heart?"

"I don't know. It's always been like that. If I like something, I only have to read it or hear it once and it sticks in my mind. But *The Little Prince* I've read lots of times. So it's not really fair."

"What do you think is the most important quality in a person?"

"A sense of humour. If you have a sense of humour – not irony or sarcasm, which are different things entirely – then you don't take yourself seriously. So you can't be catty, you can't be stupid and you can't be vulgar. If you think about it, it covers almost everything. Do you know any people who have a sense of humour?"

"Very few. On the other hand, I've met a lot of them – men especially – who take themselves a hell of a lot too seriously."

She had a moment of hesitation, then added: "My boyfriend is one of them."

"What does your boyfriend do?"

"He's an engineer."

"Pompous person?"

"No. He can make you laugh, he's nice. What I mean is, he's intelligent, he makes funny remarks and so on. But he can only joke about other people. About himself he's always tremendously serious. No, he hasn't got a sense of humour."

Another pause, then she went on, "I'd like it if you had a sense of humour."

"I'd like to have one too. To tell the truth, in view of what you've just said, I'd sell my mother and father to the cannibals just to have one. Without taking myself seriously, of course."

She laughed again and we went on chatting like that, in the car that protected us from the wind and the world. For hours.

It was past four in the morning before we realized that we ought to get back.

When we arrived outside her place, in the centre of town, the sky was already beginning to lighten.

"If tomorrow you think you still want to come out with me, phone me. If you call, I'll give you a book."

Sara took my chin between finger and thumb and gave me a kiss on the lips. Then, without a word, she got out of the car. A few seconds later she had disappeared through a shiny wooden door.

I gave myself a couple of light punches in the face, on one side and the other. Then I started up the car and drove away, music playing full blast.

Ten years later there I was alone in my empty office, with my memories and their heart-rending melody.

It was a long time since I'd been able to memorize songs, passages in books or parts of films just by hearing or reading them once.

Among the many things gone down the drain there was also that.

So I had to go home at once, hoping that among the books I had brought away with me I would find *The Little Prince*. Because at that hour there were no bookshops open and I was in a hurry, I couldn't wait till the next morning.

It was there. I turned to near the end, where the little prince is about to be bitten by the snake and is saying farewell to his airman friend.

"In one of the stars I shall be living. In one of them I shall be laughing. And so it will be as if all the stars were laughing, when you look at the sky at night . . . You – only you – will have stars that can laugh!" . . .

"And when your sorrow is comforted (time soothes all sorrows) you will be content that you have known me. You will always be my friend. You will want to laugh with me. And you will sometimes open your window, so, for that pleasure . . . And your friends will be properly astonished to see you laughing as you look up at the sky! Then you will say to them 'Yes the stars always make me laugh!' And they will think you are crazy."

18

I slept for exactly two hours.

I slipped between the sheets a few minutes before three, opened my eyes at five on the dot and got up feeling strangely refreshed.

I had no commitments that morning, so I thought I'd go for a walk. I had a shower, shaved, put on some comfortable old cotton trousers, a denim shirt and a sweatshirt. I wore gymshoes and a leather jacket.

Outside it was starting to get light.

I was already at the door when it occurred to me that I might take a book, stop and read somewhere. In a garden or a café, as I used to do years before. So I looked over the books that I'd never arranged but were there in my flat. All over the place, scattered provisionally.

I had a momentary thought that they were provisional there just as I was, but immediately I told myself that this was a banal, pathetic notion. I therefore stopped philosophizing and returned to simply choosing a book.

I picked up Arthur Schnitzler's *Dream Story*, in a cheap edition that fitted easily into the pocket of my leather jacket. I took some cigarettes, deliberately did *not* take my mobile, and left the house.

My flat was in Via Putignani, and immediately to the right as I went out I could see the Teatro Petruzzelli.

From the outside the theatre looked normal, with its dome and all the rest of it. Not so inside. One night nearly ten years ago it had been gutted by fire, and since then there it stood, waiting for someone to rebuild it. It was inhabited meanwhile by cats and ghosts.

It was towards the theatre that I turned, feeling on my face the cool, clean air of early morning. Very few cars and no pedestrians at all.

It reminded me of the time towards the end of my university days when I often used to come home at that hour.

At night I used to play poker, or go out with girls. Or simply stay drinking, smoking and chatting with my friends.

One morning at about six, after one of these nights, I was in the kitchen getting a drink of water before going to bed, when my father came in to make coffee.

"Why have you got up so early?"

"No, Dad, I've only just got home."

He looked at me for only a second, measuring me up.

"It is beyond my comprehension how you get the urge to make idiotic jokes even at this time in the morning."

He turned away and shrugged with resignation.

I reached Corso Cavour, right in front of the Teatro Petruzzelli, and continued on my way towards the sea. Two blocks later I stopped at a bar, had some breakfast and lit the first cigarette of the day.

I was in the part of Bari where the finest houses are. It was in that neighbourhood that Rossana used to live – my girlfriend in university days.

We had had a rather stormy relationship, all my fault. After only a few months it seemed to me that my freedom was, as they say, jeopardized by that relationship.

So every so often I stood her up, and if I didn't stand her up I almost always arrived late. She got mad but I maintained that those were not the things that mattered. She said that good manners did matter and I began, with a wealth of sophistical arguments, to explain to her the difference between formal good manners – hers – and real substantial good manners. Mine, of course.

At the time it didn't even remotely occur to me that I was being no better than an arrogant lout. On the contrary, as I was so good at twisting words to suit my purpose, I even persuaded myself that I was right. This led me to behave worse, including in the meaning of "worse" a series of clandestine affairs with girls of dubious morality.

I came to realize all this when we had already separated. I had several times thought back on our relationship and come to the conclusion that I had behaved like a right bastard. If I ever had an opportunity I would have to admit it and apologize.

Perhaps seven or eight years later, I came across Rossana again. In the meantime she had gone to work in Bologna.

We met at the house of some friends during the Christmas holidays, and she asked me if I'd care to have a cup of tea with her the next day. I said yes. So we met, we had tea and stayed chatting for at least an hour.

She'd had a daughter, was separated from her husband, owned a travel agency which made her a pile of money, and was still very beautiful.

I was glad to see her again and felt relaxed. It therefore came quite naturally to me to tell her that I'd often thought of when we were together and that I was convinced I'd behaved badly towards her. I just felt like telling her, for what it was worth. She smiled and looked at me in a rather strange way for a few moments before speaking. She didn't say exactly what I expected.

"You were a spoilt child. You were so intent on yourself that you didn't realize what was happening around you, even very close to you."

"What d'you mean by that?"

"You didn't so much as suspect that for nearly a year I had someone else."

I'd like to have seen my face at that moment. It must have been a pretty picture, because Rossana smiled and the sight of me seemed to amuse her.

"You had someone else? Excuse me, but in what sense?"

At that point she stopped smiling and began to laugh. Who could blame her?

"How d'you mean, in what sense? We were together."

"How d'you mean, you were together? You were together with *me*. When did you see each other?"

"In the evening, almost every evening. When you took me home. He was waiting for me round the corner, in his car. I waited in the doorway and when you'd gone I went round the corner and got into the car."

My head started spinning rather weirdly.

"And where . . . where did you go?"

"To his place, on the Walls in Old Bari."

"To his place. In Old Bari. And what did you do on the Walls in Old Bari?"

Too late I realized I had said something too stupid for words, but I wasn't connecting very well.

She realized it too, and did nothing to ease matters.

"What did we do? You mean, at night in his flat on the Walls?"

She was tickled to death. I wasn't. I had gone to have a cup of tea with an ex-girlfriend and found I had to rewrite history.

104

I discovered that his name was Beppe, that he was a jewellery salesman, that he was married and rich. The place on the Walls, to be precise, was not his home but his bachelor pad. At the time of these events he was thirty-six and had a sterling wife.

At the time of these events I was twenty-two, my parents gave me 40,000 lire a week, I shared a bedroom with my brother and – I was now discovering rather late in the day – I had a whore for a girlfriend.

I reached the coast, turned left towards the Teatro Margherita, and headed for San Nicola, passing below the Walls. Just where this Signor Beppe had his bachelor pad. Where he used to take *my* girlfriend.

By now it was daylight, the air was fresh and clean, and it was an ideal day for a walk. I continued as far as the Castello Svevo and then further still towards the Fiera del Levante, to arrive perhaps two hours and several miles after leaving home at the pine wood of San Francesco.

It was practically deserted. Only a few men running and a few others seated, preferring to let their dogs do the running.

I chose a good bench, one of those green wooden ones with a back, in the sun. I sat down and read my book.

When I finished it, about two hours later, I was feeling pretty fit and thought I'd take another ten minutes' rest before setting off for home. Or perhaps for the office, where they certainly must have begun to wonder what on earth had happened to me.

It was starting to get hot, so I took off my jacket, folded it up into a kind of pillow and stretched out with my face in the sun.

When I woke it was past midday. The joggers had multiplied, there were pairs of young boys, women with babies, and old men playing cards at the stone tables. There were also two Jehovah's Witnesses trying to convert anyone who didn't show them a sufficiently hostile front.

Time to be gone. Very much so.

19

As soon as I got home my eye fell on my mobile and I ignored it. When I went to the office in the afternoon it was in my pocket, but still turned off.

Maria Teresa engulfed me the very moment I opened the door. They'd been hunting for me all morning, at home and on my mobile. At home there was no answer and the other was always off.

Naturally – I thought – because I was in the pine wood, taking the sun, in defiance of the lot of you and without the damn phone.

That morning all hell had broken loose.

Surely I hadn't forgotten some hearing? Ah, just as well, I thought not. Lots of people looking for me? No matter, they'll call again. No, certainly I hadn't forgotten that the time limit for Colaianni's appeal expired tomorrow.

Liar! I had completely forgotten. Just as well I had a secretary who knew her job.

They'd called three times from the prison since midday? Why was that?

Maria Teresa didn't know. It was something urgent, they said, but they hadn't explained what. The last to call had been a certain Inspector Surano. He had asked me to call him back as soon as I was traced.

I called the switchboard of the administration building, asked for Inspector Surano and, after a wait of at least three minutes, I heard a low, hoarse voice with the accent of the province of Lecce.

Yes, I was Avvocato Guerrieri. Yes, I was acting for the prisoner Abdou Thiam. Yes, I could come to the prison, if he would first be good enough to tell me the reason.

He told me the reason. That morning, following visiting hours, the prisoner Abdou Thiam had put into effect an attempted suicide by means of hanging.

He had been rescued when he was already swinging from a rope made of torn-up sheets plaited together. He was now in the prison infirmary with a round-the-clock watch on him.

I said I'd be there as soon as possible.

As soon as possible is a very ambiguous concept if it is a matter of getting to the prison from the centre of Bari on a working afternoon.

However, in scarcely over half an hour I was outside the admin building and ringing the bell. Having parked the car illegally of course.

The warder in the guardroom had been alerted to my arrival. He asked me to wait and called Inspector Surano, who arrived surprisingly soon. He said the governor wanted to talk to me and we could go to him at once. I asked how my client was and he said he was fairly well, physically. He personally would accompany me to the infirmary immediately after our meeting with the governor.

We plunged into the yellowed, ill-lit corridors, in which hung the unmistakable odour of food typical of prisons, barracks and hospitals. Every so often we passed a prisoner wielding a broom or pushing a trolley. We finally entered a freshly painted corridor with potted plants in it, and at the end of this was the door of the governor's office.

Inspector Surano knocked, looked in, said something I didn't hear and then opened the door wide, ushering me in and following.

The governor was a man of about fifty-five, with an anonymous air, papery, lustreless skin and an evasive look.

He was sorry, he said, about what had happened, but thanks to the presence of mind of one of his men tragedy had been averted.

Yes, another tragedy, I thought, remembering the suicide of one of my clients – a twenty-year-old drug addict – and the rumours, never confirmed, of violence committed on the prisoners to impose discipline.

The governor wished to assure me that he had already given strict instructions for the prisoner – what's his name now? – ah yes, the prisoner Abdou Thiam to be under constant surveillance with a view to preventing further attempts at suicide or any kind of self-inflicted harm.

He felt sure that this unpleasant incident would have no consequences, let alone publicity, for the peace and quiet of the penal institute and of the prisoner himself. For his own part, he was at my disposal in case I needed anything.

In plain language, if you don't give me any trouble, it'll be better for all concerned. Including your client, who's in here and here to stay.

I would have liked to tell him to go fuck himself, but I was in a hurry to see Abdou and in addition I suddenly felt exhausted. So I thanked him for his readiness to help and asked him to have me accompanied to the infirmary.

We did not shake hands and Inspector Surano led me back the way we had come, and then along other even more dreary corridors, through barred doors and that stench of food that seemed to penetrate into every cranny.

The infirmary was a large room with about a dozen

beds, nearly all occupied. I failed to spot Abdou and looked questioningly at Surano. He jerked his head to indicate the far end of the room and went ahead of me.

Abdou was in a bed with his arms strapped down and his eyes half closed. He was breathing through his mouth.

Close by him was sitting a fat, moustachioed warder. He was smoking, on his face an expression of boredom.

Surano chose to assume an air of authority.

"What the hell are you doing smoking in the infirmary, Abbaticchio? Put it out, put it out, and give your chair to the Avvocato."

Such courtesy was new to me. Plainly the governor had given orders for me to be treated with kid gloves.

This Abbaticchio gave the inspector a sullen look. He seemed on the point of saying something, then thought better of it. He put out his cigarette and moved off, ignoring me completely. Surano told me I could take my time. When I had finished, he would himself escort me to the exit. Then he too retired as far as the infirmary door.

Now I was alone at Abdou's bedside, but he didn't seem to have noticed my presence.

I bent over him a little and tried calling his name but there was no reaction. Just as I was about to touch him on the arm he spoke, almost without moving his lips.

"What do you want, Avvocato?"

I withdrew my arm with a slight start.

"What happened, Abdou?"

"You know what happened. Otherwise you wouldn't be here."

His eyes were wide open now, staring at the ceiling. I sat down, and realized only then that I had absolutely no idea what to say.

Once down level with him, I noticed the marks on his neck.

"Did Abajaje come this morning?"

He made no answer, nor did he look at me. He closed his mouth and set his jaw. After two attempts he managed to swallow. Then, like a scene in slow motion, in the inner corner of his left eye I saw a tear – one only – forming, growing, detaching itself and coursing slowly all the way down his cheek, until it vanished at the edge of his jaw. I too had trouble swallowing.

For a time incalculable neither of us spoke. Then it came to me that there was only one thing I could say that made sense.

"You've been abandoned and you think that now it's really all up with you. I know. And you're probably even right."

Abdou's eyes, which had stayed riveted on the ceiling, now turned slowly towards me. Even his head moved, though very little. I had his attention. I started to speak again and my voice was surprisingly calm.

"In fact, as I see it, you have only one chance, and even that is a slim one. The decision is up to you alone."

He was looking at me now, and I knew I was in control of the situation.

"If you want to fight for that chance, tell me so."

"What chance?"

"We won't opt for the shortened procedure. We'll have a trial before the Court of Assizes and try to win it. That is, to get you acquitted. The chances are slight and I confirm what I said last time. My advice is still to choose the shortened procedure. But the decision is up to you. If you don't want to go for the shortened procedure, I will defend you in the Court of Assizes."

"I don't have the money."

111

"To hell with the money. If I manage to get you off, which is unlikely, you'll find a way of paying me. If they convict you, you'll have more serious problems than a debt to me."

He turned away his eyes, kept fixed on mine while I was talking. He returned to gazing at the ceiling, but in a different way. I even had the impression of the shadow of a smile, a wistful one, on his lips. At last he spoke, still without looking at me but in a firm voice.

"You are intelligent, Avvocato. I have always thought of myself as more intelligent than other people. This is not a lucky thing, but it's hard to understand that. If you think yourself more intelligent than others, you fail to understand a lot of things, until they are suddenly brought home to you. And then it's too late."

He made a motion to raise his right arm, but it was checked by the strap. I had an impulse to ask him if he wanted to be freed, but I said nothing. He started to speak again.

"Today it seems to me that you are more intelligent than I am. I thought I was a dead man and now, after listening to you, I think I was wrong. You have done something I don't understand."

He paused and took a deep breath, through his nose, as if summoning up all his strength.

"I want us to go to trial. To be acquitted."

I felt a shiver that started at the top of my head and ran all the way down my spine. I wanted to say something, but knew that whatever I said would be wrong.

"OK" was all I could manage. "We'll meet again soon."

He set his jaw again and nodded, without taking his eyes off the ceiling.

When I got back to the car, the windscreen bore the white ticket of a parking fine.

112

20

Two weeks later came the preliminary hearing.

Judge Carenza arrived late, as she always did.

I waited outside the courtroom, chatting with a few colleagues and the journalists who were there especially for my case. Cervellati, on the other hand, was not present.

He didn't like waiting for the judge outside the courtroom, mingling with the defence lawyers. So he had his secretary tell the clerk of the court to send for him when the hearing was about to begin.

La Carenza entered the courtroom, followed by the clerk of the court and a bailiff pushing a trolley loaded with dossiers. I went in too, sat down in my place at the bench on the right for those facing the judge, and opened my file, casually, just to have something to do and calm my nerves.

A few moments later I noticed that also in court was my colleague Cotugno, who was to represent the boy's parents. He was an elderly lawyer, a bit of a windbag, deaf and with murderous bad breath.

Conversations with Cotugno were surreal. He, being hard of hearing, tended to move up close. His interlocutor, whose sense of smell was usually in working order, tended to back away. As long as the size of the room and the limits of good manners enabled him to. Then he was forced to endure it.

Therefore, when I saw Cotugno sitting at the public prosecutor's bench – as is customary for counsel for the civil party – I enacted a complex strategy to avoid his breath. I half stood up, leaning on the desk before me, stretched out my arm to its fullest possible extent, and gave him my hand while maintaining this precarious stance. Plainly incompatible with any conversation. I then sat down again.

The judge told the clerk of the court to call the warders to bring in the prisoner.

At that moment Cervellati materialized on my left. He was wearing a grey suit and brown moccasins with leather tassels. He asked me what I intended to do with this trial.

I lied. My client – I said – had wanted to think about it until the last moment, so I myself would only know that morning whether or not we would ask for the shortened procedure.

Cervellati gave me a look, seemed on the point of saying something, then shook his head and sat down at his place. He hadn't believed me and he didn't look exactly friendly.

Two minutes later, through a side door, surrounded by four warders, his wrists handcuffed, in came Abdou. He was wearing khaki cotton trousers and a white shirt; over his arm was some sort of jacket. He had a clean look. He was well shaven and his shirt might have been ironed that very morning.

"Your Honour, may I have a word or two with my client before the hearing begins?"

"Certainly, Avvocato. Please remove the prisoner's handcuffs."

The eldest of the warders produced a key and freed Abdou's hands. When I came up to him he was massaging his wrists. I spoke very quietly.

"Well then, Abdou, if you've changed your mind we're still in time. Only just, but still in time."

114

He shook his head. I stood for a moment looking at him, and he gave me a straight look back. Then I returned to my seat, my heart beating faster and fear sweeping over me like a wave.

The opening formalities were quickly dispatched and then came the moment.

"Are there any requests for alternative procedures?" asked Judge Carenza.

I got to my feet, buttoning up my jacket. I darted another look in the direction of Abdou.

"Your Honour, my client and I have considered at length the possible advantages of requesting the shortened procedure, but we eventually decided together that this is a case to be submitted to a full hearing. In view of which, no, there are no requests for alternative procedures."

I sat down without looking at Cervellati.

The judge then asked the parties to formulate their conclusions.

Cervellati spoke briefly. The case was loaded with evidence against the accused, Abdou Thiam. There were proofs that as a result of the hearing would certainly lead to an affirmation of penal responsibility on all the criminal charges – the very grave, odious criminal charges – set down in the counts of indictment. The preliminary hearing could only lead to the accused being committed for trial before the Court of Assizes, to answer to charges of unlawful restraint and wilful murder. All that was needed was to supplement the charge contained under count B. In accordance with Article 423 of the code of criminal procedure, the public prosecutor intended to alter the murder charge. From simple murder to murder with aggravating circumstances.

Cervellati dictated the new charge for the records.

He had been true to his word. My client was now facing a charge which, if he was convicted, would lead him straight to life imprisonment with hard labour.

The judge asked me if I intended to apply for time for defence. This was a courtesy gesture, she was not bound to do it. I thanked her and said no, I did not so intend.

Then it was the turn of Cotugno, who was even briefer than Cervellati. He associated himself with the requests of the public prosecutor and also asked for a committal for trial.

I had little to say, because in a case like this there was obviously no chance at all of an acquittal in the preliminary hearing.

So I simply said that we had no observations to make on the request for committal.

Then the judge pronounced the ruling.

The trial of Abdou Thiam, born Dakar, Senegal, on 4 March 1968, on the charges of unlawful restraint and murder with aggravating circumstances, was fixed for 12 June, before the Assize Court of Bari.

Part Three

21

I was on my way home from the office, thinking I'd have to do a spot of shopping to avoid eating out yet again when I heard a woman's voice, slightly throaty, just behind me.

"Could you please give me a hand? I'm about to collapse."

My neighbour Margherita. It was a wonder she hadn't collapsed already. She was lugging a bursting briefcase, numerous plastic bags full of food and a long tube of the kind used by architects to carry drawings around.

I gave her a hand, meaning I took over all the shopping. So we set off walking side by side.

"Just as well I met you. A week ago I was in more or less the same straits when I met old Professor Costantini, and he offered to help me. I gave him the shopping bags and after one block he was on the verge of a heart attack."

I gave her a faintly idiotic smile. I should evidently have known who this Professor Costantini was.

"Who is Professor Costantini?"

"The one on the second floor of our building. Excuse my asking, but how long have you been living there?"

It struck me that I'd been living there for more than a year. And I didn't know any of the tenants by name.

"More or less a year."

"Congratulations! You must be a really sociable type.

What do you do? Sleep by day and go round at night in tights and a cloak and mask, ridding the city of criminals?"

I told her I was a lawyer and she, after pulling a rather wry face, said that she too, long ago, had seemed destined to become a lawyer. She had done the training, passed the exams and was even on the rolls, but then she had done a switch. Total. Now she worked in advertising and other things. However – we agreed – in a sense we were colleagues, so we could address each other as *tu*. She said that made her feel more at ease.

"I've always had trouble using *lei*. It really doesn't come naturally, I have to force it. They tried to teach me some years ago that a well-brought-up girl doesn't use *tu* with strangers, but I've always had serious doubts about being a well-brought-up girl. How about you?"

"About being a well-brought-up girl? Yes, I do have some doubts about that."

She gave a short laugh – a sort of gurgle – before speaking again.

"I can see you have doubts all along the line. You always look . . . I don't know, I can't find the word to describe it. As if you were turning over questions in your mind and didn't much like the answers. Or didn't like them one bit."

I turned to look at her, slightly disconcerted.

"Seeing that this is the second time we've seen each other, may I ask what you base this diagnosis on?"

"It's the second time *you've* seen *me*. I've seen you at least four or five other times since I came to live in this building. On two occasions we passed in the street and you literally looked straight through me. So much so that I didn't even feel inclined to say good morning. It hurt my vanity, but your thoughts were wandering."

We walked on in silence for thirty or forty yards. Then she spoke again.

"Have I put my foot in it?"

"No. I've been thinking about what you said. Wondering how come it was so obvious."

"It isn't so obvious. It's that I'm observant."

We had reached the entrance to our building. We went in together and up the few steps to the lift. I was sorry the moment had come for us to part.

"You've succeeded in arousing my curiosity. Now how should I set about having a more detailed consultation?"

She thought for a moment or two. She was making up her mind.

"Are you the kind who gets the wrong idea if you're asked to supper by a girl living on her own?"

"In the past I was a professional getter of the wrong idea, but I've given that up, I think. I hope."

"In that case, if you don't get the wrong idea and you're not otherwise engaged, this evening would suit me."

"This evening would suit me too. Are you on the sixth or the seventh?"

"The seventh. I've even got a terrace. A pity it's still too cold in the evenings, otherwise we could have eaten outside. Is nine o'clock all right for you?"

"Yes. What can I bring?"

"Wine, if you drink it, because I haven't any."

"Very good. This evening, then."

"Don't you take the lift?"

"No, I use the stairs."

She looked at me for a moment without saying anything, but with a faintly questioning air. Then she nodded, relieved me of her shopping and said goodbye.

I don't remember exactly what I did in the office that afternoon, but I do remember a feeling of lightness. A sensation I'd not had for a very long time.

I felt as I had on afternoons in May in my last school years.

Almost no one ever attended classes any longer. Those who went were the ones who had to make up for poor marks and resit exams. Very few others.

For all of us they were the first days of the holidays, and the best. Because they were in a sense illegal. According to the rules, we should have gone on attending school, but we didn't. They were days stolen one by one from the school calendar and given over to freedom.

Perhaps this was why there was that electricity, that strange tension laden with expectation, in those May afternoons suspended between school and the mysteries of summer.

Something was about to happen – something *had* to happen – and we felt it. Our time was bent like a bow, ready to shoot us who knows where.

That is how I felt that afternoon, as in those indelible memories of my adolescence.

I left the office at about half-past seven and went to a wine shop. I didn't know what we were going to eat or what Margherita's tastes were, so I couldn't get only red wine, which I would have done as a rule. I don't much care for white wine.

So I chose a Primitivo from Manduria and, just to show myself for the provincial I was, a Californian white from the Napa Valley.

When I had chosen the wine I had some time to spare so I went for a walk along Via Sparano.

The crowds milled round me and time, it seemed, had been suspended.

The air seemed full of gentle melancholy, and also a certain something I didn't quite manage to grasp.

I got home at a quarter to nine, had a shower and dressed. Light-coloured trousers, denim shirt, soft, light leather shoes.

I shut the door, holding the two bottles by the neck in my other hand, and bounced up the stairs, the image of Alberto Sordi impersonating an American in Rome.

The result was that I tripped up and only just avoided smashing everything. I couldn't help laughing, and when I knocked at Margherita's door two flights above I must still have been wearing a rather stupid smile.

"What's up?" she asked after saying hello, narrowing her eyes in puzzlement.

"Nothing, it's just that I nearly fell on the stairs, and since I'm a bit of a loony anyway I found it amusing. But don't worry, I'm harmless."

She laughed, again with that kind of gurgle.

Her flat had a good smell to it, of new furniture, cleanliness and well-cooked food. It was bigger than mine, and evidently some walls had been knocked down, because there was no hallway and one entered straight into a kind of living room with a big french window giving onto a terrace. Not much furniture. Just a kind of low cupboard that looked Japanese, a number of light wooden shelves attached to the wall, and a glass and wrought-iron table with four metal chairs. On the floor a large coconut mat and, on two sides of the room, a number of big coloured candles of varying heights, blue glass jars containing some kind of crushed stone, and a black stereo unit.

The shelves were full of books and knick-knacks and gave the impression of a home that had been lived in for some time.

On the walls were two reproductions of paintings by Hopper, *Cape Cod Evening* and *Gas*. That one of petrol pumps out in the country. They were beautiful and moving.

I said so, and she gave me a quick glance as if to see whether I was talking simply to show off. Then she nodded, gravely. Pause. Then: "Can you eat hot things?"

"I can eat hot things."

"I'll just slip into the kitchen, then, and finish getting it ready. You look around if you like, it'll be ready in five minutes. We'll chat when we're at table. I'll open the red wine because it goes with what we're going to eat. And in any case the white won't get chilled in such a short time."

She vanished into the kitchen. I began to examine the books on the shelves, as I usually do when I enter an unknown house.

There were a lot of novels and collections of short stories. American, French and Spanish, in the original languages.

Steinbeck, Hemingway, Faulkner, Carver, Bukowski, Fante, Montalban, Lodge, Simenon, Kerouac.

There was an ancient, tattered edition of *Zen and the Art of Motorcycle Maintenance*. There were travel books by an American journalist – Bill Bryson – that I liked a lot and had thought I was more or less the only person who knew them.

Then there were books on psychology, books on Japanese martial arts, catalogues of exhibitions, mostly of photography.

I took out the catalogue of an exhibition in Florence

of Robert Capa and leafed through it. Then I looked at Chatwin and then Doisneau, with his black-and-white kisses in the Paris of the 50s. There was a book on Hopper. When I opened it, I saw there was a dedication, so I quickly turned the page, embarrassed.

I read a line or two of the introduction: "Images of the city or the country, almost always deserted, in which are mingled realism of vision and an agonizing feeling for landscape, for people, for things. Hopper's paintings, beneath an appearance of objectivity, express a silence, a solitude, a metaphysical astonishment."

I put back the Hopper, took down *Ask the Dust* by John Fante and went with it onto the terrace. The air was cool and dry. I wandered around a while among the potted plants, looked down into the street, stopped to finger some strange little flowers with the consistency of wax. Then, leaning against the wall under a kind of wrought-iron lantern, I flipped through the book to the last page, because I wanted to re-read the ending.

Far out across the Mojave there arose the shimmer of heat. I made my way up the path to the Ford. In the seat was a copy of my book, my first book. I found a pencil, opened the book at the fly leaf, and wrote:

To Camilla, with love,
Arturo

I carried the book a hundred yards into the desolation, toward the southeast. With all my might I threw it far out into the direction she had gone. Then I got into the car, started the engine, and drove back to Los Angeles.

"Supper's ready."

I came to with a slight jolt and went inside. The table was laid.

The Primitivo was in a carafe, and in another like it was water. There was a tureen of chilli con carne and a dish of boiled rice. Arranged on a plate were four corncobs with some whorls of butter in the centre.

We began with the corncobs and butter. I picked up the carafe of wine and was about to pour her a glass.

She said no, she didn't drink.

"I had what they call a drinking problem. A few years ago. Then it became a *big* problem. Now I don't drink."

"Forgive me, if I'd known I wouldn't have brought the wine . . ."

"Hey, it was me who told you to bring wine. For you."

"If it upsets you, I can drink water."

"It doesn't upset me."

She said it with a smile but in a tone of voice that meant: discussion over.

All right, discussion over. I filled my glass and set to work on the corncob.

We talked very little while we ate. The chilli was *really* hot and the wine suited it to perfection. For pudding there was a date and honey cake, also Mexican.

It was scarcely a slimming meal and after it I felt the need for something strong. For obvious reasons I said nothing, but Margherita went into the kitchen and came back with a bottle of tequila gold, still sealed.

"I bought it for you this afternoon. One can't have a Mexican meal without finishing off with tequila. Take the bottle with you afterwards. And the white wine."

I poured myself a tequila, pulled out my cigarettes and then – too late – thought that perhaps she didn't like people smoking. But in fact Margherita asked for one and fetched a kind of mortar of volcanic rock as an ashtray.

"I don't buy cigarettes. If I do, I smoke them. But when I can, I bum them off someone else."

"I know the method," I replied. For many years it had been *my* method. Then my friends had begun to say no, I had become not a little unpopular and, well, in the end I was forced to buy them.

I took a sip of tequila and remained silent a moment too long. She read my thoughts.

"You want to know about my problem with alcohol."

It was not a question. I was about to say no, what was she thinking of, I was just enjoying my tequila.

I said yes.

She took a hefty drag at her cigarette before starting.

"I was an alcoholic for three years, more or less. When I got my degree my parents gave me a present of a three-month holiday in the United States, in San Francisco. It was the most fun time of my life. When I got back I realized for the first time that my future was to be a lawyer in my father's office. No. That's not exactly it, that way you won't understand it. I know now that that was my motive, but at the time I didn't realize anything, not consciously. But I felt it clearly, even if unconsciously. In short, recreation time was over and I wasn't ready to go back into the classroom. Not into the one I was destined for.

"To complicate matters, when I got back from the States I found myself a boyfriend. He was a sweet boy, eight years older than me. He was a notary, he had good manners, and my parents took to him at once. An excellent match. My parents had liked almost none of my previous boyfriends. They weren't the kind to whom they would have entrusted their only daughter for life. I had always been – how can I put it? – a bit on the lively side and a bit fickle, and this didn't go down well with them. Not that they said anything. That is, my mother sometimes said something, but they had never made any particular fuss. Or so I thought.

"However, when Pierluigi appeared on the scene it was clear that he was Mr Right. I mustn't let him get away. I began to drink soon after the beginning of my affair with him. I drank – a lot – especially in the evenings when we were out together. I drank and became more likeable. Everyone laughed at my jokes and my fiancé was obviously proud of taking me around. To show me off.

"Then we decided – he decided – that it was time to get married. I was working with my father and would soon be a lawyer, he was a notary and, let's face it, he wasn't badly off. There was no point in going on being engaged. He spoke the word and I went along with him.

"After that decision I began to drink even *before* going out. He would come to pick me up and on the intercom I'd tell him I'd need five minutes to get ready. Then I knocked back whatever I could find – beer, wine, spirits, whatever there was. I brushed my teeth to take the smell away, put on some perfume and went downstairs. We met friends and I was always so charming. And I drank. I drank the aperitif, the wine or beer with meals, and then a drop – or two, or three – afterwards. I was very fond of tequila gold, the very brand you are drinking now. But I wasn't choosy. I drank everything that came to hand. Sometimes I had the unpleasant feeling of being out of control. Sometimes I thought that maybe I ought to cut down, but for the most part I was convinced that when I decided to stop it would be no problem. Would you let me have another cigarette, please?"

I gave her the cigarette and lit one for myself. She took a couple of strong drags and went to put on a CD.
Making Movies. Dire Straits.

She took another couple of puffs before starting to speak again.

"With this jolly state of affairs we arrived at the wedding day. In my few lucid moments I was plunged into indescribable desperation. I didn't want to get married, I didn't have anything in common with that notary. I didn't want to be a lawyer, I wanted to go back to San Francisco or escape to anywhere else on earth. But there I was on a moving train and wasn't capable of pulling the emergency cord. Two or three times I thought I had plucked up the courage to tell my parents I didn't want to get married – my greatest fear was their reaction, not Pierluigi's – and that I was sorry but I thought it was better to make a decision of that kind before marriage, rather than six months or a year later.

"Then my mother would poke her head in at my door and tell me to hurry up, we had to go and choose whatever it was, the menu for the reception or the flowers for the church. So I said 'Yes, mum', knocked back a miniature bottle of liquor, brushed my teeth – I brushed my teeth the whole time – and went out. I remember that during one of these outings I left my mother in whatever shop it was and dashed off to have a quick beer in the nearest bar. Then all afternoon I was scared she might smell it on my breath.

"Can you guess how I arrived at the wedding? Drunk. I drank the evening before. To get to sleep I mixed alcohol and anxiolytics. The next morning I drank. A few beers, just to relax. Also a tot – or two – of whisky. But I brushed my teeth very, very well. On the way into church I tripped up because I was plastered. Everyone thought it was nerves. All through the ceremony I longed for the reception. To go on drinking."

She took the last puff, right down to the filter, and

then stubbed it out in the mortar, hard. I had an urge to touch her hand, or her shoulder, or her face. To let her know that I was there. I wasn't brave enough, and she went on.

"To this day I still wonder how they managed, all of them, not to notice anything. Until the marriage and for some months afterwards. Things got worse when I passed my law exams. I had sat the written papers before the wedding and a few months after it I did the orals. I came second in the final class-list. Not bad for an alcoholic, eh? I celebrated in my own fashion. When I got home I felt ill. My husband found me in bed. I had been sick several times and was stinking to high heaven. Not just of alcohol, but certainly of that also. That was the beginning of the worst phase. It began to dawn on him. Not all at once, but in the course of a few months he latched on to the fact that he had an alcoholic wife. In his way he didn't behave badly, he tried to help me. He removed all alcohol from the house and took me to a specialist in another town. To avoid scandal, of course. I promised to give up and began drinking on the sly. It's impossible to keep tabs on an alcoholic. Alcoholics are crafty liars, like drug addicts, in fact worse, because it's easier to get booze than it is 'the stuff'. One day someone saw me at ten in the morning downing a draught beer in one gulp, and they told Pierluigi. I swore I'd give up and half an hour later I was back to secret drinking. He spoke to my parents, who didn't believe it at first. Then they were forced to. We all went together to another specialist, in yet another town. Result: the same as before. Let me cut this short. This story dragged on for another year after I was found out. Then my husband left home. And who can blame him? I was going around with great bruises on my face, or grazes, because I

130

would get up in the night to have a pee, having put myself to sleep with a fine mixture of tequila or vodka and anxiolytics, and walk right into doors. Or I just collapsed on the ground. Sex, on the rare occasions we had any, wasn't a lot of fun for him, I bet. It certainly wasn't for me. All I wanted was to cry and to drink. In short, in the end he left and he was quite right.

"After he went my memories become really confused. I don't know how long it was before they grew clearer. I was in a clinic in Piedmont that specialized in addictions of every kind. There were people hooked on drugs, on pills, on gambling, and then there were us alcoholics. The majority.

"That was the toughest time of my life. In that place they were merciless, but they did help me to struggle out of the shit I'd fallen into. It's nearly five years now that I haven't had a drink. For the first two I kept count of the days. Then I stopped doing that and here I am. A lot of things have happened in these five years, but they're a different story."

I looked her in the face and didn't know what to say or do. I thought that whatever I said would be wrong, so I said nothing. So she spoke again.

"Maybe you think I tell this story to everyone I meet, right off the bat. If you come to think of it, I've practically only met you today. Is that what you think?"

"No."

"Why not?"

"I don't know. But I like to think that you don't tell it to everyone."

For once I hadn't said the wrong thing. She gave a nod, as if to say: Good.

Then we sat there talking on, deep into the night.

22

The weeks I had to wait for the trial passed swiftly.

On 12 June, around ten in the morning, the air was still cool. On my way to the law courts I saw that the liquid crystal thermometer in a computer shop read 73 degrees. Lower than the seasonal average, I thought.

The temperature seemed the only good thing to be said about that day.

The night before I had gone to bed and hadn't managed to get to sleep. At past two I had tried with pills, but they hadn't helped at all. It wasn't until about four-thirty that I nodded off, only to wake a couple of hours later. As in the worst period.

I stopped at a bar to have a coffee – a real coffee – and smoke a cigarette. I felt ghastly.

For some days I had been tortured by the thought that things were going to end in tears, for myself and, above all, for Abdou.

As the trial drew nearer I thought more and more persistently that I had made a stupid blunder in letting myself be carried away by emotion. I got to thinking that I'd behaved like a character in a second-rate novel. A kind of inferior *Uncle Tom's Cabin* set in Bari in the year 2000.

Take courage, my black friend, I, the white liberal-minded lawyer will fight in the Court of Assizes to get you acquitted. It will be hard, but in the end justice will triumph and your innocence will be proved.

Innocence? Doubts had assailed me and entrenched

themselves in my mind during those last days before the hearing began. What did I really know about Abdou? Apart from a questionable personal intuition, what was there to tell me that my client really had nothing to do with the kidnapping and death of that boy?

I now think that I was perhaps looking for an alibi for a possible – in fact probable – defeat. At that time I was not sufficiently lucid to make a hypothesis of the kind, and so my mind was simply freewheeling.

It is not a good thing for a lawyer to have these qualms before such a trial. Above all, it is not a good thing for that lawyer's client. The lawyer is in danger of cutting a sorry figure. The client is in danger of getting the chop.

In the previous few days I had talked twice with Abdou to prepare the defence. I was looking for evidence in his favour, for the hint of an alibi, something. But we found not a thing.

One morning I even made a tour of the places where the boy had disappeared and where his body was subsequently found. A rather pathetic idea, worthy of the movies; I was hoping for some intuition that would resolve everything. Needless to say, I didn't get it.

So the day of the hearing had come, the trial was about to start, and I didn't have a single witness, no scrap of evidence for the defence: nothing.

The public prosecutor would bring his witnesses, his material evidence, and would almost certainly overwhelm us. All I could hope for was to get one of those witnesses in trouble when my turn came to cross-examine.

Even if I succeeded, I would still not be sure of positive results, but I could at least play my hand.

If I did not succeed – as was more probable – in

the prison registers, beside Abdou's name and highlighted, would be stamped the words *Term of detention: permanent.*

Having smoked my cigarette right down to the filter, I crushed it underfoot and continued on my way towards the law courts.

Outside the door of the courtroom, journalists and television cameras were in waiting. A reporter from the *Gazzetta del Mezzogiorno* was the first to spot me and come up. How was I intending to conduct the defence? Did I have witnesses to call? Did I think the trial would be a long one?

I had a sick feeling but managed to control it fairly well, I think. The public prosecutor – I said – did not have proofs but only conjectures. Plausible ones, but still conjectures. In the course of the trial we would demonstrate the fact, and for this purpose, at the moment, there was no need for witnesses for the defence.

While I was saying this, the other journalists gathered round. They made a few notes and the television cameras took a quick shot of my face. Then they let me enter the courtroom.

Inside there were only a few carabinieri, the clerk of the court and the bailiff. I sat down at my place on the defence bench, on the right for those facing the court. I didn't know what to do and didn't even feel inclined to make a show of being busy. I heard the humming of the air-conditioning, which that day wasn't even necessary. A minute or two later a few members of the public began dribbling in.

Then, from the back of the courtroom, emerged the escort of warders in their blue uniforms. In their midst, Abdou. When I saw him, I felt a little better. Less alone, with less of a void around me.

They ushered him into the cage and removed his handcuffs. I went over to talk to him. More for my sake than for his, I think now.

"So, Abdou, how are things?"

"All right. I'm glad the trial has come, that the waiting is over."

"We must decide whether to ask to put you on the stand. It's something that depends largely on you."

"Is there any reason why not?"

"It can be a risk. However, if we don't ask for it, the prosecution almost certainly will, so what we have to decide is whether you want to answer questions. If you so wish you can say you don't intend to answer, and in that case they will read out your interrogation before the public prosecutor."

"I want to answer."

"Very good. Now, the judge will tell you that you can make spontaneous declarations at any time during the trial. You must thank him and then make no such declarations. Even if you have the urge to shout, don't say anything at any time without having spoken to me first. If there is something you want to say, call me, tell me what it is, and I will tell you whether it is a good thing to speak or not, and if so when. Is that clear?"

"Yes."

At that moment the bell rang to announce the entry of the court.

"Right, Abdou, we're off."

I had turned away and was starting back to my seat, the footsteps of the judges and jurors already audible.

"Avvocato."

I turned back, several steps away from the cage. The judges were already in, the jurors following.

"Yes?"

"Thank you."

I stood there motionless for a moment, not knowing what to say or do. The members of the court had already taken their places behind the big raised bench.

I gave a nod and went to my place.

23

The opening formalities of the hearing were quickly dispatched. The judge ordered the clerk of the court to read out the counts of indictment and then gave the floor to the public prosecutor.

Cervellati got to his feet, adjusted his robe with its gold cordons, put on his glasses and began to read from his notes.

"On 5 August 1999 at 19.50 hours the carabinieri of Monopoli received a telephone call reporting the disappearance of Francesco Rubino, a minor nine years old. The telephone call was made by the boy's grandfather on his mother's side, Domenico Abbrescia, who had ascertained the disappearance of the boy, who, until a short time before, had been playing in front of the villa in Contrada Capitolo, the property of the said grandparents. A search for the boy was put in hand at once, including the use of dog teams, and continued without success throughout the night. At the same time preliminary investigatory activities were set in motion, with the examination of persons in possession of the facts, of subjects resident, holidaying or pursuing commercial activities in the zone in which the disappearance took place.

"Searches continued throughout the following day and night, again without results. On 7 August the carabinieri of Polignano received an anonymous communication to the effect that in the zone lying between State Road No. 16 and the zone of San Vito, the body of a child was to be found in a well. Search promptly put in hand in that area unfortunately led to positive results, in the sense that the corpse of little Francesco was discovered. The body showed no obvious signs of violence.

"The autopsy subsequently carried out showed that death had been due to suffocation.

"The investigations carried out immediately after the finding of the body led to the acquisition of decisive evidence against the Senegalese citizen Abdou Thiam, who today stands accused.

"In the briefest of summaries, and with a view to bringing out the points on which the hearing will be based, the evidence is as follows.

"A number of witnesses have declared that on several occasions they saw the accused stop and talk to little Francesco at the Duna Beach bathing establishment.

"The proprietor of a bar in the immediate vicinity of the house belonging to the boy's grandparents – and therefore the place in which the boy was last seen alive – has reported having seen the accused pass by a few minutes before the child's disappearance. Thiam was walking in the direction of the house owned by the boy's grandparents.

"Two of Thiam's compatriots have reported, respectively, that the aforesaid did not appear on the beach – we still refer to the Duna Beach establishment – on the day subsequent to the boy's disappearance, and that in the course of those days he took the trouble to have his car washed. Clearly to get rid of all incriminating traces.

"A search of the accused's lodgings brought to light a Polaroid photograph of the boy. The importance of this evidence requires no comment. Also in the course of the search were found numerous books for children, the possession of which, in itself suspect in the case of an adult living alone, becomes a disturbing and significant element in the probative context of the matter in hand.

"Of particular significance, finally, are the results of the interrogation to which the accused was subjected during the inquiries. In view of the fact that the prosecution applies herewith to examine Thiam in the course of the hearing, I only wish to point out that the aforesaid, when asked if he knew little Rubino, denied it. Except that he provided ludicrous explanations when shown the photograph of the child found at his lodgings."

Cervellati spoke – or rather read – in his usual nasal, monotonous voice. I was expecting no surprises from his report, so I set about observing the court, one by one.

His Honour Judge Nicola Zavoianni was a personage well known in Bari society. A handsome man, nearing seventy but well preserved, an habitué of the sailing club, a great poker player and, it was rumoured, a great whoremonger. He was one of those who had never killed himself with overwork but had presided over the Assizes for a number of years and more or less knew his job. I had never taken a liking to him and had always had the impression that the feeling was reciprocated.

The associate judge was a grey, bald, short-sighted man with a shiny complexion. He came from the civil courts and it was the first time I had come across him at a trial. He hugged his gown around him in front, as if protecting himself from something. I didn't manage to get a good look at his eyes, shielded as they were behind thick lenses.

The jury was composed of four women and two men.

They all had the lost air typical of jurors at their first hearing. Two women of about fifty or sixty were seated at opposite ends of the bench. One of them reminded me obsessively of a great-aunt of mine, a cousin of my mother. I expected her at any moment to call me up to the bench and offer me sugared almonds made by the nuns.

The two men sat on the associate judge's side. One was about sixty or a bit over, with very short white hair, an old-fashioned jacket with two buttons, a black tie, slits for eyes and the look of a retired military man. He didn't look like good news. The other was a youngster, thirty at the outside. He was gazing around him with an intelligent air.

Beside the judge were the two other women. One of them – I thought at that moment – looked like a headmistress and the other, by chance seated next to the judge, was suntanned, heavily made-up, with garish lips, fresh from the hairdresser's.

I broke off my scrutiny when I realized that the public prosecutor was rounding off with the applications for evidence.

". . . I therefore request the admission of the witnesses indicated in the list, the acquisition of the documents previously indicated and the questioning of the accused, if he consents. Should the accused not intend to submit to questioning, I herewith request the attachment of the statement rendered by him in the course of the preliminary inquiries. Furthermore, since the two witnesses of Senegalese nationality are nowhere to be found, and it is therefore impossible to have them here present as witnesses, I herewith – in accordance with Article 512b – request the attachment of the statements made by them in the course of the preliminary inquiries."

140

The judge then called on Cotugno, who spoke briefly. The civil party, he said, was not involved in this trial for revenge but for justice alone. And justice is done when, responsibility having been rigorously ascertained, a penalty commensurate with the gravity of the offence is inflicted with equal rigour. He had no applications for evidence and associated himself with all the requests of the public prosecutor, whose position he fully shared.

It was my turn.

"Your Honour, ladies and gentlemen of the jury, the public prosecutor has just spoken as if he were reading out the grounds for a verdict of guilty. In the course of the proceedings, by cross-examining the witnesses, the witnesses called by the public prosecutor himself, we intend to show that the verdict of guilty, already pronounced in the mind of the representative of the public prosecution, is nothing more than a house of cards. We will demonstrate that from the first moment on, the investigations were directed not towards finding *the* culprit responsible for this horrible crime, but towards finding *a* culprit. We will show that the urgency – the justifiable urgency – of satisfying the demand for justice of the family of poor Francesco Rubino, and of the community as a whole, has led to an objective manipulation of the probative material. I wish to be clear on this point. We do not intend to maintain that the evidence has been deliberately manipulated – either by the carabinieri or still less by the public prosecutor – to the damage of my client, Signor Abdou Thiam. We do, however, intend to maintain that the desperate need to find a guilty party as soon as possible, in order to satisfy that demand for justice, gave rise in the investigations to short-sightedness, mistaken perspective, errors of method —"

The judge interrupted me.

"Avvocato Guerrieri, you have to make your applications for evidence, if you have any. Do not anticipate your harangue."

"With respect, Your Honour, I point out that I am confining myself to indicating the facts which I intend to prove, in accordance with Article 493 of the code of criminal procedure. In particular I intend to prove that a defective approach to the inquiries – arising certainly from the best intentions – has affected the quality and reliability of the probative material assembled. In any case, I have nearly finished, so, with your permission, I would like to continue."

"Avvocato, you may proceed, but stay within the limits."

"Thank you, Your Honour. I was saying, then, that the almost immediate singling out of a possible suspect, by a series of coincidences, has led the investigators to transform suspicions into conjectures and conjectures into alleged proofs in a kind of involuntary chain. The objective which we shall pursue in the course of the hearing will be to reveal this mechanism, to reverse it, to identify the defective links, the incorrect deductions, and show the substantial and grave, even though involuntary, iniquity of it.

"I have no applications for evidence to put forward at the present time, though I state in advance that in the course of some of my cross-examination I shall make use of a number of documents. Documents of which I shall subsequently request the attachment by the court. I wish to conclude by reminding the ladies and gentlemen of the jury that, in a civilized country, the defendant does not have to prove a thing. Let me repeat that: the defendant does not have to prove a thing. It is up to the prosecution to prove the

142

responsibility of the defendant beyond all reasonable doubt. I ask you to bear this in mind at all times during this trial. Thank you."

I had improvised, but when I sat down I was almost pleased. I liked the brainwave about working backwards, from presumptive proofs to conjectures to mere suspicions. And in speaking in order to convince others – the court – I had begun to convince myself. It happens in this job. It has to happen.

Perhaps we might make it. Perhaps the situation was not as desperate as I had thought that morning, and for some days before.

Perhaps.

The judge dictated for the record a brief ruling whereby he admitted the applications for evidence and adjourned the proceedings until the next day, for the beginning of the hearing. That morning, he explained to us off the record, two of the jurors had personal commitments that could not be deferred, so the adjournment was unavoidable.

The court left the room, Abdou was handcuffed again and escorted away, the public dispersed.

I put away my papers. I folded my robe over one arm, picked up my briefcase with the other and was the last to head for the exit.

24

The first witness called by the prosecution was a lieutenant of the carabinieri, the officer commanding the operations unit in Monopoli. He was a young man of twenty-six or -seven, with a pleasing air, not very military.

The judge ordered him to take the oath. The lieutenant accepted the well-thumbed sheet handed to him by the Clerk of the court and read aloud: "Conscious of the moral and juridical responsibility I am assuming with my deposition, I undertake to speak the whole truth and to conceal nothing of which I have knowledge."

"Give your full particulars."

"Lieutenant Alfredo Moroni, born in Brescia 12 September 1973, domiciled at the carabinieri station of Monopoli. I am the officer commanding the operations unit and flying squad."

"Mr Public Prosecutor, you may now proceed with your questioning."

Cervellati took a sheet of notes from the file in front of him and began.

"Now, Lieutenant, would you care to tell the court what part you played in the investigations concerning the unlawful restraint and killing of little Francesco Rubino?"

"Yes, sir. On 5 August 1999, at about 19.50 hours, the operations centre received a telephone call on the emergency number 112. It reported the disappearance of a nine-year-old boy named Francesco Rubino. The call came from the boy's grandfather, with whom he was spending the holidays because, if I am not mistaken, the parents are separated."

"Very well, Lieutenant, but avoid superfluous details. Stick to the relevant facts."

The lieutenant looked on the point of saying something in reply. He hadn't cared for that interruption. But he was a carabiniere, he said nothing, and after a brief pause resumed his testimony.

"On receipt of the message by the operations room I was personally informed and dispatched a radio patrol car to the grandparents' villa —"

"Where was the villa?"

"As I was on the point of saying, the grandparents' villa was . . . is in Contrada Capitolo, in proximity to the Duna Beach bathing establishment. Having reached the spot and spoken to the grandparents of the child, the patrolmen realized that the matter might be serious, seeing that the boy had been missing for almost two hours, so they contacted me. At that point I communicated the information to my opposite number in the police, with a view to his collaborating in the search, and then I myself went to the scene, accompanied by the personnel of the flying squad."

"How was the search organized?"

"As well as the state police I also called upon the municipal police. Of course I also reported the fact to my superiors in Bari. I ought to mention at once that the captain was on sick leave, so that I was in command of the Monopoli detachment. In any case, after the very first phase, personnel from HQ also took part in the search. The next morning we also put the dog-handling units to work."

"Did anything of relevance emerge from the work with the dogs?"

"Yes, sir. We took the dogs to the villa and started them from the point at which the boy was playing when last seen. The dogs set off confidently, crossed the square immediately outside the gate of the villa, reached the lane that leads to that particular group of villas from the Capitolo Provincial Road, went the length of that lane as far as the main road and then stopped. That is, at a point corresponding to the intersection of the lane with the main road the dogs lost the boy's scent. We took them to the other side of the road, then for some hundreds of yards in one direction and the other, with no result. The last point at which they gave a sign of picking up the boy's scent was the intersection between the lane and the main road. From this fact we deduced that the boy had boarded a motor vehicle."

"When was the boy found? And how?"

"Yes. We found the body of the boy in the vicinity of Polignano, down a well, out in the country near the coast. An anonymous message had been received by the carabinieri station at Polignano."

"What did the person say on the telephone?"

"He said that the child we were looking for was in a well, in the locality of San Vito, in the territory of the Commune of Polignano. He stated exactly at what point the well was to be found, that is, he said something in the nature of 'at such and such a milestone' . . . I don't now remember which. In any case, he mentioned State Road Number 16."

"Can you tell us if this person had any particular accent?"

It was time to intervene.

"Objection, Your Honour. Leaving aside for the

146

moment the fact that we are concerned with an anonymous telephone call, I point out that, as I understand it, the lieutenant did not receive the call in person. These questions regarding the tenor of the telephone call – granted for the sake of argument that they are admissible, but this we will discuss later – should be put to the carabiniere who received the call."

The judge said I was right and did not admit the question. The examination went on monotonously about the history of the investigations up to the moment of Abdou's arrest. The lieutenant had confined himself to coordinating operations, had not taken part in the searches, had not interrogated the chief witnesses, and was therefore from my point of view of secondary importance.

The judge said I could now put questions, if I had any.

In point of fact I had very little to ask the lieutenant, and could easily have done without cross-examining him at all. But I had to make the jury aware of my existence. I therefore said yes, I did have a few questions to ask the witness.

"So, Lieutenant, you have said that the telephone call reporting the boy's disappearance reached your operations room at . . ."

"At 19.50 hours."

"At 19.50. Thank you. And the patrol you sent out, when did that arrive at the grandparents' villa?"

"The time it takes to get from our station in Monopoli to Capitolo. I should say a quarter of an hour, twenty minutes at most."

"At what time did the child disappear?"

"How can I give an exact time . . ."

"Look here, Lieutenant, I have asked you that question because you, in replying to the prosecution, said that the patrolmen realized the child had already been missing for two hours."

"Yes, of course, I mean to say that it was my men who informed me of this circumstance."

"Would you therefore kindly tell the court, on the basis of the data in your possession, at roughly what time the child disappeared?"

"A couple of hours before, as I said."

"And therefore . . ."

"At about six, more or less."

"The child disappeared at about 18.00 and the grandfather called at 19.50. Is that correct?"

"They are approximate times."

"Yes, the child disappeared at approximately 18.00 and the grandfather telephoned at 19.50. Correct?"

"Yes."

"Have you, even informally, asked the grandfather what reason he had for waiting nearly two hours before giving the alarm?"

"I don't know why he waited. They probably went hunting around —"

"Forgive me for interrupting, Lieutenant. I did not ask you for your opinion in this regard. I asked you to state whether the grandfather said for what reason he waited for those – nearly – two hours. Can you answer that question?"

"I don't remember if he mentioned it."

"Do you remember having asked him, even informally?"

"No, I don't remember."

"It is therefore correct to say that you do not know what happened during the two hours between the child's disappearance and the report of it on the telephone."

"Excuse me, Avvocato, at that time we were busy

looking for the boy, organizing search parties and so on, not concerned with how and why the grandfather delayed reporting it, always supposing he did delay."

"Certainly, no one is disputing the correctness of your actions. I want to ask you only a few more questions. Before the public prosecutor interrupted you, you hinted at the fact that the boy's parents are separated —"

Now the public prosecutor interrupted me too.

"Objection, Your Honour. I do not see what the fact that the parents are separated has to do with the proceedings."

Cotugno also put his oar in.

"The civil party supports the objection. This is a family which has suffered a tragedy, and I cannot see what motive there may be for introducing private matters with no bearing on the question before the court."

As a rule I would not have persisted. I had asked the question simply to feel out the ground and because Cervellati had interrupted the lieutenant on that point. But now the reactions from the other side seemed to me excessive. So I thought I would push the matter a little further. To see what happened.

"Your Honour, I do not understand the strong reactions of the public prosecutor and the civil party on this point. I intend absolutely no lack of respect for the family of the child and the tragedy that has struck it. In any case, I fail to see how my question could have such an effect. My only interest is in understanding what happened during the minutes and hours after the disappearance and whether the child's parents took part in the search."

"Within these limits you may continue, Avvocato."

"Thank you, Your Honour. So we were saying that the boy's parents were – or are? – separated. Is that so?"

"So I believe."

"When did you learn of this circumstance?"

"When I went to the house."

"The child's parents were there?"

"No."

"Do you know where they were?"

"No . . . that is, I think the mother was away on a few days' holiday, and I don't know where the father was."

"How did you learn of these facts?"

"They were reported to me on my arrival by Signor Abbrescia, the grandfather on the mother's side."

"Did Signor Abbrescia tell you whether the parents had been informed of the disappearance?"

"Yes, he told me that he had got in touch with his daughter on her mobile and that she was on her way back, I don't remember where from. Or perhaps they didn't tell me. In any case, late on in the evening I saw the boy's mother, there at the villa, which we were using as a base for our search."

"And the father?"

"Look, I can't tell you about the father. I saw Signor Rubino the following day, but I don't know when he arrived or where from."

"Do you know if he was on holiday too?"

"No."

"Do you know if the grandparents telephoned the father, as well as the child's mother?"

"I don't know."

"In more general terms, do you know who informed the boy's father?"

"No."

"In any case, on the evening of the disappearance

the mother had arrived and the father not. Is that correct?"

"It is."

"Thank you, I have no more questions."

In actual fact these were pointless questions. The separation of the parents had nothing to do with the child's disappearance, with the trial or any of the rest of it. The prosecution and the civil party were probably right in objecting.

But I had very little room to move. Very little indeed. So I had to do something, even loose off shots at random, in the hope of hearing some sound, learning if in that direction there might be some way. Some track to follow.

Handbooks for lawyers would have said that this was the wrong way to set about it.

Never ask questions for which you cannot foresee the answer. Never cross-examine blindly, without having a precise object in mind. Your cross-examination must be punctiliously planned, nothing left to improvisation, because otherwise you might even strengthen the position of your adversary. And so on and so forth.

I'd really like to see the fine fellows who write such manuals conduct a damned trial. I'd like to see them in the thick of the noise, the dirt, the blood, the shit of a real trial. I'd like to see them apply their theories then.

Never cross-examine blindly.

I'd like to see them at it! Me, I was forced to go ahead blindly. And not only in the trial either.

That hearing continued with several other witnesses. There was the carabiniere who had received the call which enabled them to find the boy's body. He said that the anonymous voice was *strange*. The prosecutor wanted to know more. He would probably have liked the witness to say that the accent was *Senegalese*. The carabiniere, however, did not help him out. The accent, for him, was simply strange, which meant everything and nothing.

Then there were the dog handlers, who added nothing to what the lieutenant had said. Then the fireman who had gone down the well to fasten the sling around the boy's body and haul it up. A distressing, useless account.

Then we heard some of the habitués of the Duna Beach establishment. They knew Abdou, some had bought things from him, all of them remembered that from time to time the Senegalese stopped to chat with them on the beach. They said that they had also sometimes seen him talking to the little boy. I asked them how Abdou behaved, and they all said he was always friendly, that he had never behaved oddly. As for him and the boy, they had almost seemed to be friends.

We were to have heard the police doctor who performed the autopsy, but he wasn't there. He had sent a justification and asked to be heard during a later hearing. The judge was not sorry to get away a little earlier than expected. The trial was adjourned until the following Monday.

My fear was that by then, alas, the heat would have started. We couldn't always be so lucky with the weather, not in June.

25

A couple of weeks had passed since that evening with Margherita. In the interim we had neither seen nor spoken to one another. A strange thing had happened to me the following morning: I had felt guilty. Towards Sara, I think.

It was a strange thing because it was Sara who had left me and had been living a life of her own for over a year and a half. And yet, absurdly, for the first time I felt I had betrayed her. For the sole reason that I had enjoyed myself that evening in Margherita's company.

When we were married and living together I had done a lot of rotten things. They had made me feel uncomfortable, sometimes they had caused me to despise myself. But they had never really made me feel guilty, as I did after that evening.

I have often thought back on this phenomenon. At that time I didn't understand it. Now perhaps I do.

One grows fond even of grief, even of desperation. When we have suffered a great deal on account of a person, we are shocked by the fact that the grief is growing less. Because we think that means, yet again, that everything, really everything, comes to an end.

It isn't true, but I was not yet ready to understand this.

And I had not called Margherita. I had not called her because I was afraid of losing my grief. What strange creatures we are.

However, it was she who called me. I was in a bookshop at about half-past two in the afternoon, my favourite time. There's never anyone around, one can listen to the music and, with no people there, even catch the odour of fresh paper.

When I answered the mobile I was giving a quick reading to an essay. An old technique I acquired when I didn't have the money to buy all the books I wanted.

What was I doing? Well, I was in a bookshop. Would I care to have a cup of coffee with her? Yes, I would. In just the time it would take me to get home from Laterza's. About ten minutes. No, I didn't want the decaffeinated, a proper coffee would be fine. See you soon. Yes, I'm glad to hear from you too. Really glad.

While I was – without realizing it – hurrying home, it occurred to me that I didn't remember giving her my mobile number, that I didn't recall having talked about my sleeping problems and the decaffeinated coffee. And that I was glad she'd called me.

She greeted me by taking my hand, pulling me gently towards her and kissing me on both cheeks. A friendly, almost comradely greeting. Yet it gave me that certain feeling in the pit of my stomach, and I blushed a little.

She had me sit on the terrace, which was north-facing and therefore cool and shady. We drank our coffee and lit up cigarettes. She was wearing faded jeans and a short-sleeved T-shirt bearing the legend: *What the caterpillar thinks is the end of the world, the rest of the world calls a butterfly. Lao-tzu.*

Her face was tanned, and so were her arms, which were shapely and muscular. She had read about Abdou's trial in the paper, where it was, as they say, prominently featured. She had read that I was counsel for the defence and had called me because she wanted to know all about it. I had a slight pang of disappointment. She had called me only to learn about the trial, because she was curious. For a moment I had the temptation to stand on my dignity. It passed swiftly, I'm glad to say.

I told her. What was in the prosecutor's documents; the fact that it was a trial based on circumstantial evidence, but *lots* of evidence; of how I had been appointed, of Abajaje and all the rest of it.

I was expecting the question, and sure enough it came.

"Do you believe this young Senegalese is innocent?"

"I don't know. In a certain sense it isn't my problem. We have to defend them as best we can, whether innocent or guilty. The truth, if it exists, has to be found by the judges and jury. Our job is to defend the defendant."

She burst out laughing.

"Bully for you! What was that, the introductory lecture to a course on 'The Noble Profession of the Law'? Are you thinking of going into politics?"

I sought an adequate answer and failed to find one. She was right, and I asked myself why I had talked in that high-falutin' fashion.

"Hey, don't tell me you've taken offence? I was joking."

She peered into my face, craning forward and invading my space, and I realized that I must have kept silent more than was fitting.

"You're right, I was ridiculous. I do believe that Abdou is innocent, but I'm afraid to say so."

"Why?"

"Because I think so on the grounds of an intuition of mine, a mere fancy. I like him and therefore I think he's innocent. Because I *want* him to be innocent. And then, I'm afraid that he'll be found guilty. If I'm too convinced of his innocence and he's found guilty –

and he probably will be – it'll be a bad blow for me. Well, an even worse one for him, of course."

"Why do you like him?"

I surprised myself by answering without thinking. Discovering the answer at the very instant of uttering it.

"Because I recognize something of myself, I think."

The answer seemed to strike her, because she remained silent, looking at some spot below her on the left. She was rummaging in her thoughts, I imagined. I sat there watching her until she had finished, until she spoke again.

"I'd like to come and watch the trial. May I?"

"Of course you may. The next hearing is on Monday."

"May I read the papers first?"

I couldn't help smiling, I don't know why. I don't know why, I thought she didn't miss a trick. Always bang on. I remembered those manuals on martial arts she had on her bookshelves. I hadn't asked her why she had them, whether she practised one of those disciplines, and if so which. I did so now.

"You can read them whenever you like. I can bring them here, but perhaps it would be better if you came to the office. There's quite a pile of them. Why have you got all those books on martial arts?"

"I do a bit of aikido. Ever since I stopped drinking."

"What do you mean by a bit?"

"I'm a black belt, second dan."

"I'd like to see you at it."

"All right. Come inside."

We went in, she fetched a cassette from a cupboard, switched on the video and told me to take a seat.

The video opened with a shot of an empty gymnasium in the Japanese style, with a green tatami. I heard a voice off, saying something I didn't understand. Then into the picture came a girl in a white kimono and wide black trousers. Her hair was gathered in a ponytail. It took me several seconds to recognize Margherita. She was looking at a point outside the picture. From that point entered a man, in the same gear. He grabbed her by the lapel of her jacket, she took his hand and swivelled on her feet. She appeared to be moving in slow motion, but I still didn't understand how it was that the man was thrown with a slithering sound onto the tatami. Without pausing, but rolling onto his feet and turning, the man attacked again. His open hand chopped down towards Margherita's head. Another turn, another incomprehensible movement and the man flew into space again, his wide black trousers describing an elegant arc. There followed other sequences, in which the aggressors had sticks or knives, or attacked in pairs.

It was a hypnotic spectacle, lasting about twenty minutes. Then Margherita removed the cassette and restored it to its place. All that time she had said nothing. Even afterwards we both said nothing for I don't know how long. And yet, perhaps for the first time in my life, silence did not make me feel ill at ease. I didn't feel the urge to fill it in some way, with either my voice or some other noise. I had the impression of intuitively grasping its theme, flowing and delicate; its music, is what I thought at that moment.

When the time came for me to leave I realized that all the while, before and after the cassette, I had been looking mostly at her arms. Looking at the golden, luminous skin, the long, strong muscles. I had looked at the light blonde down on her forearms and how it was slightly ruffled when there came a gust of cooler air out on the terrace.

"You have very beautiful arms," I said when we were

at the door. Then I felt I couldn't leave things halfway, as I usually did. So I said the rest.

"You *are* a very beautiful woman."

"Thank you. And you're a very handsome man. You don't smile very often, but when you do you're beautiful. Your smile is like a child's."

No one had ever said anything like that to me.

26

Scheduled for the following Monday were the depositions of the sergeant-major who had drawn up the reports on the most important inquiries, the police doctor who had performed the autopsy and, above all, the owner of the Bar Maracaibo. The man who said he had seen Abdou pass his door shortly before the boy disappeared. It was a vital hearing, if not, indeed, decisive, so I had spent the Saturday and the morning of Sunday examining statements and consulting textbooks on forensic medicine.

On the Saturday morning I had also visited a stationer's where they made colour photocopies. The proprietress gave me a rather odd look when I told her what I needed.

However, when I left I was pleased with the job she had done and what I was taking away with me. It seemed to me that I had a few cards to play.

Margherita had come to the office on the Friday afternoon. She had read documents for more than three hours, alone in the room where we held meetings. She had asked a very puzzled Maria Teresa for a few photocopies, then at about nine o'clock she looked in to say hello. She would be away Saturday and Sunday.

With whom? I thought, though only for a second.

We'd meet on Monday morning, at half-past nine in the Court of Assizes. Love and kisses, she said as she left. Love and kisses, I'd have liked to reply. But instead I only gave her a wave, and then sat there watching her, slowly closing my hand in mid-air when she had left the room.

The weekend was still fairly cool, luckily, so working wasn't too irksome.

At about one-thirty on Sunday I thought I'd done as much as I could and decided to take a jaunt. At that time of day I could go to the sea. With the city deserted and the roads empty I could get anywhere I wanted in next to no time. I fetched a knapsack, put in a towel, bathing trunks and a book, and set off.

The city was really and truly deserted and in only a few minutes I crossed the whole centre and cruised along the seafront, passing the old Albergo delle Nazioni. The Mercedes purred smoothly along and I arrived at the motorway almost without realizing it. When I left home I'd intended to stop about twelve miles out of Bari, perhaps at Cozze or, at the farthest, at Polignano. But on the way I changed my mind and trod on the gas as far as Capitolo.

It was less crowded than I had feared, and I easily found a space in the car park of a bathing establishment which – it occurred to me as I was getting out of the car – must have been less than a mile from where the boy had disappeared.

I paid the ticket that covered parking and entrance fee, took off my shoes and set out across the sand. A strange feeling came over me. A year had gone by since the summer when I thought I was going mad. That year I had detested the blinding sunlight, I had detested the beaches, the people who seemed so relaxed while I was such a misfit wherever I went.

Now I felt like a convalescent. I looked at the people, the sea, the sand which I had detested the year before,

160

and I was amazed that it didn't hurt me just to look at it all. I felt a kind of sweet indifference and had some difficulty in imagining how, less than a twelvemonth ago, I could have been so sick.

It was a strange sensation, rather melancholy, but good.

I changed in a communal changing room, hired a deckchair and had them put it really near the waterline. The sea was just how I like it. Calm but not absolutely flat, with a breeze lightly ruffling the surface. It was fine in the sun, the heat just right for closing one's eyes and going to sleep with a book on the sand near the chair. Which is what I did, with the voices on the beach blending into the strange well-being which had enfolded me.

I dreamed, in the way one does dream in that peculiar halfway house between waking and sleeping, or else sleeping and waking.

I met Sara in the street near our home, or rather what had been our home but now was hers. She came up to me, put her arms round me and kissed me on the lips. I embraced her too, but was embarrassed. After all – in the dream – we hadn't seen each other or spoken for four years. I somehow told her this. She gave me a look and asked if I was mad, but her face was scared, as if she were about to burst into tears. I said again that we hadn't seen one another for four years and at this she really did burst into tears, desperate tears. She asked me why I said something so spiteful, and I didn't know what to do, because she seemed really and truly distressed. I grew sad, but thought that it was only a dream and wanted to open my eyes. But for an indefinite length of time I couldn't do it, and there I remained, half way between the dream and the voices on the beach.

Then I felt splashes of water on my face and chest, and heard a voice I recognized at once. Elena.

"Guido! Guido, it's been such ages!"

"Elena, what a lovely surprise . . ."

Liar, you miserable liar, was my actual thought. I had always detested Elena. Her and her beastly husband and her group of beastly friends. She had gone through secondary school and university with Sara, and was convinced of being her best friend. Sara was not of the same opinion, but didn't like to be rude. We were therefore periodically forced to accept dinner invitations from Elena, and sometimes even to ask them back.

Bending down to embrace me, she immersed me in a cloud of Opium. Wearing Opium on the beach? I felt sure that after the separation she had said a lot of things about me, none of them very flattering. Now, perfectly in keeping with her character, she embraced me, kissed me and asked what I'd been doing in all that time.

"Guido, how well you look! Have you been going to the gym over the winter? Are you alone or with a girlfriend?" Here she winked, as if to say: *You can tell me all right, I'll confine myself to putting a notice in the paper and pasting up a few hundred posters around the town.*

"Yes, you bitch, I'm alone and I want to stay that way. However, since you've turned up to get on my tits I've got something to say to you, so lend an ear. Your dinners were always a torture and, most of all, the food was vomit-worthy. I know they all said you were a great cook, but that will always remain a mystery to me. Your husband is, if possible, worse than you are. And your friends are, if possible, worse than him. One time they even suggested I join the Rotary Club. I want to tell you that I'm a *Communist*. That at so many dinners for so

162

many years you were entertaining a *Communist*. Got that?"

These and other things I would have liked to say. But obviously I replied with nauseating courtesy. Yes, I was alone; no, I had no girlfriend; yes, I really meant it; no, I had not seen Sara for quite a while. Ah, she was here at the sea on her own, was she? Were she and Mario having problems? Who wouldn't have troubles with Mario. With her too, come to that. We ought to get together one of these evenings. Her and me? Certainly, why not? Did I have her mobile number? Yes. I'm pretty certain. Ah, but I couldn't because she had a new one. Then she'd have to give it me. So, I'd call her? She could count on it? Of course she could. Of course, of course. Ciao, see you soon, kiss, Opium, kiss again and Grand Finale with a wink.

I took a dip to see how the water was and to wash off the Opium. The water was really cold. After all, we were only in mid-June and the weather had never got really hot. I swam a few strokes, felt that for my first bathe of the season that might be enough, and decided to take a stroll along the beach, by the water's edge.

The beachball players were there, but not so many of them as in July and August. I would have liked to kill them but, seeing that it was early in the season, I was willing to concede them a quick death. In July or August I would have wished them a long and painful one.

I detest beachball players, but as I walked – doing my best to get in the path of the ball as often as possible – I saw a species of creature I detest even more than beachball players. The beach-haunting pipe smoker.

I'm not exactly mad about pipe smokers anyway. I get a bit prickly when I see someone smoking a pipe in the street. I get really prickly when I see someone – as I did that afternoon – smoking a pipe on the beach, looking around him with the hauteur of a Sherlock Holmes. In bathing trunks.

As I was turning over these ideas about pipe smokers and beachball players, it occurred to me that I must really be a lot better if I had regained a little of my healthy intolerance.

At that moment there entered my field of vision a young black man with goods of all sorts hung on a kind of flexible rod balanced on one shoulder and in a large, tattered bag hanging half open. He was wearing a colourful ankle-length kaftan and a little drum-shaped hat. I stopped with my feet in the water for several seconds before I realized why I was looking at him.

When it had dawned on me, without having any particular aim in view, I decided to pay some attention to the way he worked and moved around the beach. Naturally I had no precise idea in mind. It occurred to me for a moment to ask him if he knew Abdou. But I dropped that and confined myself to watching him.

He seemed perfectly at home as he moved among the deckchairs and the towels stretched out on the sand. At almost regular intervals he gave a wave to one of the women on the beach, and they waved back. One of them called to him from a distance, but I didn't grasp the name. He turned and went up to her, smiling, dumped his stuff on the sand, shook hands and began talking. Obviously I couldn't hear what he said, but it was clear from his gestures that he was describing his wares. He stayed there more than five minutes, and in the end the woman bought a handbag. He resumed his round and I continued to follow him. With my eyes at first, but then on foot, keeping about twenty paces behind him. The scene I had witnessed was repeated several times in the course of half an hour. For no particular reason I decided to pass close by him, to get a look at him and then go away, because I'd had enough of spying on him. And just when I was close, walking beside him near enough to touch, I heard a shrilling sound inside his bag. He stopped and drew out an old Motorola mobile with the volume evidently turned full up.

He said *pronto* like the blacks in third-rate movies, that is *brondo.* Exactly like that. I thought that if he'd been Chinese he'd have said *plonto.* It wasn't a very brilliant thought, but it was precisely what passed through my mind at that moment.

The conversation was short and took place in Italian. That is, Italian of a sort.

Yes, he was working. On the beach, friend. Quite much people. Yes, friend, at Monopoli, beaches of Capitolo. He could come tomorrow, tomorrow morning. All right, friend. Ciao.

He switched off the phone and resumed his round. I stayed where I had knelt on the sand to listen to the call. An idea had just occurred to me.

And I wondered why I hadn't thought of it before.

27

"Don't you see, Guido, this is the best time of our lives. We can do whatever we like."

"Excuse me, but in what sense?"

"Sod it, Guido, you of all people. Since you've been alone you'll have gone from one screw to another with no problems. And you ask me in what sense."

"Ah, from one screw to another," I said noncommittally.

"Come off it, Guido, what the fuck's got into you? We haven't met for a year, maybe more, and you tell me nothing."

I was walking rather slowly towards the law courts, carrying two heavy briefcases containing the material I needed for the hearing. My friend Alberto had some trouble in keeping up with me, on account of being overweight and his sedentary life. We had met in the street, after more than a year. He had just turned forty, with two children and a wife who had grown fat and bad-tempered.

He owned a law firm – inherited from his father – that worked for banks and insurance companies and made a load of money. His favourite topic was *screwing*. To judge from his talk, he was a real specialist.

As a boy he had been a great charmer. One of those who is funny by nature, who always swore blue murder and made everybody laugh. But *everybody*. Because the way he did it, you just couldn't help laughing. He was someone who ought to have done a different job, maybe then he would have been happy, or something like it. Instead he had become a lawyer. Over the years the comic side of him had disappeared, along with his hair and everything else worth while. Alberto still swore but – I thought that morning – it had been a long time since he had made anyone laugh. He was a desperate man, even if he didn't know it.

"There's nothing to tell you, Alberto. I'm not going out with anyone."

"What, now that you're alone and can do what the fuck you like?"

"Yes. Life's an odd thing, isn't it?"

"Don't tell me you've gone queer, eh?" And off he went, telling me about someone I ought to have known, or at least remembered. I didn't remember him, but I didn't tell Alberto. This fellow I didn't remember – a certain Marco – was married and even had a son. At a certain point his wife had noticed a thing or two and become convinced that he had someone else. She had put a private eye on to him, and this operative had done a good job. He had discovered the intrigue and all about it. There was just one little problem. The fellow didn't have a girlfriend, he had a boyfriend. A butcher by trade.

"Don't you see, Guido, fuck it. His wife thought he was a dirty old man who was screwing some young chick and instead he was getting himself buggered by a butcher. Get that, Guido. A butcher. Perhaps he brought him horsemeat sausages for a snack . . . Don't tell me you've gone queer and get yourself buggered by, well, let's say a grocer?"

I assured him I had not gone queer and tried not to get buggered by anyone, within the bounds of possibility.

We reached the entrance to the law courts. Time for

goodbye and each to his own work. We absolutely must meet one evening along with the rest of the gang. He said some names that faintly rang a bell. For a pizza or perhaps a good game of poker. Of course, a real reunion. Yes, we'll call each other this week or next at the outside. Ciao, Guido, fucking hell it's done me good to see you. Ciao, Alberto. Me too.

He disappeared towards the lift up to the fifth floor, where the civil courtrooms were. I stood there watching him, thinking that in some far distant place lost in the mists of time we two had been friends. Really friends.

The very thought was beyond belief.

Farewell, Alberto, I wanted to say. And I did say it, quietly, but audibly enough for anyone who happened to be close by at that moment.

But no one was.

Before the hearing started I had a word with Abdou. I had to find out whether the idea that had come to me on the beach made sense and could be followed up.

It could. Perhaps we had one further chance, but I did my best to repress any enthusiasm. When you get an idea that seems perfectly brilliant it usually doesn't work, I told myself. In which case it's a let-down for you.

As had happened all too often. But not often enough to make me accept it.

Margherita arrived on the dot of half-past nine. She greeted me with a smile from the public benches. I beckoned to her to come and sit near me. She shook her head and gestured with both hands as if to say she was all right where she was. I went up to her.

"You look very fine in your robe," she said.

"Thanks. Now come and sit next to me. You've done your law exams, so it's permitted."

She gave a short laugh.

"If it comes to that, I'm even a member of the Bar Association. My father never gave up and went on paying the dues for me year after year. If I want to, I can start practising law at any moment."

"Excellent. Then come and sit by me. If you want to see how this trial is going, that's the best place to see it from."

She nodded agreement and came and sat on my right. I was glad to have her there. It gave me a sense of security.

We began with the police doctor. He confirmed what he had written in the autopsy report. He said that the boy's death had been caused by suffocation. He could not be more precise, because the causes of suffocation could be many. The boy had not been strangled, because there was no trace of the pertinent injuries. But he could have been smothered with a pillow, or by blocking his nose and mouth, or else suffocated by being kept in a very restricted space, such as the boot of a car. It was also possible – scientific literature cited several cases of the kind – that the suffocation had taken place during violent oral intercourse.

However, there were no signs of sexual violence and search for seminal fluid had given negative results. When his body was recovered, the boy was fully dressed in the clothes he had been wearing when he disappeared.

When thrown into the well the boy was already dead, because there was no water in the lungs.

I had no particular interest in cross-examining the doctor. I confined myself to getting him to state more clearly that the references to oral violence were merely the fruit of his conjectures, and that there were no objective data from which it could be inferred that that form of sexual violence – or any other – had in fact been used on the child.

After the police doctor the prosecution called Sergeant-Major Lorusso, second-in-command of the operations unit in Monopoli. Of the investigators, he was the most important witness. The reports of the main investigations had nearly all been drafted by him. I had come across him in other trials, and knew that he was a hard nut to crack. He looked like a clerk or a teacher, with glasses, thin fairish hair, and off-the-peg jacket and tie. At first sight he looked innocuous enough. But his eyes, if one managed to see them behind his spectacles, were cold and intelligent. Previously he had worked in the organized crime department in Bari, then he was involved in a story of violence inflicted on a suspect, along with a captain and another non-commissioned officer. They were all transferred, and Lorusso himself spent two years training recruits. For a cop like him that was a fitting punishment.

The examination conducted by Cervellati lasted more than an hour. The witness told of the searches for the boy, of how they had come to identify the witnesses; he spoke of Abdou's arrest, the searches of his lodgings, everything.

It was a clear and effective deposition. Sergeant-Major Lorusso was someone who knew his onions.

Counsel for the civil party, as usual, had no questions. What the prosecution did in this case was always all right with him. Then the judge called on me.

"Good morning, Sergeant-Major."

"Good morning, Avvocato." He answered without looking in my direction. He was sharp enough to know that my cordiality was aimed entirely at the jury.

170

Leave off the tomfoolery, Avvocato, and let's see what you can do. That is what was behind his "good morning". So be it, I thought.

"Would you repeat the nature of your appointment?"

"I am second-in-command of the operations unit in Monopoli."

"And what was your previous appointment?" I might as well get down to the knuckle at once, I thought.

"What has that got to do with it, Avvocato?"

Touché.

"Would you please tell the court the nature of your previous appointment?"

He hesitated a moment, seemed about to glance at Cervellati, then set his jaw briefly and finally answered.

"I was an instructor to the Carabinieri Cadet Battalion at Reggio Calabria."

"Not a position in the criminal police, if I understand rightly."

"No."

"And before that?"

At this point Cervellati intervened.

"Objection, Your Honour. I do not see the relevance of the sergeant-major's previous appointments to his deposition."

The judge turned to me.

"Avvocato, what is the relevance of the witness's previous appointments to this trial?"

"Your Honour, I need to ask these questions for purposes as under Article 194 sub-section 2 of the procedural code. The answers, as will become clear in due time, are of use to me in assessing the reliability of the witness."

The judge was silent for a moment, then the associate judge said something in his ear. At last, after another pause, he gestured to me to go ahead.

171

"So then, Sergeant-Major, what was your appointment previous to being an instructor of recruits?"

While I was asking this, Lorusso turned towards me for an instant and gave me a glare of hatred. I was about to do something not often done. I was about to violate the tacit pact of non-aggression that exists during trials between defence counsel and cops. He had realized this. If he ever got a chance, he'd make me pay for it. For sure.

"I was attached to the operations unit of the operations department in Bari, first section, organized crime."

"That is, the unit comprising the best investigators in the whole province. So if I have understood rightly you were transferred from a position in the front rank to that of . . . of an instructor of recruits in Reggio Calabria. Is that correct?"

"Yes."

"Was this a normal occurrence or was there some particular reason?"

I didn't much like what I was doing, but I had to shake his calm before going on to what really interested me.

"Avvocato, you know very well why they transferred me, and that I emerged from that business without a stain on my character."

"Would you tell us what business that was?" My tone was one of false cordiality. Perfectly odious.

The judge intervened, this time without waiting for the prosecution.

"Avvocato, take care not to abuse the patience of the court. Come to the point."

"Sergeant-Major, can you tell us why you were transferred to Reggio Calabria?"

"Because a crook caught red-handed in the possession of a kilo of cocaine with intent to peddle it, with a police record three pages long, had accused me, a captain and another NCO of having beaten him up. We were all three acquitted and that gentleman got ten years for drug trafficking. Will that do?"

"All right. You took the statements of Signor Renna, proprietor of the Bar Maracaibo, and also of the two Senegalese citizens Diouf and . . . I forget the name of the other. However, is that right?"

"Yes."

"Can you tell the court what methods you used for putting them on record?"

"In what sense, Avvocato?"

"Did you tape or videotape these statements?"

"We did not tape them. If you look carefully at those reports, you will see it in black and white that due to the unavailability of recording equipment the statements were drawn up only in summary form."

"Ah, yes, of course. So let us see if I have properly understood. You drew up the report in summary form only because the equipment for video or audio recording was not available. Is that correct?"

Lorusso realized what I was leading up to, but it was too late.

"At that moment I don't think we . . . it was an emergency situation . . ."

"I have a very simple question to ask you: in the operations unit of the carabinieri in Monopoli do you not have a tape recorder or video camera?"

"We had them, but at that moment . . . I think the tape recorder was out of order. I don't at this time remember exactly, but there was definitely some problem."

"The tape recorder was out of order. And the video camera?"

"We are not issued with a video camera."

"Excuse me, but I have here the report on the on-the-spot investigation relating to the finding of the child's body. It is stated here that 'the on-the-spot investigations were documented also by means of video-recording'. And, in fact, a video cassette is attached to the report. What have you to say about that?"

Cervellati almost shouted his objection. He was losing his cool.

"Objection, Your Honour, objection. It is inadmissible to conduct the cross-examination of a witness on the basis of how he drafted a report, whether he had a tape recorder, a pen or a computer."

"Your Honour, that it is inadmissible is the opinion of the public prosecutor. We are interested in finding out how certain statements were put on record, in order to discover whether, albeit involuntarily – since no one doubts the good faith of the investigators – I repeat, to discover whether there might have been some conditioning of the witnesses, or misunderstanding of what was actually said. Do not let us forget that the prosecution has asked for the reading of the declarations made during the inquiries of the two non-European citizens —"

Zavoianni interrupted me. He was getting rattled. He didn't like all these questions, he didn't like my procedural method and – I had always suspected it but now I was certain – he didn't like me.

"Avvocato, let us go on to something else. I have put up with a lot of totally irrelevant questions. Let us have some questions pertinent to the proceedings at last."

While looking at the judge as he spoke, I managed to steal a glance at Lorusso, who was breathing deeply, to relax.

"Your Honour, I believe it relevant to know for what motives the examination of persons in possession of

174

the facts, and in particular that of the non-European citizens whom we cannot re-examine here because they are nowhere to be found, was not fully documented."

"Avvocato, I have made up my mind. Proceed without questioning my decisions."

I compressed my lips for a moment or two. Then I started in again.

"Thank you, Your Honour. I would like you, Sergeant-Major, to tell us about the searches carried out at the defendant's lodgings."

"What in particular do you want to know, Avvocato?"

"How you set about it from an operative point of view, whether you were looking for anything in particular, what state the place was in, everything."

"I don't altogether understand your question. Operatively speaking, we searched Thiam's room, examining everything. We were not looking for any-thing in particular, but for anything that might be useful to the inquiry. It was there we found the photo-graph of the accused with the boy and the children's books, which are listed in the report."

"Did you find nothing else relevant to the inquiries?"

"No."

"Otherwise you would have taken them."

"Otherwise we would have taken them, obviously."

"Did you find a Polaroid camera, or any other kind of camera?"

"No."

"Now I would like to talk for a moment about those books. I read in the report of the search and the related seizure that Signor Thiam had in his room three novels for children in the Harry Potter series, *The Little Prince*, a fairy-tale in French, the well-known children's story *Pinocchio*, and another book for children entitled *Doctor Dolittle*. Is that correct?"

"Yes."

"Did Signor Thiam have only these books in his room?"

"I don't clearly remember now. There may have been something else."

"When you say *something else*, you mean some other books?"

"Yes, I think there were a few other books."

"Are you able to say approximately how many books?"

"I don't know. Five, six, ten."

"Would you be surprised if I told you that in that room there were over a hundred books?"

"Objection," put in the public prosecutor. "The witness is being asked for an opinion."

"I will rephrase the question, Your Honour. Are you certain, Sergeant-Major, that the books were not many more than ten or so?"

"Perhaps about twenty, not a hundred."

"Can you describe the room, and in particular whether there were any bookshelves?"

"It's nearly a year ago, however there was a bed, a bedside table . . . yes, there was a shelf beside the bed."

"Just one shelf or several, a bookcase?"

"Perhaps . . . it is possible there was a small bookcase."

"Now, I realize it is not easy after nearly a year, but I would ask you to make an effort to remember what there was in this little bookcase."

"Avvocato, I can't remember. Certainly there were books, but I can't remember what else there was."

"Sergeant-Major, you will certainly have understood that I wish it to emerge how many books there were, roughly speaking. I know the answer, but I would like you to remember."

"There were several shelves in the bookcase, and there were books, but I can't say how many."

"But you took only those indicated in the report. Why was that?"

"Because plainly they were the only ones pertinent to the inquiry."

"Because they were books for children?"

"Exactly."

"I see ... Now I would like to talk about the photograph, the one showing Signor Thiam with little Francesco. What can you tell me about this photograph?"

"I don't understand the question."

"Was it the only photograph in Signor Thiam's possession, or do you remember if there were others?"

"I don't remember, Avvocato. There were three of us carrying out the search, and I don't remember whether the photo was found by me or by a colleague."

"I would like to show you something." I took an envelope out of my briefcase, opened it unhurriedly and asked the judge permission to show the witness some photographs. He nodded.

"You see these photos, Sergeant-Major? Can you tell us in the first place whether you recognize any of the people represented?"

Lorusso looked at the photos I had given him – about thirty of them – and then replied.

"The accused is in many of them. The other people are unknown to me."

"Do you remember if these photos were in the defendant's room at the time of the search, or can you rule it out?"

"I do not remember and I cannot rule it out."

It was the moment for me to stop, to overcome the

temptation to ask another question. Which would have been one question too many.

"Thank you, Your Honour, I have finished with this witness. I request the attachment as documentary evidence of the photographs I have exhibited to the sergeant-major."

I showed the photos to Cervellati and Cotugno. They raised no objection, though Cervellati gave me a look of palpable disgust. Then I put them back in their envelope and consigned them to the judge.

Lorusso departed after taking leave of the bench and the public prosecutor. He walked straight past me, ignoring me deliberately. I could scarcely blame him.

The judge said that we would take a ten-minute break, and only then did I realize that Margherita had been next to me all the time without saying a word.

I asked her if she wanted a cup of coffee. She nodded. I would have liked to ask her what she thought of it. If she thought I had done well, and things of that kind, but then I thought it was a childish question so I didn't ask it. Instead it was she who spoke, while we were entering the bar inside the Palace of Justice, notorious for serving the worst coffee in town.

It was very interesting – she said – even if I did seem to be a different person. I had done well, but I had not been, as it were, exactly charming. Had it really been necessary to humiliate the sergeant-major that way?

I was on the verge of saying that I didn't think I had humiliated him, and in any case trials of this kind are bound to be brutal. This brutality was the cost of civil rights that we could not forgo, and in any case better a carabiniere humiliated than an innocent man convicted.

178

Luckily I said nothing of all this. Instead I stayed silent for a moment before replying. I then said I didn't know if it had been really necessary. It was certainly necessary to elicit those facts, which were important, and that maybe there was another way and maybe not. However, in those situations, that is in trials, especially tricky ones, with the media focused on them and all that, it's only too easy to show one's worst side. It was even easy to acquire a taste for it, for torturing people, with the excuse that it's sometimes a dirty job but someone has to do it.

We drank our coffee and lit cigarettes. This luckily interrupted the conversation on the ethics of lawyerhood. I said that the coffee in the law courts was also used to poison the mice. She burst out laughing and said she was glad I was able to make her laugh. I was glad too.

Then we made our way back to the courtroom.

28

The judge told the bailiff to call the witness Antonio Renna.

The latter crossed the courtroom looking about him with a cocksure air. He had the look of a peasant. A stumpy figure, checked shirt with a 70s-style collar, swarthy complexion and crafty eyes. Not at all an engaging craftiness either, rather suggesting *first chance I get, I'll cheat you.* He hoisted up his trousers by the belt with a gesture that seemed to me obscene, and took his time sitting down in the seat reserved for witnesses, shown him by the bailiff. With his back to the cage where Abdou was. He sat sprawling, filling the whole chair and relaxing against the back. He had an air of self-satisfaction, and I had a distinct urge to wipe it off his face.

Cervellati's interrogation was nothing but a kind of repeat of the one during the preliminary inquiries. Renna said exactly the same things, in the same order and more or less in the same words.

When his turn came, Cotugno finally asked a few questions, totally insignificant. Just to show his clients, the child's parents, that he existed and was earning his fee.

I was about to start my cross-examination when Margherita whispered something in my ear.

"I don't know what makes me think so, but this man's a turd."

"I know." Then I turned to the witness.

"Good morning, Signor Renna."

"Good morning."

"I am Avvocato Guerrieri, and I am defending Signor Thiam. I will now ask you a number of questions to which I ask you to reply briefly and without making comments." My tone of voice was deliberately odious. I wanted to provoke him, to see if I could find an opening so as to get in my blow. As in boxing.

Renna regarded me with his piggy little eyes. Then he addressed the judge.

"Your Honour, do I also have to answer the questions of a *lawyer*?"

"You are obliged to answer, Signor Renna." The judge's face expressed the thought that, were it in his power, he would willingly have done without me, and most other defending counsel as well. Unfortunately it was not. I, however, had gained a tiny advantage. The barman had swallowed the bait and from now on was more vulnerable.

"Well, then, Signor Renna, you told the public prosecutor that on the afternoon of 5 August 1999 you saw Signor Thiam walking quickly from north to south. Is that right?"

"Yes."

"Do you remember when it was you were heard by the public prosecutor during the inquiries?"

"He interrogated me a week later, I think."

"When were you heard by the carabinieri?"

"Before, the day before."

"Is your bar frequented by non-European citizens?"

"Quite a few. They come in for a coffee, they buy cigarettes."

"Can you tell us their nationalities?"

"I don't know. They're all niggers . . ."

"Are you able to tell us more or less how many *niggers* frequent your bar?"

"Don't know. They're the lot that go round peddling stuff on the beaches, and even in the streets. Sometimes they even hang about right outside my bar."

"Ah, they even hang about right outside your bar. But they don't interfere with your custom, do they?"

"They interfere, they interfere, and how!"

"Forgive me for asking, but if they are a nuisance, why don't you call the municipal police, or the carabinieri?"

"Why don't I call them? I call them all right, but d'you think they come?" He was thoroughly indignant now. But meanwhile Cervellati had seen what I was leading up to. A bit late though.

"Your Honour, I notice that the defence is continuing to ask every witness questions without any pertinence to the object of these proceedings. I don't see how it is possible to go ahead in this manner."

I spoke before Zavoianni could get a word in.

"I have finished on this point, Your Honour. I am going on to another."

"Taking great care, Avvocato Guerrieri. Very great care," said the judge.

"Well then, Signor Renna, I had a few other questions for you . . . ah, yes, I wanted to show you some photographs." Out of my briefcase I took a series of photocopies of colour photographs. I was deliberately clumsy about it.

"Your Honour, may I approach the witness and show him some photographs?"

"What photographs might they be, Avvocato?"

I was now about to start walking the tightrope. A wrong word on one side and I'd end up under disciplinary procedure. A wrong word on the other and I would have ruined everything I had accomplished up to that moment.

"They are photographs of non-European citizens, Your Honour. I wish to verify whether the witness recognizes any of them." In a carefully colourless tone of voice.

The judge made his usual sign to tell me I could go ahead. I hoped that Cervellati wouldn't ask to see the photos, or demand more precise information as to who were the persons represented, which was within his rights. He didn't do it. I approached the witness, photos in hand.

"Signor Renna, may I ask you to look at these ten photographs?" I felt my heartbeat accelerating wildly.

Renna looked at the photographs. He was no longer so relaxed as at the beginning. He had shifted towards the edge of his chair. Flight position, the psychologists call it.

"Do you recognize anyone in these photographs?"

"I don't think I do. There are so many of them who come by my bar, I can't remember them all."

I took the photos back and returned to my place before putting the next question.

"Nevertheless, and correct me if I am wrong, you remembered Signor Thiam perfectly well, did you not?"

"Certainly I did. He was always coming by."

"If you saw him, in person or in a photograph, you would recognize him, wouldn't you?"

"Yes, yes. He's the one in the cage."

Only at that moment did he turn round. I remained silent for a second or two before rounding it off.

"You know, Signor Renna, I put that last question to you because, of the ten photographs you looked at, two show the face of Signor Thiam, the defendant. But you said you didn't think you recognized any of them. How do you explain this fact?"

A coup of this order is very rare in a trial, as indeed in life. But when it comes off, the feeling it gives is almost indescribable. I felt time slow down, and the tension in the air and on my skin. I felt Margherita's eyes on me, and I knew there was no need to ask her if I'd done well. I had.

"You just let me see those photos again . . ." Renna addressed me as *tu*, and not because we had suddenly become friends. It sometimes happens like that.

"Don't worry about the photos. I assure you that two of these photos represent the defendant, as the court will be able to verify shortly, when I produce them. From you I wish to know how you explain – if you can explain – the fact that you were not able to recognize Signor Thiam."

Renna replied angrily, almost lapsing into dialect.

"Explain, explain. Why they're all the same, these niggers. How can I tell, after a year . . . I'd like to see you, Avvocato, I'd just like to see you . . ."

Stop there, stop there, I told myself, feeling an almost overwhelming urge to ask another question and triumph. Or else blunder. *Stop there.*

"Thank you, Your Honour, I have finished with this witness. I ask to produce the photographs, or rather the photocopies, used during the cross-examination. The two showing the defendant have a note on the back. The others are of subjects quite extraneous to the proceedings and are taken from various periodicals."

Cervellati wanted to ask a few additional questions, as was his right by law. However, the very fact that he made use of that right meant he was showing signs of weakening.

He made Renna repeat his account, made him clarify

the fact that a year ago it had all been fresh in his memory, and that since then he had not seen the accused, either in person or in a photograph. He patched together a few fragments, but we both knew it would not be easy to rid the minds of the jury of the impression they had received that morning.

29

The next hearing – on Wednesday, 21 June – Margherita did not attend because she had a job to finish. She had told me she would try to be there for Abdou's interrogation the following week.

That morning the boy's parents and grandparents were heard. Cervellati and Cotugno questioned them at length about insignificant details. They could have done without it.

I put only a few questions, to the grandfather. Did he have a Polaroid? He did, and he remembered taking shots on the beach last summer. It was possible – though he didn't remember it – that the boy had kept some. In any case, he couldn't say where those photos had got to.

Of the parents I asked nothing, and while I was watching them during Cervellati's examination I grew ashamed of having put those questions about the separation to the carabinieri lieutenant.

They were more or less my age. He was an engineer and she a physical education teacher. They answered the questions identically, behaved in the same way. Lifeless, not even angry. Nothing.

Abdou spent the whole hearing clutching the bars of the cage, his face pressed between them, his eyes riveted on those witnesses, as if longing to attract their attention and tell them something.

But those two didn't look anyone in the face, and when their deposition was over, they went away without so much as a glance at the cage in which Abdou was locked.

They no longer cared about anything, not even that the presumed author of all that destruction was punished.

The thought occurred me that if we had had a child when Sara had brought the matter up, it would now have been about six years old.

The trial was adjourned until the following Monday, for the examination of the defendant and any possible applications for additional evidence before the closing argument.

I left the courtroom, cool as it was with its air-conditioning, and was enveloped in the damp and deadly heat of June. It had arrived, even though late. I loosened my tie and unbuttoned my collar on my way down the broad central steps of the law courts.

I walked homewards with a strange buzzing in my head. I feared a return of my trouble a year before, and it occurred to me that since that time I had never used a lift.

My thoughts began to get muddled, fear was encroaching. I might have been in a scene of one of those disaster movies where the hero is fleeing desperately before the waters flooding an underground tunnel.

In a strange way this idea helped me. I told myself I no longer wanted to run away. I would stop, I would hold my breath and let the wave sweep over me. Come what may.

I did exactly that. I mean I really stopped in the street, took a deep breath and stood there holding it for several seconds.

Nothing happened, and when I let it go I felt better. Much better, with a brain that was functioning again, lucidly, as if it had been cleansed of old incrustations and piles of rubbish all in one go.

It was then that I had the idea of passing by the office before going home. I had decided to try something.

On my way to the office I began breathing by forcing my diaphragm down, as I used to before a boxing match. Trying to empty my mind and to concentrate on what I had to do.

I reached the street door, got my keys from my briefcase, opened the door and dropped the keys back in. I rebuttoned my collar and reknotted my tie. Then, instead of heading for the stairs as I had done for about a year, I pushed the button and called the lift. While it was on its way down I felt my heartbeat quicken and heat surge to my face.

When the lift arrived I told myself that I mustn't think and I mustn't hesitate. I opened the metal outer door, then the two inner flaps. I entered, closed the metal door, closed the inner ones, looked at the panel of buttons, placed the first finger of my right hand on number eight, shut my eyes and pressed.

I felt the lift jerk upwards and thought the test wouldn't work if I kept my eyes shut. I opened them wide as I felt my breath coming short, my arms and legs weaken.

When the lift reached the eighth floor I remained motionless for a short while. I told myself that it was no good if I couldn't stay there another ten seconds without moving, even at the risk of someone calling the lift.

I counted. A hundred and one. A hundred and two. A hundred and three. A hundred and four. A hundred and five. A hundred and six. A hundred and seven. A

188

hundred and eight. A hundred and nine. There I stopped, my hand hovering near the knob of one of the inner doors. I had pins and needles all over my body, but really fiercely in that hand and arm.

I had stopped time in its tracks.

A hundred and ten.

Slowly I opened one flap. Then the other. Then I opened the metal door. Without leaving the lift I looked out at the broad slabs of marble paving the landing. I knew I mustn't put a foot on the cracks between them. I must be careful to tread from one slab to the next. I remembered that was exactly what I had always thought coming out of that lift ever since I had used it.

I thought: what the hell.

And I put the first foot right between two slabs. I was not concerned about the second, but turned to close the lift doors with intense concentration. First the two inner flaps, then the metal door, which I pushed to gently until I heard it click.

I stayed there leaning against the wall of the landing for maybe ten minutes. I held my briefcase in front of me with both hands, my arms stiff. From time to time I swung it to and fro. I looked into space with half-closed eyes and, I think, a slight smile on my lips.

When enough time had passed I pushed myself away from the wall. I recalled how a year before I had met Signor Strisciuglio, and thought now of knocking at his door. To tell him how it had all ended.

But I didn't. I stepped back into the lift, which no one had summoned in the meantime, and left the building.

High time to get home.

30

When I was a child and they asked me what I wanted to be when I grew up I always said "a sheriff". My idol was Gary Cooper in *High Noon*. When they told me there weren't any sheriffs in Italy, but only policemen, I promptly replied that I would be a policeman sheriff. I was a good child and wanted to hunt down wrongdoers one way or another.

Then – I must have been about eight or nine – I witnessed the arrest of a bag snatcher in the street. As a matter of fact I don't know if he was a bag snatcher or a pickpocket or some other kind of petty crook. My memories are slightly vague. They only become clear for one short sequence.

I am with my father walking along the street. There is a rumpus behind us and then a skinny youngster rushes past us like greased lightning, it seems to me. My father clasps me to him, just in time to prevent me being knocked over by another man, also running. He is wearing a black sweater and yelling out as he runs. Yelling in dialect. He is yelling to the boy to stop or else he'll kill him. The boy doesn't stop of his own accord, but perhaps twenty yards further on he crashes into a pedestrian. He falls. The man in the black sweater is on top of him and now a third man is coming up, bigger and slower on his feet. I wriggle free from my father and get near them. The man in the black sweater strikes the boy, who from close up looks little more than a child. He hits him in the face with his fists, and when the other tries to protect himself, he tears his hands away and starts hitting him again, yelling in dialect, "You son of a whore. Go fuck your mother. Damn you, you fucking bastard." And another smash on the head with his clenched fist. The boy cries out, "Stop it, stop it", also in dialect. Then he stops shouting and bursts into tears.

I watch the scene, hypnotized. I feel physically sick and also ashamed at the sight of it. But I can't tear my eyes away.

Now the other man, the big one, comes up. He has a placid look and I think he's going to intervene, to put an end to that horror. He stops running five or six yards from the boy, who is now huddled on the ground. He covers that distance at a walk, panting hard. When he is standing right over the boy, he takes a deep breath and kicks him in the stomach. Only one kick, but really hard. The boy stops weeping even. He opens his mouth and stays that way, unable to breathe. My father, who until then has also been petrified with horror, steps forward to intervene, says something. Of all the people around, he is the only one to make a move. The man in the black sweater tells him to mind his own bloody business. "Police!" he barks. But they both stop hitting the boy. The big man lifts him, grasping him by the jacket from behind, and forces him onto his knees. Hands behind his back, held by the hair, handcuffed. This is the most obscene memory in the whole sequence: a helpless boy at the mercy of two men.

My father pulls me away and the scene fades.

From then on I gave up saying I wanted to be a sheriff.

That episode had occasionally come to mind over

the years. Sometimes I told myself I had become a lawyer as a sort of reaction to the disgust I had felt. Sometimes, in moments of self-glorification, I had even believed it.

The truth, however, was quite different. I had become a lawyer by sheer chance, because I had found nothing better to do or wasn't up to looking for it. Which comes to the same thing of course.

I had enrolled in law school because I hoped to gain time, because my ideas were none too clear. When I graduated, I sought to gain more time by parking myself in a law firm while waiting for my ideas to clarify.

For some years after that I thought I was working as a lawyer only until I got my ideas clear.

Then I gave up thinking this, because time was passing and I was afraid that if I did get my ideas clear I would be forced to draw some unpleasant conclusions. Little by little I had anaesthetized my emotions, my desires, my memories, everything. Year after year. Until the time when Sara showed me the door.

Then the lid blew off and from the pan emerged a lot of things I had never imagined and didn't want to see. That no one would want to see.

Every man has reminiscences that he would not tell to everyone, but only to his friends. He has other matters in his mind that he would not reveal even to his friends, but only to himself, and that in secret. But there are other things which a man is afraid to tell even to himself, and every decent man has a number of such things stored away in his mind.

Dostoyevsky. *Notes from Underground.*

It isn't good when those stored-away things come out. All at once.

I reflected on all these things, and others, while working through piles of routine matters in the office. I checked on expiry dates, wrote simple deeds and, above all, made out some bills. I had to, in view of the fact that defending Abdou would not make me a rich man. The room was cool, thanks to the air-conditioning, whereas outside the heat had set in, for keeps.

I finished at about seven. My room is north-facing and has a big window to the left of the desk. Looking out, I noticed the sun on the terrace of the building opposite, then I lent an ear to the faint buzzing of the air-conditioning and the muffled music coming from the apartment below.

Such awareness was unusual for me and made me feel good. It occurred to me that I wanted a cigarette, but not in the usual way. I wanted to do things with calm. I picked up the packet lying on the desk and held it in my hand for a while. I popped one out by tapping with two fingers on the bottom end and took it directly between my lips. I remembered the infinite number of times I had made that series of gestures like an automaton. I felt that now I was able to look into the void without being overcome with dizziness. Able not to tear my eyes away. I felt a kind of shiver pass through my whole body and simultaneous exaltation and sadness. I had a vision of a ship leaving harbour for a long voyage. I put a match to the cigarette and felt the smoke strike my lungs as another sequence of memories burst upon me. But they held no terror for me now. I could tell you exactly what I thought at each puff of that cigarette.

They were eleven in number. When I stubbed out the butt in the little glass bowl I used as an ashtray I knew that after the trial was over there was something I must do.

Something important.

31

On the Friday morning, having dropped in at the law courts for a preliminary hearing, I went to see Abdou in prison. His interrogation was fixed for the following Monday and we had to prepare for it.

The warder in charge of the register ushered me into the interview room and, with what seemed to me a malevolent smirk, closed the door. The heat was suffocating, worse than I'd expected. I removed my jacket, loosened my tie, unbuttoned my collar, and finally decided that I was not a prisoner, that there was no rule that said I had to stay shut in there gasping for breath, so I opened the door. The warder in the corridor gave me a nasty look, seemed about to say something, but then let it go.

I leaned against the doorpost, half in and half out of the room. I took out a cigarette but didn't light it. Too hot even for that.

I felt the shirt sticking to my back with sweat, and into my brain burst a thought straight from the recesses of my childhood.

What you need is talcum powder.

When we were sweaty as children, they sprinkled us with talcum powder. If you made a fuss, because you thought you were too grown up for talcum powder, you were told that you might catch pleurisy. If you asked what pleurisy was, you were told that it was *a serious illness.* The tone in which they said this put paid to any wish to ask again.

Thinking thus, I realized that it was the second time in as many days that I had remembered childhood things. This was odd, because usually I *never* thought about my childhood. Whenever anyone asked how my childhood had been, I always answered at random, sometimes saying I'd had a happy childhood, sometimes that I'd been a sad little boy. Sometimes, when I wanted to make an impression, I said I'd been a *strange* child. It gave me an aura of glamour, I thought. We special people have often been strange children, was the implication.

The truth was that I remembered next to nothing of my childhood and had no wish to think about it. I had occasionally tried really hard to remember, and it made me sad. So I gave up. I didn't care for sadness, I preferred to avoid it.

Now I looked with amazement at these fragments of memory popping out from goodness knows where. They made me slightly melancholy and gave me a sense of astonishment and curiosity. But not sadness, not what had previously made me look away.

I meditated on this further change in me, and a really cold shiver ran up my spine to the roots of the hair on the nape of my neck and down my arms. Even in that heat.

I lit that cigarette.

I saw Abdou arriving from way down the corridor.

He came up to me and gave me his hand, with a motion of his head that looked to me like a little bow. It seemed only natural to reply in kind, but then I felt embarrassed.

He had a newspaper with him, and stood aside for me to enter the room.

We sat down, both of us avoiding the ever-present, broken-seated armchair. Abdou handed me the newspaper with a kind of smile.

"What is it?" I asked.

"It talks about you, Avvocato." The tone of his voice had changed.

I took the paper. It was three days old. It mentioned the hearing of the previous Monday and there was even a photo of me. I hadn't seen it, let alone read it: for a year now I hadn't bought the papers.

KEY WITNESS WAVERS IN LITTLE FRANCESCO'S DEATH TRIAL

A dramatic hearing yesterday in the trial of Senegalese citizen Abdou Thiam for the kidnap and murder of little Francesco Rubino. Evidence was given by several of the key witnesses for the prosecution, including Antonio Renna, owner of a bar in Capitolo, the seaside district of Monopoli from which the child disappeared.

In the course of the preliminary inquiries Renna stated that he had seen the accused passing his bar, very close to the scene of the disappearance and only a few minutes before the disappearance itself. Interrogated in court by the public prosecutor, the witness confirmed these statements with a great show of confidence.

The sensation occurred in the course of the spectacular cross-examination conducted by the counsel defending the Senegalese, Avvocato Guido Guerrieri. After putting a number of apparently innocuous questions, from the answers to which there emerged, however, a patently hostile attitude on the part of Renna towards non-European immigrants, Avvocato Guerrieri showed the witness a number of photographs of black men, asking him if they portrayed anyone he recognized. The bar owner said no, and it was then that the defence counsel played his trump card: two of those photographs were in fact of the defendant, Abdou Thiam. The very person whom the witness Renna had with such confidence declared having seen pass his bar on that tragic afternoon. The photographs were attached by the court as documentary evidence.

Public Prosecutor Cervellati was forced to re-examine the witness with a view to explaining the details of his deposition. The witness explained that he had not seen the accused since the year before, when the events took place, that he was certain about his statements and had not recognized the accused in the photos because it was so long ago and the photographs were badly printed. The latter were, in fact, imperfectly reproduced colour photocopies.

The re-examination conducted by the public prosecutor to some extent repaired the damage, but it is unquestionable that in the course of this trial Avvocato Guerrieri has scored several points in his favour in what is undoubtedly a very difficult trial for the defence.

Interrogated before the bar owner were the police doctor and Sergeant-Major Lorusso, the detective who conducted the inquiries. The cross-examination of Lorusso also had its tense moments, when the defence hinted at shortcomings and oversights in the course of the searches carried out at the lodgings of the Senegalese.

The trial continues tomorrow with the parents and grandparents of the little boy. Fixed for next Monday is the interrogation of the accused and then, except in the event of eventual applications to produce fresh evidence, the trial will proceed to the closing argument.

I read the article twice. *Spectacular cross-examination.* I could not suppress a feeling of childish pleasure at reading those words and seeing my photograph in the paper. Occasionally during other trials I had got a mention and even had my photograph printed.

But in this case it was different. I was the protagonist of the whole article.

When had they taken that photo? It wasn't very recent, perhaps a couple of years old, but I couldn't remember the occasion. I looked fairly good in it, even though, all told, I thought I looked better in real life.

After a second or two of such reflections I felt a complete idiot, put down the paper and turned to Abdou.

He was watching me. From his expression it was clear that now he was convinced that we would pull it off. He had read the paper and was now thinking that perhaps he had been lucky, that he was in the hands of the right lawyer. I asked myself whether I had better tell him that despite the fact that things had gone well in the hearing, the odds were still heavily against us. I concluded that there was no reason to do so. I therefore only nodded and gave a slight shrug. It could mean anything or nothing.

"Right, Abdou. We must now put our minds to the next hearing. Your interrogation."

He nodded and said nothing. He was attentive but it was not up to him to talk. It was up to me.

"I am now going to tell you how the thing works, and how you must behave. If something I say is not clear to you, please interrupt me and tell me so at once."

Another nod. "Of course."

"You will first be examined by the public prosecutor. While he is asking you questions, look him in the face. Attentively, not with an air of challenge. Do not answer until he has finished the question. When he has finished, turn towards the bench and speak to the court.

Never get into an argument with the public prosecutor. Is that clear?"

"When the prosecutor is speaking I look at him, when I am speaking I look at the judges."

"OK. Obviously the same thing holds true when you are questioned by the counsel for the civil party, or when I question you myself. You must make it clear to the court that you are listening to the questions before answering them. Is that clear?"

"Yes."

"Wait for the questions to end before answering. Especially when I am doing the questioning. We must not seem to be putting on an act, with every question and answer memorized. You see what I'm trying to say?"

"It must not seem like an act between us two."

"OK. Don't sit on the edge of your chair. Sit well back. Like this." I showed him how. "But don't sit like this." And I showed him again, slouching back, sprawling, knees crossed and so on.

"The idea's clear enough, isn't it? You mustn't give the impression of wanting to run away, by sitting on the edge of your chair, but nor must you give the impression of being too relaxed. We'll be talking about your life, the fact that you might go to prison for a great many years, and so you can't be relaxed. If you seem relaxed, it means you're putting it on and they will realize that. Maybe unconsciously, but realize it they will. You follow me?"

"Yes."

"When you don't understand a question, or even if you are unsure of having understood it, don't try to answer. Whoever has put the question, ask him to repeat it."

"Very good."

"Then, before going on would you like to repeat to me what I've said so far?"

"I must look in the face whoever is asking me questions. When the question is finished, I turn, look at the court and answer. If I don't understand a question, I must ask for it to be repeated, please. I must sit like this."

He sat as I had told him to. I smiled and nodded. He didn't need things said twice.

At that point I delved into my briefcase and took out the copy of his interrogation by the public prosecutor and various other papers. Having made clear how he must conduct himself, we now had to talk about what he would have to say, of how he was to explain what he had already said, and of the applications for additional evidence that I would have to put forward after his interrogation.

I was in the prison until three o'clock, with the heat becoming more and more insufferable. When we shook hands at the moment of parting, I felt we had really done everything we could.

I went home, had a shower, put on light trousers and a sweater. I made a salad, ate it, and smoked a couple of cigarettes, seated in an armchair and drinking a whizzed-up American coffee. At about half-past four I started for the office. I tried to buzz Margherita from the front door but she wasn't at home. I was disappointed, but thought I would ring her later, when I'd finished work.

At the office I saw a few clients, had a visit from my accountant, got through the correspondence, and having done that told Maria Teresa that she could pack up early for the day. I looked down at a sheet of paper on the desk before me. When I looked up again she was still there. I regarded her with a slightly questioning smile. She was not a beautiful girl, but she had lovely blue eyes, intelligent and humorous. She had been working for me for four years and in the meantime was studying for a law degree. She wanted to be a magistrate.

"Is there something?" I asked, still with that smile.

For her part, she seemed to be searching for words.

"I wanted to tell you that I'm glad . . . I'm glad that you're better. I've been very . . . very worried."

I was dumbstruck. Never since we had known one another had we so much as hinted at personal matters. After four years I didn't know who she really was, that girl, whether she had a boyfriend, what she thought and so on. I was simply not expecting her to say anything of that sort, even though I well knew that she realized what had happened to me. It was she who spoke again.

"I would have liked to do something to help you, when you were so ill, but you were so withdrawn. I was worried, I thought it might come to a bad end."

"Bad end?"

"Yes, don't laugh. I thought of people who commit suicide and then their friends and acquaintances say they were depressed, for some time they had been so changed, and things of that sort . . ."

"You thought I might kill myself?"

"Yes. Then these last months things have begun going better and I've been glad. Now they're going much better and I wanted to tell you. That I'm glad."

I didn't know what to say. The things that came to my lips were all banalities, and I didn't want to utter banalities. Whole worlds pass close by us and we don't notice. I was moved.

"Thank you," was all I said. Then I quickly got up, circled the desk and gave her a kiss on the cheek. She blushed, just a little.

"So . . . see you Monday."

"Yes, Monday. Thank you, Maria Teresa."

I had to finish preparing for Abdou's interrogation and also sort out a few technical questions regarding my applications for additional evidence. I therefore went on working until past eight, then shut up everything and went out. There was still some daylight left and a slight breeze had sprung up. The temperature was comfortable and I felt euphoric. I had done my duty, it was summer and it was Friday. For the first time for ever so long I had the weekend feeling, and a wonderful feeling it was. I wanted to do something to celebrate.

I tried calling Margherita on her mobile but it was off or didn't make the connection. I tried calling her on the intercom but she wasn't at home. I was disappointed, but only slightly.

I wondered what to do and came up with an answer at once. I went upstairs, packed a small bag, took a few books, got into the car and headed south. I was off to the sea.

I reached Santa Maria di Leuca around eleven and took a room in a small *pensione* right on the seafront. I had dinner and then went for a long walk up and down the front, sitting on a bench every so often to smoke a cigarette, watching the people and enjoying the cool night air. About half-past one I went to bed. I fell asleep at once, waking at nine o'clock on the Saturday. I couldn't remember when I had last slept so soundly. Perhaps when I was twenty or a little more.

Those two days were nothing but bathing, sun, eating, reading, sleeping and watching people. Scarcely a single thought. I watched the people on the beach, in the restaurants, and in the evening in the streets. I spent hours just watching people, without worrying that they were watching me too and might be speculating about me in one way or another. On Saturday morning on the beach I made friends with a woman from Lecce, about sixty-five and somewhat fat, in a blue flowered bathing costume, fortunately one-piece. She was nice, she told me about her husband, who had died three years before, and how she had been in a really bad way for five or six months and thought that her life was over because they had been married when she was twenty-two and she had never been with another man. Then she had begun to think that perhaps her life was not over, and that there were a few things she had always wanted to do but for one reason or another had always put off doing. So she started going to origami classes, which was one of those things she had always wanted to do, because when she was little her grandmother used to make her the loveliest toys by folding, cutting and colouring paper. Her grandmother had promised to teach her when she was bigger. But her grandmother had died when she was seven and hadn't been able to teach her. So she had learned origami and become very good at it – she showed me so by making a penguin, a seal and even a reindeer before my very eyes – and she'd taken a fancy to doing other things too, and had done them. For example, coming to the seaside on her own, or travelling, since luckily she didn't have money troubles and so forth. And you know, young man, when you have a lot of things to do, you haven't got time to think that your life is over, or how long you've got left, or that you're going to die and all that. You'll die anyway, so . . . While she was saying all this she started worrying in case I got sunburnt and handed me a bottle of lotion, advising me to put some on. I did so, and just as well, because the sun was scorching and I'd certainly have got burnt, spending all day on the beach. She wanted to know about me, and I surprised myself by telling her about my troubles, something I'd never done with anyone. Apart from the bearded psychiatrist, and even that with scant success. She listened without comment, and this pleased me too.

The next evening after supper I went to a kind of piano bar and stayed there listening to music until late. I made friends with the waiter, who was studying physics and worked weekends to make a little money. He told me that there were two girls at a nearby table, in a dark corner, and they had asked who I was. The student told me they were pretty and, if I wanted, he would take them a message. He said it pleasantly enough, not vulgarly. I said thanks, but no, perhaps some other time, and he looked rather surprised. I tipped him when I left. Maybe he thought I fancied men, but I didn't care.

That night too I slept like a log and woke up relaxed and happy. I spent the Sunday on the beach reading, jumping into the water, and smearing myself with the lotion the origami lady had given me.

At seven, with the sun still warm, I had a last dip, went by the *pensione* to pick up my bag and headed back to Bari.

I was a few miles from home when the mobile buried in my bag gave the sound it makes on receiving a message. I was curious, because it was a long time since I'd received any. So I pulled in to a service station, got out the phone and tried hard to remember how to read them. After a while I succeeded. The message read: *It would take too long to explain now. So don't try to understand. But I needed to tell you, now, that meeting you has*

205

been one of the most wonderful things that has ever happened to me. M.

I was stupefied for a moment or two, staring at those words, then I set off again for home. A few minutes later I felt like switching off the air-conditioning and lowering the windows. The mistral was getting up, sweeping the damp air before it.

I don't know if it was the wind that gave me the shivers on my skin, still warm from the sun, as I drove homewards with the windows down. From the loud-speakers came the voice of Rod Stewart singing "I Don't Want to Talk about It" and I was thinking about the words of that message, and many another thing besides.

I don't know if it was the wind that gave me those shivers on my skin.

32

The hearing began nearly an hour late, for reasons unspecified. I had a suspicion that before the court entered there had been some animated discussion in camera, because when they filed in and took their places their expressions were tense. The only exception was the buxom woman on the judge's left. She still wore the same look of superiority and simulated concentration that she had, with admirable consistency, maintained throughout every hearing. The attitude she evidently considered *comme il faut* for a member of the jury in a Court of Assizes.

If I was not mistaken and there had been an argument, it must chiefly have been between the judge and the associate judge. This I inferred from the way they were sitting. The judge had ostentatiously turned away from his associate, even to the point of shifting his chair. As for the latter, he was staring straight ahead of him and polishing his spectacles nervously and almost obsessively. They exchanged not a single word during the entire hearing.

It struck me that these were not the ideal conditions for a hearing of such moment. I also thought, quite irrationally, that the judge had already made up his mind to convict Abdou. This feeling weighed on my mind the whole morning.

Margherita had not come, but nor had I expected her to.

I can't say exactly why I was convinced that I wouldn't be seeing her that morning. In fact, I don't know if there was any reasoning behind it. But certain it is that I didn't expect to see her, only a few hours after that message.

Abdou was allowed out of the cage, unhandcuffed, and accompanied to the seat reserved for witnesses. Behind him, half a pace away, two warders.

The judge began by asking him if he confirmed the fact that he had no need for an interpreter. Abdou nodded, and Zavoianni told him that he could not confine himself to gestures but must say yes or no, speaking close to the microphone. Abdou said no, he didn't need an interpreter, he could understand.

The judge then asked whether he intended to answer questions, and Abdou said yes in a firm voice and speaking right into the microphone. Then the public prosecutor took the floor.

"First of all, Thiam, did you know little Francesco Rubino."

"Yes."

"But when you were interrogated you said you didn't know him, you remember?"

We were off to a flying start. I leapt to my feet for the first objection.

"Objection, Your Honour. This question is inadmissible. If the public prosecutor intends to impugn the defendant on the grounds of his previous statements, he must do so by declaring which document he is referring to and giving a full reading of the statements he intends to question."

The judge was about to say something but Cervellati got in first.

"I am referring to the record of his interrogation before the public prosecutor dated 11 August 1999. I will read it with a view to the impugnment, so that the defence will have nothing to complain about. So then . . . in the course of that interrogation you said word for word that —"

"Objection, Your Honour. The prosecution cannot affirm that my client said something *word for word* when he is referring to a report in summary form, such as is the one in question. In the interrogation cited by the public prosecutor – which is the first and the only one to which Signor Thiam has been subjected – use was not made of shorthand typing or any other form of recording."

This was not a genuine objection, but it enabled me to get across to the court from the start an important item of information: that the first – and indeed the only – time that Abdou had been questioned, there was no recording equipment, no video camera, no shorthand typist.

The judge overruled the objection and told me that he didn't like the way in which we had begun. I would have liked to say I didn't either, but I refrained. I simply thanked the judge and Cervellati resumed.

"I will read this statement: 'I am not acquainted with any Francesco Rubino. This name means nothing to me.' "

"May I explain? I knew the little boy by the name of Ciccio. That's what I called him. Everyone on the beach called him that. When I heard the name Francesco Rubino I didn't realize that it was Ciccio. For me the boy's name was Ciccio."

"In the course of that interrogation, however, at a certain point you admitted you knew the boy, did you not?"

"Yes, when I saw the photograph."

"You mean to say, when you were challenged with

the fact that a photograph of the boy had been found in your room?"

"When they showed me the photograph . . . yes, the one I had at home."

"Then it is correct to say that you admitted knowing the boy only when you realized that we had found the photograph —"

He was going too far.

"Objection. That is not a question. The public prosecutor is trying to draw conclusions and he cannot do that at this point."

Unwillingly, the judge sustained my objection.

"Signor Cervellati, please confine yourself to questions. Leave conclusions for when it comes to your final speech."

Cervellati resumed his questioning but he was plainly getting nettled, and not only at me.

"Well, Thiam, are you able to say where you were on the afternoon of 5 August 1999?"

"Yes."

"Tell the court."

"I was returning from Naples by car."

"What had you gone to Naples to do?"

"To buy goods to sell on the beaches."

"I have a question to raise, concerning the same document as before. I read from the text: 'On the afternoon of 5 August, I believe I went to Naples . . . I went to visit some fellow countrymen of mine, whose names I am, however, unable to indicate. We met, as on other occasions, in the neighbourhood of the Central Station. I am unable to provide useful indications for the identification of these fellow countrymen of mine and I am unable to indicate anyone in a position to confirm that I was in Naples that day.' You understand, Thiam? When you were interrogated, in

August of last year, you said you had been to Naples but you did not mention the purchase of goods etc. You only said you had gone to visit your fellow countrymen, whose particulars you were, however, unable to supply. What can you tell us on this point?"

"I went to buy goods. And I also went to buy hashish. I didn't mention these things because I didn't want to involve the people who sold me the goods and the hashish. And I didn't want to involve my friend who kept my goods and the hashish at his place."

"Who is this friend of yours?"

"I don't wish to say."

"Very well. This will serve in the assessment of the reliability of your story. What were you going to do with the hashish?"

"We bought it in a group with other African friends, to smoke it together."

"What quantity of hashish had you bought?"

"Half a kilo."

"And you expect us to believe this story? To believe that in order not to reveal the possession of hashish and counterfeit goods, you did not defend yourself on a charge of murder?"

"I don't know whether you believe my story. However, when I was interrogated I was very confused. I didn't understand exactly what was happening and I didn't want to involve people who had nothing to do with it. I didn't know what to do. If I'd had a lawyer I might have —"

"During that interrogation you *had* a lawyer!" Cervellati almost shouted. He was really losing his cool. I had no need to intervene.

"I had a lawyer appointed by the court. We didn't exchange a word before the interrogation and afterwards I never saw him again. If you asked me what he looked like I wouldn't be able to tell you."

"Very well," said Cervellati, trying to control himself and turning to the court. "I must not argue with the accused. Listen, Thiam, you said you went to Naples that day. Describe the events of the day in detail."

"The day I went to Naples?"

"Yes."

"I set off early in the morning, at about six. I got to Naples around nine. I went to a depot in the neighbourhood of the prison at Poggioreale, where I get my goods, and I loaded up the car. Then I went to a place really close to the station, where my friends were who had the hashish, and I bought it. I had the money we had put together in Bari —"

"Why did you have to go to Naples to buy the hashish? Can't it be got in Bari?"

"You can find stuff in Bari, but it's mostly grass, that is marijuana, which comes from Albania. But I had to go to Naples anyway for my goods. These friends in Naples have very good stuff and let me have it cheap, at cost price."

"What price do your pusher friends ask you?"

"A million lire for half a kilo."

"Which you then peddled in Bari."

"No. I didn't peddle it. We bought it cooperatively and then divided it up to smoke it ourselves."

"What time did you get back to Bari?"

"In the afternoon. I don't know exactly what time. When I unloaded the car at my friend's place it was still daylight."

"And of course – you've already told us – you don't want to tell us the name of this friend."

"I can't."

"Is there anyone who can confirm the story you have told us in this courtroom today?"

"A witness?"

"Yes, a witness."

"No, I cannot call anyone. What's more, I have been in prison for nearly a year, and I don't know if the people in Naples, or even my friend in Bari, are still in Italy."

"Very well. We therefore have only your word for it. In any case you can exclude the possibility of having gone to Monopoli, to Capitolo, that evening."

"No."

"You can't exclude it?"

"I mean I didn't go. When I finished unloading, I stayed in Bari. It was late and I wouldn't have found anyone on the beaches."

"You say you didn't go to Monopoli that evening. In that case, how do you explain the fact that Signor Renna – the proprietor of the Bar Maracaibo – declares that he saw you passing in front of his bar that very evening at about six o'clock? Are you of the opinion that Signor Renna has not told the truth? Do you think that Signor Renna has some reason for hostility towards you?"

"I don't understand. What is the meaning of 'hostility'?"

"Is it your opinion that Renna is accusing you falsely because he wishes you harm? Has he something against you?"

I was on the point of objecting, but Abdou answered first, and answered well.

"That is not what I said. I did not say that he is accusing me *falsely*. I know he is mistaken, but that is a different thing. To accuse falsely is when someone says something he knows is not true. He is saying something untrue but I think he believes it to be true."

"In the days following 5 August did you take your car to be washed?"

"Yes, after my trip to Naples. I took it to be washed at that time."

"Why?"

"Because it was dirty."

I seemed to perceive the trace of a smile on the lips of some of the bench. Those who remained deadly serious were the judge, the associate judge, the buxom woman who appeared to be embalmed, and the elderly man who looked like a retired officer. I remained very serious indeed. So did Cervellati, who continued his examination for a few more minutes, asking Abdou about the photograph of the child and a handful of other things.

Counsel for the civil party put a few questions, just to show he was there, then the judge gave me permission to proceed.

"Signor Thiam, could you tell us what work you did in Senegal?"

"I am a primary-school teacher."

"How many languages do you speak?"

"I speak Wolof – my native language – Italian, French and English."

"Why did you come to this country?"

"Because I couldn't see a future in my own country."

"Are you an illegal immigrant?"

"No, I have a residence permit and also a licence to sell goods. However, I also sold counterfeit goods. That's the illegal thing I did."

"How long did you know little Francesco?"

"I met him last summer . . . no, I mean the summer before . . . in 1998."

"Why did you have that photograph of the boy?"

"He gave it to me himself . . . the boy and I were friends. We often used to talk . . ."

"When was it given to you?"

"Last year, in July. The boy said that if I went back to Africa I could take it with me as a memento. I told him that I wouldn't be going back to Africa, but he gave it to me all the same."

"When was the photo taken?"

"The very day he gave it to me. His grandfather had a Polaroid camera and was taking photographs. The boy chose one of them and gave it to me."

"I would now like to turn to another matter. I see you speak very good Italian. I would therefore like to ask you something. Can you tell us the meaning of the sentence: 'I expressly renounce any time for defence'?"

"I don't know what that means."

"That's odd, Signor Thiam, because it's a phrase you appear to have pronounced during your interrogation by the public prosecutor. Would you care to read it?"

I went up to Abdou and showed him my copy of the record. I was expecting Cervellati to raise an objection, but he stayed seated and said nothing.

Abdou peered at the document, as I had told him to last week in prison. Then he shook his head.

"No, I don't know what it means."

"Excuse me, Signor Thiam, but did you not say that you renounced any time for you to prepare for your appearance and interrogation?"

"I don't know what this means."

That was the place for me to stop. The message, I thought, had got across. The record of Abdou's interrogation had been drafted pretty casually, and now the court knew it. I could change the subject and get on to the decisive point.

215

"You have said that on 5 August you went to Naples but that there are no witnesses who can confirm this fact. Is that right?"

"Yes."

"Have you got a mobile telephone?"

"I had one. When they arrested me they confiscated that too."

"Of course, it is on file in the report. When you went to Naples did you have that mobile with you?"

"Yes."

"Do you remember whether you made or received any calls that day?"

"I think so. I don't remember exactly, but I think so."

"Can you tell us the number of that mobile telephone?"

"Yes. The number was 0339–7134964."

"I have finished, Your Honour. Thank you."

The public prosecutor had no more questions and requested the attachment of the document used for his assertions. I made no objections. The judge said that after half an hour's break would be the time to put forward any applications for additional evidence. The court would decide whether to accept or reject them and we would agree on the dates for further hearings.

My feeling was that I was seriously in need of coffee and a cigarette.

33

The bar in the law courts had little tables like the ones in the snack bars of the 1970s. I got my cup of coffee at the counter, then went and sat at one, alone and with the intention of spending half an hour without thinking of anything or talking to a soul.

I lit a cigarette and sat there watching the people coming in and out of the bar. Peaceful.

There I was when in came a suntanned, stylish, bejewelled woman with the air of one who spends a lot of her time between the gym and the beauty parlour. She was making for the counter when she spotted me and stopped. She was looking in my direction with the beginnings of a smile on her face, as if she expected some sign of recognition. I glanced to right and left, to see if it was really me she was looking at. Behind me was impossible, because I was right against the wall. However, I was the only one at the tables, so it really was me she was looking at.

Noticing the way I acted, she came nearer. Her expression had changed a little. I imagine she thought I must be extremely short-sighted or extremely dim-witted.

"Don't you recognize me?" she said at last.

I craned towards her, and a doltish smile spread over my face while I hunted for something to say. Then I did recognize her.

From fifteen years before, or perhaps more. I had only just graduated. I couldn't remember what she was doing at that time, but certainly something quite different. Maybe studying medicine, or maybe I was confusing her with someone else.

We had gone out together for a couple of months, or perhaps less. She was older than me, by five years or so. So now she must be about forty-five. What was her name? I couldn't for the life of me remember her name.

"Magda. I'm Magda. How come you don't recognize me?"

Magda. We'd gone out together for two months fifteen years before.

What did we do? What did we talk about?

"Magda. Forgive me. I don't wear specs because I'm too vain and then I make this sort of a fool of myself. I'm a little short-sighted. How are you?"

"I'm well. And you?"

There followed an absurd conversation. I remembered almost nothing about her, so I was cautious, trying to avoid any more gaffes. She told me she was in the law courts for work reasons. The way she said it implied that I knew what her job was. But I hadn't the foggiest and while she went on talking – about separations, the single life, holidays, how we absolutely must meet again one evening with a series of persons whose names meant nothing to me – I felt sucked into a surreal maelstrom.

I recovered only when we parted, with hugs and kisses.

Ciao, Magda. When we meet again I'll pluck up the courage to ask you what we talked about, nearly every evening for two whole months, fifteen years ago.

The judge asked the public prosecutor and counsel for the civil party if they wished to produce any additional evidence. They both said no. Then he turned to me with the same question. I got to my feet and before speaking adjusted my robe, which, as usual, was slipping off my shoulders.

"Yes, Your Honour. We have applications in accordance with Article 507 of the code of criminal procedure. A short while ago the court heard the examination of the defendant. He stated that he was registered as the owner of a mobile telephone. This fact, moreover, has already emerged from the documents in your possession, because among the papers on file is the report of the confiscation of the instrument in question and the relative card, corresponding to the number 0339–7134964, the property of the defendant. The defendant stated that he took this telephone with him on that trip to Naples, and that he probably made and received calls on that occasion. You certainly know as well as I do that the use of a mobile phone leaves a trace which is preserved on a magnetic support by the telephone company, in this case Telecom. It is possible to acquire mobile-phone records showing the numbers of incoming and outgoing calls, the time and duration of each call and, above all, the area in which the telephone user was at the time of the call.

"Having said that, I think I need not make any further explanation of what importance may attach to the acquisition from Telecom Italia of the records relative to the use of the mobile telephone number 0339–7134964 on the day of 5 August 1999. It is true that we have no witness who can confirm the alibi of the defendant. The outcome of the mobile-phone records, however, might be far more telling than any witness. The location of the instrument in question at a precise time of day might provide evidence decisive

219

to the outcome of the trial. In conclusion, therefore, in accordance with Article 507 of the code of criminal procedure, I request an order of attachment of the mobile-phone records relative to the subscriber number 0339–7134964 for the day of 5 August 1999. I have nothing more to add. Thank you."

The judge kept his eyes on me for several moments after I had finished speaking. He was about to turn to the associate judge when he must have remembered that they had had a quarrel a couple of hours earlier. At least, I was convinced that for some reason or other they had quarrelled. There's no doubt that Zavoianni was turning towards the other judge and stopped half way. So suddenly that he had to strike an attitude, resting his chin on his hand with a thoughtful air. He had moved like a character in a farce and for some moments remained quite unnaturally motionless. Then he addressed the public prosecutor.

"Does the prosecution have any observations to make about this application by the defence?"

"Your Honour, I have many doubts not only about the absolute necessity, but even concerning the relevance to the present trial of this request on the part of the defence. These doubts may be summed up in a few words. Who is to say whether on 5 August 1999 this mobile phone was at Thiam's disposal? It is true that it was found in his possession at the time of the search. But this is of little significance. The search took place some days later, and we know that in certain circles – such as that of drug pushers, with which the accused has told us he is familiar, if not actively involved – it is common practice to pass around mobile phones, as it is with weapons and other things. In the absence of proof that this instrument was available to Thiam

220

at the date on which the unlawful restraint of the child took place, the evidence requested is without relevance.

"I might add a consideration of a purely procedural nature. Article 507 permits the taking of additional evidence when the need for it has emerged in the course of the proceedings. In this case the evidence could easily have been requested in the introductory phase, but the defence did not so act, whether from negligence or some other reason we do not know. In any case the request is late, and in this respect also it must be rejected."

"Does the civil party have any observations?" said the judge.

"We concur with the considerations put forward by the public prosecutor."

"Your Honour," I put in, "may I be permitted a brief objection to the observations made by the prosecution?"

"As you well know, Avvocato, objections are not admitted at this stage."

"Your Honour . . ."

"Avvocato, not a word more. I repeat, not a word more."

Thus saying, he rose to retire. One by one the members of the jury rose to follow him. The associate judge remained seated. I got the impression that he clenched his teeth for a moment. Then he too got up and was the last to leave the courtroom.

The wait was a long one. Usually decisions of that kind, regarding applications for additional evidence, are taken directly in the hearing, or after only a few minutes of consultation in camera. But not that day.

The hours went by without anything happening. I chatted a bit with the clerk of the court, who told me he didn't understand the reason for the delay. I told him that I didn't either, but it wasn't true. They were out that long because the court was in fact divided between those who had already decided to convict Abdou and those who wanted to understand things better. If the first lot won, and my application for the attachment of the phone records was rejected, I might as well save myself the trouble of disputing the case. Abdou was already done for. Only if the others won was our hat still in the ring.

From where he was in the cage, Abdou asked me what was going on and I lied to him, saying that the wait was perfectly normal.

I had an urge to call up Margherita, but I didn't.

For no reason I could put my finger on, there came to mind an ancient Turkish proverb that goes more or less like this: "Before you fall in love, learn to walk on snow without leaving footprints." Now why did that come to mind?

I felt terribly alone and, hell and dammit, I was on the verge of tears. After months, just then of all times, just there of all places.

No. Please, no!

I made for the courtroom door, just in case I should make a spectacle of myself, and anyway to have another cigarette. I had already put it to my lips when the providential ringing of the bell tore through my thoughts.

I returned to my place, put on my robe, and realized I still had the cigarette dangling from the corner of my mouth even when the court had filed back in and taken their seats and the judge was beginning to read the ruling.

I lowered my eyes to my desk, half closing them, blurring the papers lying there. I listened.

"The Court of Assizes of Bari, pronouncing on the application for the taking of additional evidence put forward by the defence of the accused Abdou Thiam, observes as follows.

"The defence of the accused – in accordance with Article 507 of the code of criminal procedure – applies for the attachment of the mobile-telephone records relative to the telephone traffic of mobile number 0339–7134964 for the day of 5 August 1999, on the double presupposition that the necessity for the aforesaid attachment has emerged in the course of the proceedings (and in particular from the examination of the accused) and that in any case the above-mentioned attachment is absolutely necessary to the ascertainment of the truth.

"The public prosecutor objects, maintaining the non-relevance (or at any rate the absence of absolute necessity) and the tardiness of this request.

"In fact – as the public prosecutor observed – the application could well have been made at the time of the introductory exposition, because the elements to make it were at that stage already in the possession of the defence.

"Technically, therefore, the application is to be considered tardy."

The judge paused, or so it seemed to me. I stayed stock still, eyes cast down, head bent. A moment or two later I realized I had been holding my breath.

"From another point of view, however . . ."

However! They'd granted it.

"From another point of view, however, we have to point out, in accordance with the judicial principles of the Court of Appeal, that the presiding judge is obliged not to neglect the fact that the primary purpose of a criminal trial cannot be other than to search for the truth. Within this perspective we cannot accept methods or decisions which unreasonably obstruct such ascertainment of the course of events as is required to arrive at a just decision.

"This said, we are bound to stress the fact that the evidence requested is to be considered as potentially decisive. From the attachment of the mobile-telephone records there could in fact emerge a real and proper alibi, in the case of the accused being located in a place incompatible with the hypothesis of his responsibility for the facts set down in the indictment.

"For these motives the Court of Assizes of Bari orders the attachment of the mobile-telephone records relative to the telephone traffic of subscriber number 0339–7134964 for the day of 5 August 1999 from 06.00 to 24.00 hours.

"It furthermore orders the presence of the officer responsible for Telecom (Bari Branch), or another employee of the company expressly empowered, to explain the precise meaning of the records before the court.

"It charges the criminal police with the execution of this order within five days.

"It postpones the taking of evidence and the closing argument until the hearing of 3 July.

"The court is dismissed."

When I reopened my eyes and looked up, the court had already left.

One week and it would all be over. One way or another.

34

During that week there were some strangely normal days. I worked as normal, attended my normal hearings, received clients, pocketed a few fees – which was all to the good – and so on and so forth.

I didn't concern myself with Abdou's trial. I had to wait for the mobile-phone records to arrive anyway, because on the result of that inquiry depended the line I would take in my final speech. Until then it was pointless to re-read documents or prepare for the closing argument.

On Thursday afternoon Margherita called me on my mobile. I had heard nothing from her since the message on Sunday evening. I hadn't called her, or tried her on the intercom. I don't know why. Something had held me back.

Would I care to go out for a drink after supper? Yes, I would. Should I buzz her from down below or knock at her door? Ah, she was going out earlier and could we meet up somewhere, fairly late on. How would Via Venezia suit me? In front of the Fort at about half-past ten? Fine by me. See you later, then.

Her tone of voice was a little puzzling, and worried me slightly.

From that moment on, the afternoon dragged by. My thoughts wandered and I kept looking at my watch.

I left the office at about eight, went home, had a shower and change of clothes, and started off long before the appointed hour. I whiled away the time in one way or another, and headed towards the Fort at about ten.

I walked up the slope of Via Venezia, crowded as it always was at that hour in summertime.

Mostly with groups of youngsters. They exuded a mixture of deodorant, sun cream and mint-flavoured chewing gum. A few bronzed fifty-year-olds with twenty-year-old girls in clouds of perfume. Very few of my age. I wondered why, just to give my mind something to toy with.

I reached the Fort at least ten minutes early, but I felt better simply because time had passed. I leaned my back against a wall and lit a cigarette, waiting.

She arrived at about twenty to eleven.

"So sorry. It's been a rough day. In a rough week. And that's only to mention this week."

"What's happened?"

"Let's walk, is that all right?"

We headed north, still on Via Venezia. The further we got from the area of the Fort, the more the crowd thinned out. Smaller groups, couples, a few solitary walkers, a uniformed policeman or two on duty.

We walked together without speaking until we drew level with the Basilica of St Nicholas. A fellow with a Corsican mastiff passed right by us and the huge dog stopped dead to sniff at Margherita's legs. She stopped too, stretched out a hand and stroked the dog's head. The owner was amazed that the ferocious creature allowed itself to be touched like that, and by a stranger too. It was the first time such a thing had happened, he said. Did the lady have a dog? No, she didn't. She'd had one, but it had died years ago.

The dog and its owner went on their way and we sat on the low wall facing the right-hand side of the basilica.

"How's it been going for you these last few days? How about the trial?" she asked.

"Well, I hope. Monday next we may see the end of it. And how about you?" Tentative.

She paused, then spoke as if I hadn't asked any question at all.

"In the places where they teach you to knock off drink they also explain how to resist the temptation to backslide. In the first year after treatment an awful lot of people relapse, and even after that it's very frequent. It was something they told us over and over again. There will be difficult moments – they told us – when you will feel depressed, you will have a terrible nostalgia for the past or fear of the future. At those times you will feel the urge to drink. An urge you feel you can't resist, that will sweep over you like a wave. But it's not irresistible. It seems so to you because at that moment you are weaker. But it really is just like a wave. A wave of the sea only submerges you for a second or two, even if when you are under water it seems like eternity. You come out easily enough if you don't panic. So remember – they said – that at such moments you have only to stay calm. Don't give way to panic, remember that your head will soon come out from under because the wave has passed. When you are struck by the overwhelming impulse to drink, do something to make the seconds or the minutes pass, or however long the crisis lasts. Do exercises, run two miles, eat a piece of fruit, call up a friend. Anything that makes the time pass without thinking."

I remained silent, fearful of what was coming next.

"It has happened to me several times, as it has to everyone. Aikido has helped me. When the wave came, I put on my kimono and went through the technical moves, trying to concentrate only on what I was doing.

227

It worked. When I finished training I'd forgotten the urge to drink.

"With time those moments have become rarer and rarer. For at least two years I hadn't had one."

I lit the cigarette I'd been holding between my fingers for several minutes. Margherita went on in the same tone of voice, gazing at some indeterminate spot before her.

"There's someone in my life, there has been for nearly three years. He doesn't live in Bari, and maybe that's why it has worked for so long. We see each other at weekends, either he comes to me or I go to him. Last weekend he came here. I had already mentioned you. Casually, as one might normally, and at first he didn't mind. Or if he did he didn't say so."

She turned slightly towards me, took my cigarette and smoked quite a lot of it before giving it back.

"However, I don't know how, but the discussion cropped up again last Saturday. That is, not so much a discussion as a jealous scene. Now, I should tell you that he is *not* a jealous person. He's quite the opposite. So I was taken aback and reacted badly. Very badly. We had been together, in a word we'd made love . . ."

I felt a stab in the guts. Instant fog in the brain for I don't know how long before I could grasp what she was saying again.

". . . and then I told him that I'd never have expected him to say such things. That I was disappointed in him and so on. He got back at me by calling me a hypocrite. I was lying when I said that you were just a friend. Lying not just to him but to myself, which made me even more of a hypocrite. And I was reacting so violently just because I knew he was right. We argued most of the night. In the morning he said he was leaving me. That I must get my ideas straight, and

228

try to be honest with him and with myself. After that we could talk about it again. He went off and I stayed put, sitting on the bed, my mind in a turmoil. Unable to think. The hours passed like a hallucination, and of course I got the urge to drink. A mad craving, such as I'd never had since I gave up. I tried putting on my kimono and doing some training, but there was no drive behind it. I had only this craving to drink, to feel good, to drown the turmoil in my head, to shuffle off responsibility and duty and effort, the whole bloody lot. Shit!

"So I went downstairs, got in the car and drove to Poggiofranco. You know that big bar that's open round the clock, I can't remember what it's called, where they sell wines and spirits?"

I knew the bar and nodded. My mouth was dry, my tongue stuck to my palate.

"I went in and asked for a bottle of Jim Beam, my favourite. At that point I felt calm. Deathly calm. I went home, got a big tumbler and went out onto the terrace. I sat down, broke the seal of the bottle – you know that lovely snap when you open a new bottle? – and helped myself to three fingers of bourbon, for a start. I did it slowly, watching as it poured into the glass, the colour of it, the reflections. Then I raised the glass to my nose and breathed in deeply.

"I sat for a long time staring at that glass, with thoughts whirling in my head. You're a naughty girl. You've always been one. You can't fight your own destiny. It's useless. Several times I raised the glass to my lips, looked at it and put it back on the table. I was sure I'd drink it in the long run so I might as well take it slowly.

"Darkness fell and there I still was with that glass of bourbon. I felt like filling it some more. I put it down on

229

the table and poured, very slowly. Halfway, two-thirds, right to the brim. And still I went on pouring.

"Very gradually the liquid began to overflow, and I watched it dribbling down the outside of the glass, then spreading over the table, dripping onto the floor.

"When the bottle was empty I set it down on the table. I took the glass between finger and thumb and slowly tipped it, without lifting it. It began to empty. Very, very slowly. As it emptied, I tipped it more. Finally I turned it upside down."

I passed my hands across my face, breathing at last. I realized my jaws were aching.

"At that point I got up, fetched a bucket and floor-cloths and cleaned everything up. I put the rags and empty bottle into a bin-liner, went downstairs and threw the lot into the rubbish. I wanted to call you, but it didn't seem right. I had to deal with this on my own, I thought. So I just sent you that message."

She stopped abruptly. We were silent for a long time, sitting on that wall. I was burning with questions. About him, of course. What had happened after that evening? Where had she been today? Had they met again, and talked, and so on?

I asked none of them. It wasn't easy, but I didn't ask a single question. All the time we were sitting there and after, walking across the city to our building. Until the moment came to part, at her door. Then it was she who spoke.

"What do you think of me, after what I've told you?"

"What I thought before. It's just a bit more complicated."

"Would you like to come in?"

"No, not this evening. Don't misunderstand me, it's just that —"

She interrupted me, speaking quickly. Embarrassed.

"I don't misunderstand you. You're right. I oughtn't even to have said it. Did you say the trial ends on Monday?"

"Most likely. It depends on one last check-up ordered by the court. If certain documents arrive in time, then we should wrap it up on Monday."

"Will you be speaking in the morning?"

"No, I don't think so. Almost certainly the afternoon."

"Then I'll almost certainly manage to come. I want to be there when you speak."

"I'd like you to be there too."

"Then . . . goodnight. And thanks."

"Goodnight."

I was already on the stairs.

"Guido . . ."

"Yes?"

"I did go to him afterwards. I told him he was right. About the hypocrisy – mine – and all the rest."

She paused briefly, and when she spoke again there was an unfamiliar timidity in her voice.

"Did I do right?"

I took a deep breath and felt a knot dissolving in the pit of my stomach.

I told her yes, she had done right.

35

The mobile-phone records arrived punctually on the fifth day after the hearing during which they had been ordered. I was assured of this by the carabinieri sergeant who had carried out the court order. He was a friend of mine, so I had called him up to find out. On his assurance I went to the law courts to examine them.

It was Saturday, 1 July. The Palace of Justice was deserted and the atmosphere slightly surreal.

The door to the Assize Court chancellery was closed. I opened it and found no one inside, but at least the air-conditioning was working. I therefore entered, closed the door behind me and waited for someone to come back and let me see those records.

After a quarter of an hour a clerk arrived at last, a little titch of about sixty whom I didn't know. He gave me a vague look and asked if I needed anything. I did need something and told him what. He appeared to reflect upon the matter for a while before nodding thoughtfully.

The search for the documents was a laborious business and pretty exasperating, but one way or another the little man finally managed to unearth them.

From the mobile-phone records it emerged that Abdou had certainly told the truth about his trip to Naples. The first call was at 9.18. It was an outgoing call from Abdou's mobile to a number in Naples, and had lasted two minutes fourteen seconds. At the time of the call Abdou was already in Naples or the immediate vicinity. There followed four other calls – to Naples numbers and to mobiles – always from within the Naples area. The last was at 12.46. Then nothing happened for more than four hours. At 16.52 Abdou received a call from a mobile. At that time the area was Bari city. The call after that was at 21.10. It was an outgoing call from Abdou's mobile, still from Bari. Then nothing more.

I sat there thinking over the result of that inquiry. Certainly it was not decisive and it failed to sew up the trial. There was a gap of more than four hours, and smack in the middle of those four hours the child had disappeared. What emerged from the phone records did not exclude the possibility that Abdou, returning from Naples, had gone on to Monopoli, reached Capitolo, kidnapped the boy and done God knows what else.

I got up to leave and noticed that the little man had sat himself down on the other side of the chancellery, with his chin on his hands, his elbows on the desk and his gaze lost in space.

I wished him good day. He turned his head, looked at me as if I had said something extraordinary, then turned away again and gave a vague nod. Impossible to say if he had replied to my greeting or had still been elsewhere, talking to some ghost.

The air outside was scorching. It was midday on Saturday, 1 July and I was bound for the office to shut myself in and prepare my speech for the defence.

I was in for a long weekend of it.

36

The hearing began on the dot of nine-thirty. The court took note of the arrival of the mobile-phone records, and we all agreed that we did not require explanation from an expert in order to understand the data. For our purposes, what was written in those records was clear enough. The Telecom engineer who had presented himself for the hearing was thanked and told his services were not required.

Immediately afterwards the judge went through the last formalities and called upon the prosecution. It was nine-forty.

Cervellati got to his feet, pressing down on the table and shoving back his chair. He adjusted his robe, glanced at his notes, then raised his head and addressed the judge.

"Your Honour, ladies and gentlemen of the jury, today you are called to give judgement on a very horrible crime. A young life, a very young life, brutally cut off, as the result of an act so iniquitous that we are unable to grasp the motive or the measure of it. The consequences of this iniquity are tragically irremediable. No one can restore this child to the love of his parents. I cannot, you cannot, no one can.

"You, however, have a great power, an all-important power, of which I hope you will make good use. Of which I am sure you will make good use."

I thought: now he is going to say they have the power, and also the duty, to see justice done. To see to it that the author of such a heinous crime does not get away with it, due perhaps to some cavil or quibble.

"You have the power to see justice done. And this is a power of great moment, because it brings with it the *duty* of doing justice. In the first place to the family of the little victim. But thereafter to all of us who, as citizens, expect a response when such abominable things occur."

It was one of his favourite dictums in the Court of Assizes. I think he was convinced that it impressed the jury. Anyway, he continued in this vein and after a little my attention began to stray.

I heard his voice like a background noise. Every so often I followed his drift for a minute or two and then my thoughts went rambling off again.

He spoke of what had taken place in the course of the trial, in a monotonous drone read long chunks of the records and explained exactly why the evidence advanced by the prosecution was totally convincing, bar nothing.

One of the most tedious closing speeches I had ever heard, I thought, as I leafed through my file just for something to do.

But at a certain point he came to speak of the evidence of the bar owner, the heart of the whole trial.

He re-read Renna's statements – but not his answers to *my* questions – and commented on them. I forced myself to listen carefully.

"So we must ask ourselves, *you* must ask yourselves: what reason did the witness Renna have for bringing false accusations against the defendant? Because the question, in fact, is very simple and the alternative is clear. One hypothesis is that the witness Renna is lying, thereby paving the way for an innocent man to be sentenced to life imprisonment. Because he is well aware of the consequences of his testimony, but nevertheless persists in it, despite the difficulties we saw in the course of his cross-examination. If he is lying, thus accusing an innocent man of a crime punishable by life imprisonment, he must have a reason. Indeed, a ferocious and ignoble personal antagonism, because only hatred of such a kind could explain so aberrant an action.

"Is there any proof, or even the suspicion, of such destructive hatred on the part of Renna with regard to the defendant? Naturally not.

"The other hypothesis is that the witness is telling the truth. And if there is nothing to tell us that the witness is lying, we have to recognize the fact that – in spite of approximations, errors, understandable moments of confusion – he is telling the truth.

"The effect on the outcome of the present trial is obvious. For do not forget that the accused denies being at Monopoli, at Capitolo, that afternoon. And if he denies it when in fact he was present in those localities – and we can assert it with complete confidence because we are told it by a witness who has no cause to lie – then the explanation is one and one only and, unhappily, is there for all to see."

I made a note of this concept too, because it had a sense to it that had to be confuted explicitly.

Cervellati continued, following the proceedings in chronological order, and finally came to discuss the mobile-phone records.

He said what I expected him to say. The verification requested by the defence had not only failed to prove the innocence of the defendant, but, on the contrary, provided further material in favour of the prosecution.

Because that gap of four or so hours with no telephone calls, during which the instrument was probably

236

switched off, was an item of circumstantial evidence worth exploiting. And Cervellati exploited it. There was a degree of verisimilitude – a high degree, he said – in the hypothesis that the defendant, having returned to Bari from Naples, had gone on to Capitolo, having already formed a plan of action. Or perhaps in the grip of a "raptus", or brainstorm. It was probable that he had switched off his mobile phone so as not to be disturbed during the heinous deed. And this, better than any other hypothesis, explained the absence of calls between five and nine o'clock that evening.

I took notes on this part of the speech as well. It was an insidious argument and might well influence the jury.

There followed a hypothetical reconstruction of how Abdou might have put his plan into effect, basely and craftily exploiting the little boy's trust in him.

What had occurred after the kidnapping could be easily imagined. The child, realizing what was happening, had tried to resist the attempted violence. Maybe he had tried to escape, and this had sparked off the lethal reaction of the accused. It is probable that no signs of sexual abuse had been found because the situation had got out of hand before such abuse – which was certainly the defendant's object – had taken place.

In conclusion the public prosecutor explained why the only adequate punishment for such a crime was life imprisonment. It was the most convincing part of his whole speech, because life imprisonment was in fact the just penalty for the perpetrator of such a crime.

While this thought was in my mind Cervellati went through the ritual request for a verdict of guilty.

"For the reasons previously stated, therefore, I ask you to affirm the criminal responsibility of the defendant for all the offences of which he stands accused and

237

therefore to sentence him to imprisonment for life with isolation by day for a period of six months, together with the application of the additional penalty of perpetual debarment from holding public office."

I took a deep breath, glanced at my watch and realized that almost two hours had passed.

The judge said there would be a short break before counsel for the civil party was called. Subsequently there would be an hour for lunch, and when the hearing resumed I would have the floor. Following any further discussions, the court would retire to consider the verdict.

The courtroom emptied out and I too got up to go and have a smoke. Only Cotugno remained behind, putting the finishing touches to his speech.

Outside, a woman journalist I had never seen before asked me what I thought of the prosecution's request for a sentence of guilty.

What I thought of *that* was that rarely had I heard such an idiotic question. I was sorely tempted to give expression to this opinion, but of course I didn't. I said nothing, just shrugged my shoulders, shook my head and spread my hands slightly, palms uppermost. I went off, fishing out my cigarettes while the girl stared after me a bit nonplussed.

I felt fairly calm. I had no wish to look through my notes. I had no wish to do anything further until the moment came for me to speak. In any case, I didn't feel I needed to.

This was a new sensation for me. I had always arrived breathless at important appointments, in my studies, my work or anything else. I had always left things until the last moment, the last night, the last revision; and afterwards I had always had the feeling of having stolen something and got away with it. I had managed to cheat the world yet again. Yet again they hadn't managed to catch me out, but within myself I knew I was an impostor. Sooner or later someone would find me out. Sure to.

That morning I felt good. I knew I had done everything in my power. I was afraid, but it was a healthy fear, not the fear of being caught out, of everyone realizing I was a fake. I was afraid of losing the case, afraid that Abdou might be convicted, but not afraid of losing my dignity. I didn't feel I was an impostor.

Cotugno spoke for a little more than an hour. He used a lot of adjectives and adverbs and succeeded in saying absolutely nothing.

In the lunch hour I went up to the sixth floor, to the Bar Council. I needed to consult a dictionary to check on an idea that had come to me while Cervellati was speaking. I found the sole employee locking everything up and on the point of leaving, but I managed to persuade her that it was an emergency. She let me into the library, where I quickly looked up what I wanted and made a few notes. Then I thanked her and left.

I would have liked at that point to take a short stroll, but the heat out of doors was intolerable. So I went to the bar, ordered a smoothie and a croissant, sat at a table and whiled the time away.

When the moment came I returned to the courtroom, took off my jacket and put on my robe. Almost simultaneously the bell rang, the door opened and in filed the court. I remained standing as I watched them, arms folded, weight on my left leg. They all seated themselves and so did I. Silence reigned.

"I call on the defence," said the judge curtly.

I was just getting to my feet when I noticed some of

the court looking at a spot immediately behind me. I felt a gentle squeeze on my left arm, just above the elbow. I turned and saw Margherita. She was slightly out of breath, and there were beads of sweat on her upper lip. She flashed a smile at me, and sat down on my right without a word.

I made a brief pause before beginning.

"Your Honour, ladies and gentlemen of the jury, as the public prosecutor has already said, this trial is concerned with the most horrible and unnatural of crimes. The violent death of a child, with its aftermath of immeasurable, incomprehensible sorrow for the parents of that child.

"If our defence has in some way unintentionally been lacking in respect for that sorrow, I ask for their pardon."

The judge looked at me without fondness. He thought that starting that way was just an expedient to curry favour with the jury. I was so sure he thought it that I felt compelled to tell him I knew, and that I didn't care a hoot.

"It may be thought that this is just a rather shabby way of gaining the sympathy of the court. Or at least of the jury. It would not be absurd to think this, because we lawyers often get up to such tricks. And anyway, everyone is free to think of it as he pleases. Not least because criminal cases are not debated and decided on the basis of the charm of the defence counsel or the prosecutor. Thank goodness. Cases are decided – if I may state the obvious – on the basis of positive proofs. If they are present, the verdict is guilty. If they are lacking – or even if they are merely insufficient or contradictory – the verdict is not guilty.

"We therefore have to ask ourselves on the basis of what criteria we can affirm that the evidence in a case is sufficient, enabling us to convict the defendant, or else insufficient or contradictory, in which event we must acquit him.

"In our consideration of these matters we may confidently start from the manner in which the public prosecutor proposed them.

"The public prosecutor – and I made an exact note of his statement – said: 'There is a high degree of verisimilitude in the hypothesis that the defendant arrived in Bari from Naples, went on to Monopoli, having already worked out his criminal design in detail, or in the grip of a raptus, or brainstorm, reached Capitolo, probably switched off his mobile so as not to be disturbed, seized the child' etc. From this 'high degree of verisimilitude' the public prosecutor deduces an important, if not indeed decisive, item of evidence – in order to maintain the defendant's guilt and to ask you to sentence him to prison for life.

"Therefore, to verify how well founded and reliable is the line of argument adopted by the prosecution, we have to ascertain the meaning of the word 'verisimilitude'."

I paused, picked up the sheet on which I had earlier made a note in the library, and read: "Verisimilitude, we read in the most authoritative dictionary, is 'the appearance of being true or real . . . the likeness or resemblance to truth, reality or fact'.

"And under the heading 'truth' we read this definition: 'conformity to fact; agreement with reality'. And under the heading 'appearance': 'apparent form or look, especially as distinguished from reality'. We also find an explanation of the phrase 'It looks real' as being used of something artificial that imitates reality to perfection. What looks real is therefore something artificial, something which imitates reality.

"Do you remember the definition of 'verisimilitude'? The word used by the public prosecutor? It refers to something that looks true or real, that imitates reality but does not correspond to it. Something, in short, to be distinguished from reality. By using this term the prosecutor implicitly and unconsciously admits that he cannot use the words 'true' or 'real'. You see clearly how in the very words of the speech for the prosecution there lurk its irredeemable short-comings."

At this point, as I expected, Cervellati lost his cool and protested to the judge. It was unacceptable that the defence should be permitted to pour scorn on the function of the public prosecutor with cheap sophistical arguments. The judge did not appreciate the interruption and reminded the public prosecutor that the defence could say what it liked, short of personal abuse. Cervellati attempted to add something, but the judge told him, brusquely this time, that he could make his comments on my speech – if he so wished – when the time came for his response. That was that, he said, and he would tolerate no more interruptions. He turned to me and invited me to proceed. I thanked him, carefully avoided making any reference to the interruption, and went ahead.

"What we have said briefly about the meaning of these key words – truth, reality, the appearance of reality – therefore offers us an interesting approach to interpreting the arguments used by the public prosecutor and the psychological premises underlying those arguments.

"A trial, however, is not based on a psychological interpretation of what the public prosecutor says. Neither, in order to verify whether his reasoning is right or wrong, is it based on an analysis of what the public prosecutor has said. Because the public prosecutor might have followed a wrong line of reasoning and arrived nonetheless at correct conclusions. That is, it might be right to pronounce a sentence of guilty. In spite of the public prosecutor's mistaken reasoning and on the basis of a different, more correct line of argument."

Cervellati got to his feet, dumped his robe on his chair and ostentatiously left the room. I showed no sign of noticing.

"It is therefore not enough to single out the defects in the prosecution's argument. We have to ascertain whether the evidence assembled does or does not enable us to formulate a judgement corresponding to the truth. We do not wish to shirk this task. But before we tackle it I wish to repeat one concept.

"It is a concept which I would like you to bear in mind throughout these proceedings and, above all, when you are in camera. To bring in a verdict of guilty it is not enough to say that a certain version of the facts, a certain hypothetical reconstruction of the facts, is likely, or even very probable. You must be able to say that this reconstruction is the truth. If you can do that, then it is right for you to send the defendant to prison. For life.

"The hypothesis put forward by the prosecution in this trial runs as follows: on 5 August 1999 Abdou Thiam unlawfully restrained Francesco Rubino, a minor, subsequently causing his death by suffocation.

"Can we assert, on the basis of the evidence provided, that this hypothesis is true? That is, can we assert that this is a correct description of how events happened *in fact and truth*, and not just a mere conjecture as to how they *might* have occurred?"

I paused as if I had lost my thread, glanced down

and passed the first two fingers of my right hand across my brow. After a moment or two I looked up towards the bench, still without speaking. There was dead silence. Everyone was looking at me, expectant.

"Let us examine this evidence together. And in particular let us examine the statements of the witness Renna, proprietor of the Bar Maracaibo. To avoid any misunderstandings, I would like to say at once that I agree with the public prosecutor in saying that this witness is telling the truth. Or to be more precise, this witness is not telling lies."

Another short pause to give them time to wonder what I was aiming at.

"Because a lie is an assertion made in the awareness that it is contrary to the truth, and I am convinced that Signor Renna did not make assertions in the awareness that they were contrary to the truth. In saying that he saw Abdou Thiam pass his bar on just that afternoon, at just that time, Signor Renna thinks he is telling the truth. And in fact he would have no reason to bring false accusations against the defendant.

"To be sure, it emerged from his examination that he has, to put it mildly, no particular liking for the non-European citizens who gravitate towards the area of Capitolo and the vicinity of his bar.

"I want to read you a brief passage from that cross-examination. We are speaking of the non-European citizens whom Signor Renna calls 'niggers'. Counsel for the defence asks whether these persons interfere with Renna's custom.

"The witness replies, 'They interfere, they interfere, and how!'

" 'Forgive me for asking, but if they are a nuisance, why don't you call the municipal police, or the carabinieri?'

" 'Why don't I call them? I call them all right, but d'you think they come?'

"In short, Signor Renna – he tells us so himself – does not like the presence of the non-European citizens at Capitolo and in the vicinity of his bar. He would like the strong arm of the law to intervene and move them on, but this doesn't happen. He is somewhat incensed.

"All this, be it clear, does not mean that he has deliberately told us untruths about Signor Abdou Thiam.

"But setting aside his liking for – or dislike of – 'niggers', and his unsatisfied demand for the strong arm of the law to act in some way against these 'niggers', has Signor Renna told us the objective truth? Can we affirm beyond any reasonable doubt that the version provided by this witness corresponds to the truth of the actual facts with which we are concerned?

"One element of doubt may be inferred from the little experiment with the photographs, which you will remember. Renna failed to recognize the defendant in a photograph, in fact in two photographs, which you have in the records and can verify for yourselves as to their likeness to the defendant. The very man who is here in court and, above all, the person whom the witness declares he knows well and whom he saw pass his bar that August afternoon.

"Does this mean that Renna invented the lot, that he is telling lies? Certainly not. The fact that he doesn't like 'niggers' and that he sensationally failed the photographic test does not mean that he knowingly lied.

"When he says he remembers that that afternoon Abdou Thiam passed his bar, without his usual bag, walking quickly in a southerly direction, the witness Renna is telling the truth.

245

"In the sense that he does in fact *remember* this sequence of events and fixes it on that afternoon. To be more precise, he tells us what he believes to be the truth. The really interesting thing – and this introduces us to the fascinating subject of how the memory functions – is that Renna believes that that is the truth, because he *remembers* those events, even if they never happened. Not in the terms of his account."

Pause. I needed these notions to settle in the minds of the court, and especially of the jury. I made a pretence of rummaging in my notes until about ten seconds had passed. Just time for them to wonder what was coming next.

"Now I want to tell you about a scientific experiment into the functioning of the memory and the mechanism by which memories are produced. A team of American psychologists, at Harvard University I believe, set out to test the reliability of childhood memories. A number of children of nine or ten years old were told a story by their elder brothers or sisters, who were instructed in what to say. The story was that at the age of four or five they had escaped an attempted kidnapping. They were told that they had been in a supermarket with their mother, and at a moment when her attention was distracted a stranger had seized them by the hand and made for the exit. Their mother had realized what was happening, had started shouting and had put the would-be kidnapper to flight.

"The episode had never in fact occurred, but a few months after being told the story the children not only thought they remembered it – and really in a certain sense they *did* remember it – but in telling the story they even added details that were not there in the original version.

"Were these children lying? That is, were they saying untrue things in the awareness of doing so? Certainly not.

"Did these children give an account of things that had really happened? Certainly not.

"It is an acknowledged fact – and one of the most important objects of study in modern forensic psychology – that both children and adults make mistakes about the source of their memories and are convinced that they remember contexts, facts and details which have in fact been suggested by others. Deliberately, as in the case of the experiment I have recounted to you. Or involuntarily, as in many situations in everyday life and also, at times, during criminal investigations.

"On the basis of these considerations we can give an answer to the question put by the public prosecutor in the course of his speech, regarding the reliability of the witness Renna. The public prosecutor asked himself, and above all he asked *you*: what reason did Renna have for lying and therefore falsely accusing Abdou Thiam?

"We can answer that question with perfect confidence: no reason at all. And in fact Renna did not lie. Between lying – that is, knowingly uttering falsehoods – and telling the truth – which is giving an account of the facts as they really and truly happened – there exists a third possibility. A possibility which the public prosecutor did not take into consideration, but which you must take into very close consideration. That of a witness who gives a certain version of the facts in the erroneous conviction that it is true.

"We are here concerned with what might be defined as involuntary false witness."

They seemed interested. Even the judge and the

military-looking juryman. The pair who – I was convinced of it – had already decided to find Abdou guilty.

"There are many ways of building up involuntary false witness. Some are deliberate, as in the case of the experiment with children that I told you about. Others are themselves involuntary and often prompted by the best intentions. As in this case.

"Let us together try to reconstruct what happened in the inquiry which led to the indictment of Abdou Thiam, and therefore to this trial. A little boy disappears and two days later his dead body is found. It is a deeply disturbing event, and those whose task it is to put the investigations in hand – the carabinieri, the public prosecutor – feel it is their urgent, their pressing duty to discover the culprits. There is justifiable eagerness to satisfy to the demand for justice provoked by such a horrible crime. By questioning the child's relatives, and other persons who knew him well, the carabinieri discover this apparent friendship existing between the boy and this African pedlar. It is something strange, unusual, that arouses suspicions. And also the feeling that perhaps they are on the right track. Perhaps it is possible to satisfy that demand for justice and to placate that anguish. The investigation is no longer groping in the dark; it now has a possible suspect and a theoretical solution. This redoubles the efforts made to find confirmation for this theoretical solution. This is how things stand when the witness Renna is heard for the first time, by the carabinieri. The investigators are understandably excited by the possibility of solving the case, and they realize that the statements of this witness could well constitute a decisive step. It is at this stage that we see the construction of the involuntary false witness.

"Attention please, I beg of you. I am very far from saying that there was any deliberate manipulation of the inquiries. And even less am I speaking of the grotesque hypothesis of plots on the part of the investigators to the detriment of the defendant. The question is, at one and the same time, both simpler and more complex, and to explain what I wish to say I will borrow a famous phrase of Albert Einstein's. The phrase, if I remember rightly, goes more or less like this: 'It is the theory that determines what we observe.'

"What does this mean? It means that if we have a theory – a theory we like, that we are satisfied with, that seems to us good – we tend to examine the facts in the light of that theory. Rather than objectively observing all the available data, we look only for confirmations of that theory. Our very perception is strongly influenced, is indeed determined, by the theory we have settled on. As Einstein said in speaking of science, it is indeed the theory that determines what we succeed in observing. In other words, we see, we hear, we perceive what conforms to our theory and simply pass over all the rest. There is a Chinese saying that expresses the same concept in a different way. The Chinese say: 'Two-thirds of what we see is behind our eyes.'

"We have all had experience of how our very perceptions are determined by what, for the most varied reasons, is in our heads or, as the Chinese would put it, behind our eyes.

"Have you never bought a new car and suddenly, driving along, you notice dozens of the same model on the roads? Where were they before?

"Perception filters, the psychologists call them.

"Paraphrasing Einstein, who, I imagine, must be turning in his grave at my intrusion, we can state that it is the investigatory hypothesis that determines what the investigators see. But not only that. It determines what they look for. It determines the questions they ask. It determines the manner in which they draw up their reports. And all this does not in the least imply bad faith.

"Allow me to repeat: all these things I have mentioned can produce errors in the investigations – and it is the business of the trial to correct such errors – but they do not in the least imply bad faith.

"If anything, in a case such as this, we are faced with an excess of *good* faith.

"Let us therefore return to what we were saying a few minutes ago. The investigators want to solve this dreadful crime. They want to do it for the best reasons and with the best intentions. They want to do it for the love of justice. They want to do it quickly, so that the perpetrator of such a horrible deed remains at liberty – and in a position to strike again – for as short a time as possible. In this state of mind they find a track to follow and single out a possible suspect. Not fantasies, mind you, or hypotheses used as pretexts. The track was a good one and the suspicions with regard to Abdou Thiam were plausible. On the basis of this good track, the investigators set off in pursuit of the man they considered to be the probable culprit.

"From that moment on the carabinieri and the public prosecutor have a theory which – as we learn from Einstein – will determine what they see, how they will act with witnesses, what they will ask them, how they will draw up the records and even *what* they will record. In perfect good faith and eagerness to see justice done.

"You will now understand the reason for those questions put by the defence to the carabinieri sergeant-major regarding the manner in which the report was drawn up. Because if I make a complete record – complete, that is, with tape recording, stenotyping and so on – there is no difficulty in understanding what happened during that examination. Everything is on record – questions, answers, pauses, the lot – and we have only to read the transcription or listen to the tape recording. If the examiner has involuntarily influenced the witness, we can verify the fact simply by reading. Then each of us can come to his own conclusions.

"If the report is a mere summary, such a verification is impossible. And if the summarized report is that of the very first contact between the investigators and the witness, the risk of involuntary manipulation of the witness's statements and memories is very high indeed.

"Would you like a little example of how this can happen?

"I am the investigator and I have before me someone who might be an important witness, perhaps a decisive one. I have strong suspicions of a certain subject, Abdou Thiam.

"I ask the witness: Do you know Abdou Thiam? The name means nothing to me, perhaps you could show me a photo. Here's a photo, do you know him? Yes, yes. He's one of those niggers who often hang about outside my bar. They're such a nuisance. Did you see him pass your bar on the day the little boy disappeared?

"The witness pauses, thinking back. The investigators feel they are nearing a solution.

"Think hard. The afternoon of the child's disappearance. It's a week ago.

"It seems to me I did. Yes, he must have passed by. Seems to me it was certainly him.

"At this point the sergeant-major dictates this for the records, because he wants to get it down in black and white before the witness changes his mind. Which happens all too often, alas. He dictates it to the lance-corporal at the computer. He dictates it in his bureaucratic jargon, not in the language used by the witness."

From my documents I selected the copy of Renna's first statement and read from it.

"In the report concerned we find expressions such as 'in the management of the aforesaid commercial premises I am assisted by . . .' and so on. Obviously these are not the words of the witness Renna. Obviously we do not know what questions were addressed to Renna. We do not know because we are given only the answers. What were the questions put to the witness? Were they questions which influenced him? Were they leading questions, that is, questions so put as to suggest or prompt the expected answer? Were they questions which, quite involuntarily, created a memory?

"There is no need for bad faith. It is enough to have a theory to confirm and our brain does the rest on its own, perceiving, working out, setting down in the records in such a way as to adapt the facts to fit the theory. Creating, or shall I say assembling, a false memory.

"I say 'false' not because Renna invented anything or the carabinieri with criminal intent suggested a false story for him to tell. It is simply that in the course of the first interrogation Renna's memories were reprogrammed in the light of the investigatory theory adopted, for which no objective verification was sought, but only confirmation. Those memories were reprogrammed, and how this happened in concrete fact we shall never know. Because the interrogation of this witness was not taped, only summarized in writing. In the manner which we have seen.

"Would you like to know how far it is possible to influence the reply of a witness, or even modify his memory, simply by putting the question in a different way? Let me tell you of another experiment, this time carried out in Italy. Three groups of psychology students – not children, not uninformed persons, but students of psychology who knew they were being submitted to a scientific test – these students, I say, were shown a film sequence. In this sequence a woman was seen leaving a supermarket with a trolley. A young man approached the woman from behind, seized a handbag lying on top of the trolley and made off with it. The three groups were asked to give an account of what they had seen, but in answer to different questions. The first group was asked 'Did the thief barge into the woman?' The second group was asked 'In what way did the aggressor push the woman?' The students of the third group were simply asked to tell what they had seen. Needless to say, in the film there had been no push and no barging.

"I think you will already have guessed the result of the experiment. Among the students of the third group – those who had simply been asked to give an account of the facts – only 10 per cent or just over spoke of a bump or any kind of physical contact between the aggressor and the woman. Of the students of the first group only 20 per cent spoke of a shove. While in the second group – to whom the most strongly suggestive question had been put – almost 70 per cent of the answers spoke of the non-existent contact. As in the case of the children, moreover, all those who spoke of it embroidered their accounts with details about the manner, the violence and the direction of this non-existent shove.

"Need I say more? Do we have to waste more words in explaining how far the manner of conducting an interrogation can influence not only the answers but the very reconstruction of the memories of the person being interrogated? I think not.

"We have now understood how vital it is to know which questions – and in what order, at what speed, in what tone of voice – have been put to a witness in his most important deposition, which is his first.

"In this case this vital information is denied us, because in the carabinieri report we only read: 'Witness replied.'

"Replied to what question? What questions?"

I raised my voice slightly. It was not my practice, but the jury were beginning to tire, and just as I was approaching the crucial point. I simply had to keep them alert.

"We have said that if we do not know what the question was, we cannot say if the reply is genuine, or has been influenced or even manipulated. We will never be able to say because of that examination, that first examination of the witness Renna, all we have is a brief summary. We can only make conjectures. But in making them there is one fact we must not overlook. A fact that occurred before our eyes, during a hearing, in this trial. And that fact is the cross-examination of Renna. In the course of which we learned a series of very important things on the basis of which to assess the reliability of this witness. Which does not mean to assess whether the witness is lying or is telling his *subjective* truth. It means to verify how far his account corresponds with the *objective* course of events.

"I will summarize these points. Signor Renna does not like non-European citizens and wishes the police would do something about them. Signor Renna does not know Abdou Thiam very well if – having two photographs of him in his hand and being in the same courtroom – he fails to recognize him. Signor Renna, finally and consequently, doesn't have much of a memory for faces and does not find it easy to distinguish between one non-European citizen and another. From his point of view 'they are all niggers', to use the very words he used himself in replying to a question from the defence."

I was about to launch one of the decisive offensives, so I paused once more and gave the court at least twenty seconds. They had to wonder why I had stopped speaking and give me all the attention they could, after so many hours in the courtroom. When I started again, I pitched my voice higher. It had to be clear that we had reached the climax.

"And on the basis of the statements of this witness, these statements from a dubious source – dubious on account of what we have said concerning the first interrogation by the carabinieri – the public prosecutor is asking you to inflict a sentence of imprisonment for life.

"Bear in mind that to inflict not life imprisonment but even a single day in prison, you must *not* apply the criteria of verisimilitude, you must *not* apply the criteria of probability. Even supposing that in this case and with reference to the content of Renna's deposition we are entitled to speak of verisimilitude or probability. You must apply the criteria of certainty. Absolute certainty!

"We may speak of certainty in the reconstruction of an occurrence when every other alternative hypothesis is implausible and must therefore be rejected. Is that the case here? Is it implausible to think, for example, that Renna saw someone else that afternoon, not Abdou Thiam, in view of the fact that for him 'niggers'

255

are all alike? Is it implausible to think that this witness was in some way mistaken? This witness who – mind you – failed miserably before your eyes to recognize the photographs. Could he not be mistaken? Can you with untroubled mind entrust your entire decision, and the whole life of a man, to the declarations of a witness whose fallibility has been revealed before your very eyes?"

A pause. Seven, eight seconds.

"And please take note: even if against all the evidence you still choose to maintain that Renna's account is reliable, this would not amount to proof of the defendant's guilt.

"Because the other evidence against him isn't worth the paper it's written on."

And I went on to examine the statements of the two Senegalese, the results of the searches and all the rest of the evidence.

I spoke of the mobile-phone records. Even if we agreed to speak in terms of the famous "verisimilitude", I said, the prosecution's reconstruction didn't hold water. In fact it was almost grotesque. The prosecution held that the defendant had returned from Naples in the grip of a raptus, and had gone to Capitolo with the insane intention of kidnapping, violating and killing little Francesco. In that case he was mad. Because only madness could account for such preposterous behaviour. In which case, why had he not been subjected to any psychiatric examination? If to explain his behaviour it was necessary to fall back on mental illness, then this illness should have been ascertained. Otherwise that hypothesis remained simply an attempt to influence the court.

I raised all these points fairly briefly. The jurors were tired, and I was convinced that when the moment came to decide they would primarily discuss Renna's evidence.

So I began to wind up. To end at the point from which one started gives the idea of completeness and lends strength to an argument. So I believe.

"Verisimilitude or veracity, ladies and gentlemen. Probability or certainty. The choice ought not to be difficult. But instead it is. Because if on the one hand there is the perception – which I am sure we all share – that this trial has produced no answer, on the other hand there is the feeling of dismay at the idea that a horrible crime can remain unpunished, without a known culprit. It is an intolerable idea, and one that brings with it a very grave risk."

At that moment Cervellati re-entered the courtroom. He sat down and propped his head on his right hand, using the hand as a kind of barrier. Between him and me. His gaze was ostentatiously directed at a point in the courtroom high up on the left. Where nothing was.

It was the position closest to turning his back on me that was physically possible with the tables and chairs arranged in parallel rows.

I thought he was a turd and carried on.

"The risk is that we may try to rid ourselves of this anguish by finding not *the* culprit but *a* culprit. Anyone at all. Someone who has suffered the mischance of getting ensnared in the proceedings.

"Without – having – done – a – thing. Let me repeat that: without – having – done – a – thing.

"Some may not share the categorical tone of my statement. Very well. Everyone is entitled to doubts. I am the defending counsel and for many reasons I am convinced of the innocence of my client. You have the right not to share this certainty. You have a right to your doubts. You have a right to think that

Abdou Thiam could be guilty, despite what his counsel says.

"He could be guilty. Despite the absurdity of the reconstruction put forward by the prosecution, you have the right to think that the defendant could be guilty.

"He *could* be. In the conditional.

"Verdicts of guilty, however, are not written – cannot be written – in the conditional mood. They are written in the indicative, they affirm certainties. Certainties!

"Can you make affirmations of certainty? Can you say it is *certain* that the witness Renna was not mistaken? Can you say that at the end of this trial you are left with no reasonable doubt?

"If you can say all this, then convict Abdou Thiam."

I had raised my voice and I became aware that this time I was not play-acting.

"Sentence him to life imprisonment and nothing less. If you can say that there is not a single doubt, that you are absolutely certain, then it is your *duty* to sentence this man to prison for ever. You must have the courage to do it. The great courage."

For an indefinable time everything hung in the air. Until I heard my voice once more. Low now, and with a crack in it.

"If, however, you do not have this certainty, then you require even more courage.

"In order not to suppress your doubts in the name of summary justice, and therefore to acquit, you will need enormous courage. I am confident that you will have it.

"Thank you for hearing me out."

I sat down, scarcely able to believe that I had really finished. From behind me on the public benches came a murmur of voices. I sat with lips compressed and head slightly bowed, staring dumbly to my left at the grain of the wood on my desk.

I heard the judge speaking and his voice seemed to come from far away. He asked the prosecution and the civil party if they had any responses. They said no.

Then he asked Abdou if he wished to make a concluding statement, before the court retired in camera. As was his right by law. The murmur died and there were a few seconds of silence. Then came Abdou's voice speaking into a microphone inserted between the bars of the cage. It was quiet but firm.

"I want to say one thing. I want to thank my lawyer because he has believed I am innocent. I want to tell him he did right, because it is true."

The president gave an imperceptible nod. "The court will retire," he said.

He got to his feet, and almost at once the others did likewise.

I got up too, mechanically. I watched them disappear one by one through the door and only then did I turn to Margherita.

"How long did I speak for?"

"Two and a half hours, more or less."

I looked at my watch. It was a quarter past six. It seemed to me I had spoken for no more than forty minutes.

We stood for a while in silence. Then she asked me why I didn't take off my robe. I did so and laid it on the desk, while she regarded me with the expression of one who wants to say something and is searching for the way, for the words.

"I'm not very good at paying compliments. I've never really liked doing it, and I think I know why. In any case, that doesn't matter now. What I wanted to say was that . . . well, listening to you was . . . extraordinary.

I'd like to give you a kiss, but I don't think this is the time and place for it."

I said nothing, because I was at a loss for words, and what's more I had a lump in my throat.

A journalist came up and complimented me. Then another, and then the girl who had asked me what I thought of the prosecutor's request for a verdict of guilty. I felt a pang of remorse at not having been kinder to her earlier.

While the journalists jabbered on at me without my listening, Margherita gave a gentle tug at my sleeve.

"I must dash. Good luck." She raised her left fist to her brow and briefly bowed her head.

Then she turned and made off, and I felt lonely.

37

The first defence I conducted on my own, shortly after qualifying, had to do with a series of frauds. The defendant was a large, jolly fellow with a black moustache and a nose laced with broken veins. I had a feeling he was not a teetotaller.

The prosecutor made a very short speech and asked for two years' imprisonment. I made a long harangue. While I was speaking the judge kept nodding, and this gave me confidence. My arguments seemed to me cogent and unanswerably persuasive.

When I finished I was convinced that in a matter of minutes my client would be acquitted.

The judge was out for about twenty minutes, and when he returned he pronounced exactly the sentence the prosecution had asked for. Two years' imprisonment without remission, because my client was a habitual criminal.

I didn't sleep that night, and for days afterwards I asked myself where I had gone wrong. I felt humiliated, and persuaded myself that the judge for some unknown reason had it in for me. I lost faith in justice.

It never occurred to me for one moment that there was an obvious explanation for the matter: that my client was guilty and the judge had been right to convict him. This was a brilliant intuition that only came to me long afterwards.

However, that experience taught me to treat my

trials with due detachment. Without getting emotional and above all without nursing any expectations.

Getting emotional and nursing expectations are both dangerous things. They can do harm, even great harm. And not only in trials.

I thought about this now while the courtroom was emptying. I thought I had done my job well. I had done everything possible. Now I had to feel unconcerned about the result.

I ought to go out, go to the office or take a stroll, even go home. When the court was ready the clerk of the court would call me on my mobile – he had asked for my number before he left the courtroom himself – and I would return to hear the reading of the verdict.

This is the usual practice in trials of this kind, when the court is expected to remain in camera for many hours, or even for days. When they are ready, they call the clerk and tell him what time they will re-enter the courtroom to pronounce the verdict. The clerk in turn calls the public prosecutor and the counsels and at the established hour there they all are, ready for the final scene.

In short, according to practice I should have left.

But instead I stayed put, and after gazing around the empty courtroom for a while I approached the cage. Abdou rose from his bench and came towards me.

I took hold of the bars and he gave me a nod of greeting and the ghost of a smile. I nodded and smiled back before I spoke.

"Did you manage to follow my speech?"

"Yes."

"What did you think?"

He didn't answer at once. As on other occasions, I had the feeling that he was concentrating on finding the right words.

262

"I have one question, Avvocato."

"Tell me."

"Why have you done all this?"

If he hadn't done so, sooner or later I would have had to ask myself that question.

I was searching for an answer, but I realized I didn't want to talk through the bars. There was no question of them letting Abdou out for a chat in the courtroom. Against all regulations.

So I asked the head of his escort if I could go into the cage.

He stared at me in disbelief, then turned to his men, shrugged as if abandoning all hope of understanding, and ordered the warder with the keys to let me in.

I sat on the bench near Abdou, and felt an absurd sense of relief as I heard the bolt slide home in the door of the cage.

I was about to offer him a cigarette when he pulled out a packet and insisted on my taking one of his. Diana Red. The prisoners' Marlboro.

I took one, and after smoking half I told him I had no answer to his question.

I told him that I thought it was for a good motive, but I didn't know exactly what that motive was.

Abdou gave a nod, as if satisfied with my answer.

Then he said, "I'm frightened."

"So am I."

And so it was we began to talk. We talked of many things and went on smoking his cigarettes. At a certain point we both felt thirsty and I called up the bar on my mobile to place an order. Ten minutes later in came the boy with the tray, and passed two glasses of iced tea through the bars. Abdou paid.

We drank beneath the bewildered gaze of the warders.

At about eight o'clock I told him I was going for a walk to stretch my legs.

I had no wish to go home or to the office. Or into the centre of town among the shops and the crowds. So I ventured into the district round the law courts, towards the cemetery. Among working-class tenements which emitted the smell of rather unsavoury food, run-down shops, streets I'd never been along in all my thirty-nine years of living in Bari.

I walked for a long time, without an aim or a thought in my head. It seemed to me I was somewhere else entirely, and the whole place was so ugly that it had a strange, seedy allure to it.

Darkness had fallen and my mind was completely distracted when I became aware of the vibration in my back trouser pocket.

I pulled out the mobile and on the other end heard the voice of the clerk of the court. He was pretty agitated.

Had he already called once and got no answer? So sorry, I hadn't registered. They'd been ready for ten minutes? I'd be there at once. At once. Just a minute or two.

I glanced around and it took me a while to realize where I was. Not at all close. I would have to run, and I did.

I entered the courtroom about ten minutes later, forcing myself to breathe through my nose and not my mouth, feeling my shirt stuck to my back with sweat, and trying to look dignified.

They were all there, ready in their places. Counsel for the civil party, public prosecutor, clerk of the court, journalists and, despite the late hour, even some members of the public. I noticed that there were a number of Africans, never seen at the other hearings.

As soon as he saw me, the clerk of the court went through to inform the court that I had arrived at last.

I threw on my robe and glanced at my watch. Nine fifty-five.

The clerk returned to his seat and then, in rapid succession, the bell rang and the court entered.

The judge hurried to his place, with the air of a man who wants to get some disagreeable duty quickly over and done with. He looked first right, then left. He assured himself that the members of the court were all in position. He put on his glasses to read the verdict.

Eyes lowered, half closed, I listened to my thudding heart.

"In the name of the Italian people, the Court of Assizes at Bari, in accordance with Article 530, Paragraph One, of the code of criminal procedure . . ."

I felt a charge throughout my body and my legs turned to jelly.

Acquitted.

Article 530 of the code of criminal procedure is entitled "Verdict of acquittal".

". . . finds Abdou Thiam not guilty on the grounds that the accused has not committed the offences with which he is charged. In accordance with Article 300 of the code of criminal procedure it decrees the cessation of the precautionary measure of detention in prison at present in force against the defendant and orders the immediate discharge of the aforesaid unless detained on other counts. The court is dismissed."

It is hard to explain what one feels at such a moment. Because it's really hard to understand it.

I stayed where I was, gazing towards the empty bench where the court had sat. All around were excited voices, while people patted me on the back and others grasped my hand and wrung it. I wondered what so many people were doing in a courtroom of the Bari Assizes on 3 July at ten o'clock at night.

I don't know how long it was until I moved.

Until among the babble of voices I distinguished that of Abdou. I took off my robe and went to the cage. In theory, he should have been released at once. In practice, though, they had to take him back to the prison to go through the formalities. In any case, he was still inside there.

We found ourselves face to face, very close, the bars between us. His eyes were moist, his jaw set, the corners of his mouth trembling.

My own face was not very different, I think.

It was a long handshake, through the bars. Not in the usual way, like businessmen or when you are introduced, but gripping thumbs with elbows crooked.

He said only a few words, in his own language. I didn't need an interpreter to tell me what they meant.

38

I left Margherita a message on her mobile the very evening of the verdict, but we didn't manage to meet until the next afternoon.

She called by my office, and we went and sat in a bar. We talked very little about the trial. I had no wish to, and she realized that and soon stopped asking questions. We were both of us in a strange state of mild embarrassment.

When we got back to the street door of my office I made an effort to say what I had in mind.

"I really rather wanted to ask you out to dinner. Please don't say no, even if it's not much of an invitation. I'm out of practice."

She looked at me as if she wanted to laugh, but she didn't say a thing.

"What about it?" I asked after a moment.

"As a matter of fact it was a pretty rottenly put invitation, but I'd like to reward your good intentions."

"You mean you accept?"

"I mean I accept. This evening?"

"Not this evening. Tomorrow if you don't mind."

She narrowed her eyes and gave me a rather puzzled look, so I felt bound to say more.

"There's something I have to do this evening. Something important. I can't put it off. I can't go out with you unless I've done it first."

Still the same puzzled look for a moment. Then she nodded and said that was fine.

Till tomorrow then.

Till tomorrow.

I got home from the office, had a shower, put on some shorts and made a smoothie. I wandered for a while from room to room. Every so often I stopped to look at the telephone. I scrutinized it from a distance.

After a little of this I sat down in an armchair. The telephone was in front of me and I had only to reach out and pick up the receiver. Instead I simply sat staring at the instrument.

No need to rush, I thought.

In any case, before you phone you have to run through the number in your head. The number is 080 . . . 5219 . . . that is 080 . . . 52198 . . . No, it's 52196 . . . No it isn't.

I couldn't remember it! Ridiculous. It wasn't even two years and I couldn't remember the number. Yet a few months before I'd known it by heart. So really it was only a few months, and I'd forgotten it.

All right, no use fretting. Such things happen.

I looked up Sara's name in the phone book but it wasn't there.

For a moment I didn't know what to do. Then inspiration struck and I looked up *my* name. There it was. At the old address, I mean. Where I lived now the phone was in the landlord's name.

I went on staring at the phone for a bit longer, but I knew that time was running out.

I hope she'll be the one to answer. If it's the same man as last time, what shall I say? Good evening, I'm the ex-husband or, rather, still the husband though separated. Yes, you've understood rightly, *that* little shit. I would like to speak to Sara, please. My dear sir, don't be so crude. You'll bust my face in if I ring again? Be careful how you talk, I am a boxer. Ah, you are a master of full-contact karate? Well, I only said it for a lark.

I punched the number hard, quickly, without thinking. Only way to do it.

After three rings she answered.

She didn't seem surprised to hear my voice. In fact, she seemed pleased. Yes, she was well. I was well too. Yes, I was sure, I was as fit as a fiddle. No, it was just that I seemed to her a trifle strange. Meet this evening? That is, in a couple of hours, after a couple of years? She complimented me for still being able to surprise her, which she said wasn't easy. I was glad about this – no, really glad – so, apart from that, could we meet? For dinner, or for a drink afterwards. Very well. Would she like me to come and fetch her or might that create some embarrassment? Laughter. OK, I'd come for her at ten. Should I call her on the intercom or would she meet me downstairs? No, better on the intercom … Another laugh. All right, I'll buzz from downstairs. See you then. Ciao. Ciao.

I dressed quickly and quickly left the house. The shops shut at eight.

I made good time, and was back home by half-past. It remained to fill up the time until ten. I read a little. *Zen in the Art of Archery*. But it wasn't the right book for the occasion. So I thought I'd listen to a little music. I was about to put on *Rimmel*, but then thought that even though quite alone I ought to avoid pathos. Better to go out at once.

I changed, just to while away a few more minutes, then went downstairs, little shopping bag in hand.

I wandered about the streets until dead on ten, when I pressed the bell at Sara's place. She answered, in the way I knew so well.

I'll be right down.

Down she came and gave me a kiss on the cheek and I gave her a kiss on hers. If she saw my little shopping bag she gave no sign of it. We walked as far as the car and I drove to a restaurant by the sea, near Polignano.

We didn't exchange many words while we were in the car, nor did we exchange many during dinner.

She was waiting for me to say why I'd wanted to see her. I was waiting until we'd finished eating, because one has to be patient and do everything at the right time. It seemed to me I'd understood this fact, among other things.

So we shared a big lobster dressed with olive oil and lemon, and drank chilled white wine. Every so often we caught each other's eye, said something of no consequence and went on eating. And every so often she gave me a mildly questioning look.

When we had finished I paid and asked her if she'd like to go for a stroll. She would.

As we walked I began to speak.

"I've been through a very . . . a very singular experience. A number of things have happened to me . . ."

I paused. It wasn't a great start. In fact it was a lousy one. She said nothing. She was waiting.

We walked, both staring straight ahead, among the boats of a little harbour.

"Do you remember saying that sooner or later one has to pay up?"

"I remember. And you said that before that you'd get out from under. If they wanted, they could sue you."

Smiles, both of us. That's exactly what I'd said. If they wanted, they could sue me. I expected Sara to say I had always been a dab hand at wriggling out of paying. She would have been absolutely right, but she didn't say it. And I went on.

"One of the things that has happened to me is that I haven't managed to wriggle out of it this time, not as quickly as before. So they caught me and made me pay up all the arrears. It hasn't been a lot of fun."

I sat on the side of a boat, very near the water. She sat on another, facing me. I had reached the most difficult part and I couldn't find the words.

"So in all this at a certain point I realized that . . . well, if I was settling all my debts, there was one that I absolutely couldn't leave unpaid."

She watched me with her head tilted slightly to one side, her eyes fixed on mine. I felt the urge for a cigarette, lit one, and waited for the smoke to hit my lungs before I spoke again.

Then, in the first words that came into my head, I said everything I had to say. She listened without a single interruption, and even when I had finished she didn't speak at once. To be certain I had really and truly finished. I wasn't sure, because of the darkness, but it looked to me as if her eyes were moist. Mine were, and I needed no light to tell me so. When she did speak, I knew that I had done the right thing, that evening.

"Today you have given me back every day, every single minute we were together. So many times, before we separated and since, I've thought that with you I'd thrown away nearly ten years of my life. Then I rebelled against this idea and banished it from my mind. Then it came back. It seeméd as if it would never end, this anguish. But this evening you have set me free. You've given me back my memories."

There was a kind of smile on her face now.

I tried to smile too, but instead I felt tears coming. I made some effort to hold them back, but then felt it didn't matter a damn. So my eyes filled with tears and then overflowed, all the tears I had, in silence.

271

She let me get over it, then passed two fingers gently beneath my eyes.

And then I gave her my present. It was a watch, a man's watch with a leather strap and a big face. Just like one I had had years before. She used to steal it from me because she liked it so much. Then, away on some trip, I lost it and she was upset. Much more than I was. I often thought of giving her another the same but never did. Just as I had never done lots of other things.

She put it on without a word. And then it was time to go home.

I stopped the car some way from her door, where there happened to be a free space. I switched off the engine, turned towards her, and didn't know what to do. Sara, on the contrary, did know. She hugged me tightly, almost violently, her chin on my shoulder and her head against mine. This for several seconds before breaking away. Thank you, she murmured before opening the car door and walking away.

Thank *you*, thank *you*, I said to the empty car as she disappeared into the doorway.

39

I didn't sleep that night. I didn't even try to go to bed. I sat on the balcony and listened to the sounds from down in the street. I lit four or five cigarettes, but I didn't smoke much of them. I let them burn down slowly between my fingers while I gazed at the windows and balconies opposite, the antennae on the roofs, the sky.

A little before dawn the mistral got up and the very first gusts made me shiver.

They say the mistral lasts for three days or for seven, so I knew that for three days or for seven it wouldn't be hot. Not too hot anyway.

I had always loved the summer mistral because it cleansed the air, swept away the mugginess and made one feel freer. It seemed to me appropriate that it should arrive that very morning.

I thought of the old accounts that were closed and the new things beginning. I thought I was afraid, but that for the first time I didn't want to run away from my fear or hide it. And it seemed to me a tremendous and a wonderful thing.

I watched the light creeping into the sky and the grey clouds that were so strangely out of place in the month of July.

In a short while I would get up and go walking in the still-deserted streets. I would sit at a table in the open, at a bar on the seafront and have a cappuccino. I would watch the streets gradually changing as the day advanced. I would have another cappuccino and smoke a cigarette and then, when it was broad daylight, I would go home. And I would sleep, or read, or go to the sea, and spend the day doing only what I wanted to do.

I would wait until evening came and only then would I ring Margherita. I didn't know what I would tell her, but I was sure I would find the words.

I thought of all these things and more as I sat on the balcony.

I thought I would not have exchanged that moment for anything.

Not for anything in the world.